W9-DGW-673

Secrets
at
Spawning Run

Sally Roseveare

Cover Art by
Carolyn R. Egan

ISBN 0-7414-2308-1

Published by:

INFINITY
PUBLISHING.COM

1094 New DeHaven Street, Suite 100
West Conshohocken, PA 19428-2713
Info@buybooksontheweb.com
www.buybooksontheweb.com
Toll-free (877) BUY BOOK
Local Phone (610) 941-9999
Fax (610) 941-9959

Printed in the United States of America

Printed on Recycled Paper

Published April 2005

DEDICATION

This book is dedicated to
my loving and supportive husband
Ronald N. Roseveare,
who fell asleep reading the
first page of the first draft.
On the following pages is
the 35th revision of
Secrets at Spawning Run.
I hope, dear Ron,
this version will keep you awake.

and

To the many dogs—past and present—in my life
who have given me unconditional love
and never-failing loyalty.

ACKNOWLEDGMENTS

My deepest gratitude to Marilee Earle, Carol and Jerry Downey, Betsy McLean, Ron Roseveare, Jr., Lou and Bob Womack, and Nancy Fitzgerald for reading my manuscript in its various stages and offering helpful suggestions and critiques; to Derek Lee of Scuba Schools of Virginia for his technical advice; to Mary Lou McDonald for her valuable input; to Karen Wrigley for her suggestions and encouragement.

Special thanks to good friends Marilyn Fisher, Wanda Garner (who convinced me to put my stories on paper), and Janet Shaffer. Without you three ladies, our monthly meetings and your support, I may not have continued. I wish you great success with your books.

The Lake Writers, sponsored by the Smith Mountain Arts Council, allowed me to bounce ideas—some good, many bad—off them and offered constructive criticism and encouragement. Many of these talented folks are published authors themselves; others will soon be published.

Becky Mushko—fellow Lake Writer, author of three published books, newspaper columnist, winner of numerous contests and awards—became my "literary midwife." I laughed and learned every time she scrawled "Aarrgghh!" and "Cliché!" and "Passive Voice!" (among other things) across my pages. Thank you, Becky. If any portions of the book still need fixing, the fault lies not with Becky or with any of the people listed above. I am a stubborn Southern gal who occasionally ignores excellent advice.

To Carolyn Egan, friend and artist, thank you for the original art work for the book cover. From the moment I started believing *Secrets at Spawning Run* would actually be published, I hoped you would be available to do the cover. You didn't let me down.

CHAPTER ONE

Tuesday, January 13

Luke followed the overturned boat's anchor rope into the depths of Smith Mountain Lake, slid his gloved hand down the rope until he hit a knot, then flipped on his underwater light. He didn't like winter diving in Virginia, disliked wearing the necessary dry suit instead of a wet suit, but at least visibility was better than in summer. And he knew that winter temperatures and forty-degree water always slowed the decomposition and bloating of victims' bodies.

He found the body suspended several feet above the bottom of the lake, the anchor rope twisted around the dead man's ankle, the anchor partially buried in the mucky bottom.

Luke forced himself to pay attention to the task ahead of him. Relaxing his guard for even one second in this man-made lake with its underwater secrets could make him a victim also. He'd tag the boat, the police would take over, and his job would be finished.

On shore, spectators who'd gathered to watch were saying the victim most likely had committed suicide. Luke had heard them talking while he put on his diving gear, but he didn't believe the man had killed himself. Luke had this gut feeling about the man's death, kind of a sixth sense that said. . . .

*Well, it's out of my hands, anyhow, none of my business.
A damn shame, though. I bet all the poor guy wanted was to
catch a striped bass.*

Late that afternoon, three hundred fifty miles south of
Smith Mountain Lake, Aurora Harris stood on the River
Walk in Augusta, Georgia, and tossed a red Frisbee to a
black Lab. She tripped on a tree root and fell. The dog
galloped back to her, licked her face. Laughing, she pushed
the Lab away. She stood and plucked dead leaves out of her
blonde hair, and brushed twigs and dirt from her Land's End
jacket.

A man stepped out from the shadow of a century-old live
oak tree and whistled. The dog barked a greeting and Aurora
smiled. The man walked toward them.

"Sam, what a wonderful surprise!" Aurora pulled her
camera from its case. "Do you have time to help me get
some shots of King catching the Frisbee?"

"Aurora, I have bad news." Sam took her hands in his.
He watched her bright smile disappear and tears well in her
eyes.

"It's happened, hasn't it? I knew this day would come,
but I hoped I'd have more time with her."

Sam wrapped his arms around his wife. A single tear ran
down his cheek. He didn't bother to wipe it off. "It's not
Margaret, Aurora."

"Not Mother? Uncle Charlie, then?"

"No."

Aurora pushed away from Sam, her green eyes searching
his blue ones. "Not Dad. Sam, don't tell me it's Dad."

"My darling Aurora, I'm so sorry."

"But Mom's the one who's sick. Not Dad. He's healthy
as a horse."

"It was an accident, Aurora." Sam refused to accept the
cops' theory that Jack killed himself. He hoped no one would
suggest such a thing to Aurora. She'd miscarried five months
ago, and now this. He wondered how much more his wife
could endure.

"How . . . ?"

"Jack apparently went fishing. Seems a couple of fishermen found his fishing cap snagged on a log near the shore and his rowboat turned over. Somehow Jack's ankle became twisted in the anchor rope, and. . . . "

"No! I don't believe it. Dad was always so careful in his boat. There must be some mistake."

"No, Aurora. There's no mistake."

CHAPTER TWO

Thursday, April 15

Why couldn't she shake this feeling of danger? She wanted to run, to escape, but she couldn't go back to Augusta now. Aurora steered her Jeep into the driveway at 210 Spawning Run Road and drove past the barn and paddocks. Today the cedar and stone house on the wooded knoll didn't beckon her, didn't promise the usual warm, uplifting thoughts of family and friends. She dreaded opening the front door of her parents' house at Smith Mountain Lake, Virginia.

"This would be easier if Sam were with us, King. I wonder where he is. He should have met us at the funeral. Hope he's not still in Japan." She parked near the flagstone walkway.

King whined and licked her face. His thick, black tail beat staccato-fashion against the back of the passenger seat.

"You know where we are, don't you?" King barked. Aurora opened the door and watched her dog leap from the car and race down the steep hill to the lake.

Aurora stared at the house. She didn't want to go inside. She wanted to leave, drive back home to Augusta. Today would be the first time she'd entered the house since her father's funeral three months earlier. And here she was, back for her mother's funeral. At least her mother's death was expected. A blessing, some folks said.

Hooking her purse over her shoulder, she blinked back tears, then pulled the house keys from the pocket of her black linen jacket, picked up a bag of groceries and an open can of Sprite, and walked toward the house. With shaking hand, she unlocked the door. Instead of the closed-up, stuffy house smell she expected, familiar scents of her dad's Sir Walter Raleigh pipe tobacco and her mother's lavender and rose potpourri greeted her. She could almost feel the presence of her parents.

She set the grocery bag and the soda can on the kitchen counter and looked around the room. *Someone's been in the house. I can feel it.*

Nothing seemed out of place, and yet. . . . *Something's wrong, different. But what?* She crossed into the large living room, turned, and stared at the floor-to-ceiling bookshelves flanking the massive stone fireplace.

"Someone's moved the books!" she said aloud. "They're no longer in alphabetical order by author or in their correct section!" She ran a finger along the books' spines, pulled *The Black Arrow* by Robert Louis Stevenson from the reference section and stuck it back in with the classics. The skin on the back of her neck tingled.

She hurried to the kitchen door and called, "King, come!" The Lab grabbed a stick and bounded up the hill.

"Good boy. We're going to check out this house, see if anyone's hiding inside."

They searched every room. Two antique vases rested on the living room mantel as they had for over twenty years, but not in their usual spots. On the kitchen counter, the Kitchenaid mixer faced the wall. Her mother had always turned it toward the kitchen. "The counter just looks tidier that way," her mother had said. Aurora knew her dad hadn't changed it. He probably never even used the mixer after his wife moved into the nursing home three years ago. If he had, Aurora would have noticed when she closed up the house after his funeral.

Clack! Clank-clink! She jumped when she heard the noise behind her and whirled around.

"That's a relief! I guess I didn't close the door all the way, and the wind blew the Sprite can off the counter. I half expected to see an axe murderer standing there. That can made lots of noise when it hit the tile floor, didn't it, King?"

King licked up the few drops of Sprite dripping from the can and sniffed around for more. "Come on, boy, we still need to check the basement. I'll mop the floor later." She set the can in the sink, then left the kitchen. King followed.

Aurora opened the basement door, flipped on the light, and peered down the steps. She and King stood motionless as she strained to hear the slightest sound. Then with King leading, she started slowly down the stairs. A board squeaked under her foot, and she jumped. She stopped and listened. Her heart pounded. She reached the bottom step and glanced around her dad's tidy workshop. Satisfied that no one was hiding in the basement, she went back up the stairs and closed the door. *I know I have to deal with the memories in the basement, but not until tomorrow.*

King whined and Aurora let him outside. She mopped up the mess caused by the spilled soda, then made several more trips to the car for her cameras, luggage and the rest of the groceries. After putting the perishables away and opening a few windows to freshen the house, she stepped out the door to inhale the essence of the lake she loved so much. *Why can't I stand being in this house? Got to get over that, stop dwelling on my grief.*

When she heard King's high-pitched bark, Aurora went back inside, snatched a mystery novel from her tote bag, then hurried along the winding path to join her dog at the dock.

"King?"

The Lab, trembling with the anticipation inherent in all good hunting dogs, teetered on the edge of the dock. Aurora scanned the lake's surface. Less than five feet away a water bird struggled on its side. Aurora recognized the bird as a pied-billed grebe—a chunky, brown, duck-type bird with very little tail, a dark ring around his short bill, a black patch on his throat. And this one needed help.

Oblivious to King's barking, another grebe farther from the dock squawked to her mate. Aurora unlocked the boathouse storage shed and grabbed a long-handled net. She leaned out over the water to scoop up the frightened bird, but he flapped out of her reach.

"Fetch, King!"

King hit the water with a splash. When his head and shoulders surfaced, he swam straight toward his quarry. Panicked, the grebe screeched and tried to swim away, but King caught it. With the bird firmly in his mouth, King swam back to the dock. He dropped the grebe in Aurora's outstretched hands and shook water from his black coat. Then he stretched out next to her feet.

"Good boy, King. Good boy."

Sitting on the dock, Aurora cradled the terrified grebe between her thighs while she examined the bird's body. Something was twisted tight around his neck and one of his legs. "You poor thing. Every time you try to paddle with your feet, the pull on your neck chokes you and causes you to topple over. Ouch! Don't peck me again, okay? I'm trying to help you.

"A necklace? That's weird. Bless your heart, how'd you ever get yourself all tied up like this?"

Despite his struggling, Aurora managed to free the bird's leg. Then she worked on unwinding the necklace from around his neck. "Whew, that was trickier than straightening out a knotted ski rope! Hope you make it, sweetie." She placed the exhausted bird in shallow water and moved away. Aurora worried that the released grebe wouldn't respond to the throaty calls from his mate, but finally the bird slowly swam toward deeper water and the other pied-billed grebe.

"Don't go dressing up again with bangles and beads, okay?" Aurora hollered. She thought about running back up to the house to get her camera, but worried that the bird might need more help. She couldn't risk leaving until she was sure he was okay.

As she watched from the dock, Aurora wondered if the grebes had a nest hidden, if there were eggs or chicks to be cared for. She waited until both birds dived below the surface. When they popped back up, she smiled and yelled, "Yes!"

She picked up the necklace from the dock and fingered it. *How did the grebe get the necklace? Did someone accidentally drop the necklace in the lake? Threw it away, maybe? Did a woman wearing the necklace fall into the lake and drown? Was the woman's body under the dock?* Aurora shivered.

Stop it. You're letting your imagination run away with you again. That's what Sam would think if he were here. "Surely there's a simple explanation," he'd say. And he'd probably be right.

She hung the necklace on a peg in the storage shed and dragged a lounge chair onto the dock. Aurora settled down to read, but couldn't concentrate on her book. Instead, she watched the pair of grebes diving and swimming in the cove. She decided she'd take time to canoe the shoreline, try to spot their nest before she returned to Augusta. The early evening wind whipped her hair. She looked up at the dark clouds whizzing across the sky and frowned.

King tugged on her shirt. "I know. It's getting dark, we're about to be hit with a bad storm, and I bet you're ready for your supper." Aurora returned the lounge chair to the storage shed, took one last glance at the grebes, and climbed the path to the house.

Huge raindrops pelted her seconds before she opened the door, and a sharp clap of thunder echoed across the cove. "Darn, I left my book on the dock," she said and dashed back outside. "Stay, King!" she commanded as the door banged shut behind her.

Angry gray waves slammed against the dock pilings. Dark storm clouds cast eerie shadows over the dock. Despite the rapidly cooling air, beads of perspiration dotted Aurora's forehead. She bit her lip and tasted fear. *What's wrong with me? This is the home I grew up in; there's nothing to be afraid of.*

As she leaned over to retrieve her book, something moved in the water close to the dock. Instinctively, Aurora flattened her back against the gray boathouse wall. A black bass boat glided silently into the boathouse. She heard muffled voices, then a splash. The boat exited the boathouse as quietly as it had entered.

Aurora exhaled, then took a deep breath. She was scared. Her fear, which started when she left Augusta at 4:00 this morning, had intensified with each passing mile. Now this same fear almost controlled her. Another roll of thunder made her jump as jagged lightning sliced through the sky. Clutching her book, she ran back up the hill to the security of the house.

She heard the telephone ringing when she opened the door. Her hand shook as she answered.

"Hello?"

"Susie-Q, how's my favorite girl?" said the familiar voice on the other end of the line.

Aurora smiled at her husband's pet name for her. "Sam, I can't even begin to tell you how good it is to hear your voice. How am I? Physically, I'm fine. Emotionally, I'm a basket case. I wish you were here with me. Are you back in Augusta or still in Japan?"

"I'm in Augusta now, just walked in the front door." He paused, then asked in a gentle voice, "How'd your mother's funeral go?"

"As well as any funeral, I guess." She reached into a cabinet and took out a glass. "The folks at St. Stephen's were wonderful. The choir sang Mom's favorite hymns, the same ones they sang at Daddy's funeral—'Hail Thee, Festival Day' and 'Amazing Grace.' The ladies of the church came through with a wonderful reception afterwards, too. I kept looking for you, knew you'd be with me if possible. When you didn't come, I prayed you were safe." She filled the glass with tap water and sipped it.

"I wanted to be there, but my flight from Japan was delayed. Don't know why, but after we boarded, the plane sat on the tarmac for a couple of hours. I think it was some kind of security problem. Then all passengers were ordered back to the terminal. We re-boarded three hours later. Once we finally took off, an engine quit about thirty minutes into the flight and forced the pilot to return to Tokyo. And, of course, I missed my connection from D.C. to Roanoke. I'd planned to rent a car and drive in for Margaret's funeral. So sorry I couldn't be with you. Are you all right?"

Aurora jumped at a crack of thunder. The lights blinked.

"Aurora, are you there?"

"Yes, I'm here. We're having a bad storm. What were we talking about?" She pushed a strand of wet hair away from her face.

"I asked if you're okay. You know, okay with the funeral and all. Are you?"

"As well as can be expected, I guess. But Mom's death is hitting me harder than I ever dreamed it would. And I don't understand it. We both know she's better off now." Aurora swallowed a sob.

"I've always believed the survivors suffer more than their loved ones who've died. Margaret's gone to a better place, honey."

"Your theory may be true in most cases, but I think Dad suffered more than I'm suffering. I think drowning would be the most horrible death of all. Or maybe fire."

"But not in Margaret's case, Aurora. You know that."

"Yes, you're right, of course."

"There's something else, Sam. Someone's been in the house."

"What?"

"I said someone's been in the house."

"How do you know?"

"The books on the bookshelves in the living room are out of order, and several other things in the house have been moved around. And I sense it. I know someone's been in here."

"Are you and King locked safely inside now?"

"Yes." She leaned over and locked the dead bolt on the kitchen door.

"Was anything taken?"

"I don't think so."

"I'll bet you a long, passionate kiss that the cleaning service moved things around, probably took all the books off the shelves to dust, too. They have a key."

"I know, but after Dad's funeral, I called and told them to stop coming."

"They just forgot, Aurora. Erase it from your mind." Sam added, "Guess it wouldn't hurt for you to call and ask if anyone cleaned the house, though. Say you want your key back."

"I really don't think the cleaning service was here. After all, things were never out of place when they came on a regular basis before. But I'll call them tomorrow."

"Good."

"Let me tell you what King did today."

"What'd he do?" Sam was glad she'd changed the subject.

She recounted the grebe's plight and subsequent rescue. "King has such a gentle, soft mouth that the bird's feathers weren't even ruffled. You trained our dog well."

"Wouldn't be much of a retriever if he damaged the goods, now would he?"

"That's true. But why would a necklace be on a duck? What do you think?"

"That's not something you see every day, I'll admit. The necklace is costume jewelry, right?"

"Well, yeah. At least I assume so. I want you to see it, tell me what you think."

"Where is it?"

"I left it in the storage shed on the dock. I was concerned about the grebes, and then the storm came up and I forgot about the necklace. Besides, I know very little about jewelry. You know that."

Sam laughed. "Yeah, I surely do. I remember every time I bought jewelry for you. Seems to me you kept only one pair of earrings—I think they were one-carat diamonds—and always returned the other gifts. Then you bought cameras and special lenses. It took me a while to finally learn that you prefer practical presents." Sam chuckled. "I think your favorite present was the year I inundated you with rolls of 16mm film."

"Can you blame me? Rolls of 16mm film are expensive. Besides that, you only get about two minutes and forty seconds of filming per roll. Thanks again for getting me the film."

"You're welcome, Susie-Q. Now back to the necklace. My guess is someone accidentally dropped it from a boat, and the luckless grebe, attracted to something shiny, investigated and got himself in a bind—literally. Good thing you found him."

"King found him. King's the hero here, Sam, not I." She reached down and patted the Lab's head.

Sam and Aurora chatted a few minutes longer. When King whined and pulled on her wrist, Aurora laughed. "I need to feed our canine hero. We walked up from the dock to fix his supper, but the thunderstorm hit as soon as I came inside, and I rushed back down for my book. Still haven't fed him.

"One other thing before we hang up, though. Sam, when I ran down to the dock to get my book, a black fishing boat—I think there were two men on board—went in the boathouse. It made me uneasy. Any thoughts on that?"

"I think fishermen were seeking shelter from the storm."

"But they didn't stay long; they were in and out in seconds. Don't you think that's odd? And I heard a splash, too."

"Susie-Q, you need to curb that vivid imagination of yours. They were probably fishermen trying to find shelter from the storm, then figured they could outrun it. I wouldn't worry. After all, you have King there to protect you."

"You're right, I guess. Will you call me tomorrow?"

"You know I can barely go more than a day without hearing your voice."

"I'm glad."

"I love you and I'll talk to you tomorrow. 'Bye."

"'Bye, Sam."

An hour later, the rain still beat against the three skylights in the living room. Aurora finished her microwave dinner and cleaned up the few dirty dishes. She lit the gas logs in the fireplace and settled down on the cream colored, overstuffed sofa with her novel. She was glad she had retrieved it before the deluge began. She pulled a blue and white crocheted afghan over her legs to ward off the damp, spring chill from the storm. Tonight she'd escape into fantasy. Tomorrow she'd deal with reality and face the memories lurking in this house.

King nudged Aurora's leg, then stretched out on the hearth rug.

Friday, April 16

With the sunrise came a clear, fresh dawn. The wet leaves on the trees sparkled in the early morning light, and the ripples on the lake danced and shimmered. Aurora leaned over the deck railing and admired the view of mountains and water.

Aurora's dad Jack, an architect with a head for business, had recognized the lake's potential and invested heavily in lakefront property in 1970. A few years later, he built a two-story cottage and, for a decade, his family spent their summers and weekends at the lake. They moved there permanently when Aurora was ten years old. Over the years, Jack added rooms to the home, but the rambling, friendly house still radiated the original cottage warmth and charm.

"What a paradise," Aurora said to King as her fingers caressed the big Lab's head. "This lake never loses its hold on me. Why did I stay away so long?"

She turned and went inside for her first cup of coffee. She never saw the black boat glide into her boathouse.

Her breakfast was simple: half a grapefruit (no sugar), a bowl of Total cereal with skim milk, and a second cup of strong, black coffee. At 33, Aurora was slim, attractive, and health conscious. Even though she yearned for a plump, jelly-filled doughnut, she knew she'd better resist the impulse. She'd learned from experience what too many sweets would do to her 5'5" frame, especially her hips.

After breakfast, Aurora donned a pair of faded jeans, white T-shirt, and a teal sweat shirt with yellow Lab puppies printed across the front. She stared at her reflection in the mirror. Big green eyes with flecks of golden brown stared back at her. *You're stalling. Time to get on with it, old girl.*

"King, come," she called. She opened the basement door. When they reached the bottom of the stairs, she looked around. She hadn't been in her father's workshop since he'd drowned; yesterday she'd gone only to the bottom of the stairs. Arranged neatly on the wall to the left hung his drills, hammers, screwdrivers, and hand saw. Another section housed his three power saws. His wood planer stood nearby, ready for use. She noticed his lathe that could turn twelve-inch thick pieces of wood. He'd made it himself.

Aurora ran her fingers over a picture frame crafted from curly maple. On the workbench an unfinished frame waited for her father to add his final touch. *I didn't know you'd finished a frame for me and started another. Oh, Dad, why were you so careless in that damn boat?*

When she was a junior in college, her film production professor urged Aurora to produce a commercial for the owner of an apple orchard. Only five minutes long, the film was well received by the customer—he liked the quality of her work and the price—and earned her an "A" in her film production class. Her mother suggested that Aurora start a tradition of needlepointing a scene from any film work she produced, so Aurora had painstakingly transferred one of the shots from the commercial to fabric. She soon learned she'd not inherited her mother's ability to do exquisite needlepoint; it was too complicated, required great concentration, and made her nervous. So she adapted that first design of apple blossoms from the Shenandoah Valley for cross-stitch and discovered she could relax while working on the design. With the completion of that first project, her dad had surprised her with a handsome, curly maple frame. From then on, Jack supplied his daughter with frames, always of curly maple and always with a short message intricately routed in the back of the wood.

Her mother's suggestion turned into an enjoyable and lucrative side business for Aurora. Once she finished a cross-stitch design from a promotional film, commercial, or travelogue, Aurora photographed it, selected the correct amount and colors of floss, printed directions, and produced cross-stitch kits. Soon the kits became hot items; gift and needlework shops located in areas where the travelogues were filmed gladly stocked the kits.

Aurora stayed in her dad's shop for almost an hour. Reminiscing and fingering tools whose wooden handles shone with the patina of years of use, she felt calm for the first time in months. Unable to face her dad's death, she'd been furious with him, angry that he'd been so careless in the boat, that he'd drowned and left her to care for her mother alone. She'd depended on his love and support to help her accept the loss of her unborn baby five months before he died. Emotionally, she'd had no real closure since her dad's death until now. She climbed the stairs and gently shut the basement door. No more suspicions, no more emotional ghosts, no more anger—just fond memories.

Now she would deal with her mother's death from Alzheimer's disease four days ago. Aurora finished reading the many cards and letters she'd received, then picked up her pen and started writing thank-you notes. She wondered if her mother had known somewhere in the deep recesses of her mind that her husband had died.

"Of course not," the nurses assured Aurora when she broached the question. But she wasn't sure, and now she'd never know.

At 10:30, Aurora pushed herself away from the desk and stretched. *I need a break. The thank-you notes can wait a while longer.* She hurried to the bedroom and changed into an old blue swimsuit. She picked up her camera bag, called King, and walked down to the lake while the Lab raced ahead of her.

She held onto the ladder and stuck a bare foot in the water. *Brrr. I should have known the lake wouldn't be warm enough for a swim until mid-May or later. To be honest, I don't think I could swim in the lake even if it were warm. Dad drowned here. His precious lake killed him.* Aurora blinked back a tear and spread her thick towel across the green lounge chair. She stretched out to let the sun warm her.

King brought her a stick and barked until she said, "Fetch, King," and hurled it into the water. She laughed when he returned with the stick a minute later and shook. Droplets of cold water sprayed her. After touching Aurora with his nose, King flopped down beside her.

Lying there on the dock, Aurora reflected on the past ten years and how their lives—hers and Sam's—had changed. Eight years ago they were living in Roanoke, only an hour's drive from the lake, when Sam accepted an engineering design job in Augusta, Georgia. The job promised a tremendous opportunity for Sam's career, and Aurora was thrilled at the chance to experience a new lifestyle. Besides, she reasoned, Augusta was only a six or seven hour drive from the lake; she could visit her folks and the lake every month or two.

When they were settled in Augusta, Aurora started her own business. With excellent references and film clips of her work in Roanoke to present to potential clients, Aurora's business soared. Within two years she was recognized as one of America's top producers of travelogues and promotional films.

Five years ago Aurora and Sam bought a wonderful old Craftsman-style house two blocks off Highland Avenue in Augusta. Aurora fell in love with it the minute she walked through the front door. The one-story house had huge rooms, a screened porch, and a large fenced-in back yard for King, then two months old.

When her dad saw the house, he exclaimed, "It's an authentic Craftsman bungalow, Aurora, built between 1905 and 1929, and it's in great shape!"

Aurora grinned at her dad's enthusiasm. "So you really like it?"

"Like it? I love it. You kids bought yourselves a real gem."

For a few months, life seemed storybook perfect. Then her mother's behavior, temperament, memory all changed. On her way to a church meeting—at the church she'd attended for over thirty years—Margaret made a wrong turn and ended up 25 miles away in Rustburg, Virginia. A convenience store employee called Jack to come pick her up.

"I must be losing my mind," Margaret had said to Aurora when they talked on the phone that night.

"No, Mom. You're just not concentrating," Aurora had answered.

But a few weeks later when she questioned her father, he admitted his wife's memory had been bad for nearly a year and was getting worse fast. "Aurora, I'm worried. She's forgetting things. Last Thursday she tried to refill the same prescription three times in one day. The pharmacist called me and asked what was going on. And this week she called the dentist office four times to make an appointment to have her teeth cleaned. I guess I've been covering up for her because I don't want to admit that something is wrong."

"Dad, you've got to take her to a doctor. Maybe it's something simple that medication can fix," Aurora had said.

But it wasn't something simple. The diagnosis was Alzheimer's disease.

Caring for his wife at home worked well in the beginning. Then Margaret left a frying pan filled with bacon grease on a lit burner. Jack extinguished the fire that developed, but not before the cabinets above the stove were charred.

"Margaret, you could have burned the house down. What were you thinking? You could have been killed!" Jack had said.

"I'm so sorry, Jack. Do you still love me?"

"Of course I love you, sweetheart," he'd said as he cradled her in his arms. "I'll always love you."

Concern for Margaret's safety, plus the need for constant supervision, took their toll on Jack. Aurora pleaded with him until he hired round-the-clock help to assist with his wife's day to day needs.

Early one morning three years ago, Jack looked out the bathroom window and couldn't believe what he saw. Margaret, wearing a pale blue cotton nightgown, stood alone at the end of the dock as her frantic, pajama-clad caretaker ran screaming down the hill toward her. Margaret smiled sweetly, waved, then turned and stepped off the dock into water fifteen feet deep. The caretaker couldn't swim. Jack, wearing only his jockey shorts, dashed barefoot to the water, dived in, and hauled Margaret back to shore. The next week he moved her into a nursing home.

Looking after Margaret had been difficult for Jack, even though Aurora tried to come home every two weeks to help. Then last May a glorious thing happened; Aurora discovered she was pregnant. The thought of having a precious baby in the family helped ease the stress during the tough times with her mother, but Aurora miscarried four months into the pregnancy. Still grieving for her unborn child, Aurora was devastated when her dad drowned five months later.

After Jack's funeral, Sam told his wife, "You are not running back and forth to Lynchburg to look after your mother. Aurora, this is just too much for you."

So Aurora moved Margaret from the nursing home in Lynchburg to one in Augusta. Even though she no longer spoke or recognized anyone, Margaret seemed calm.

Aurora was in a meeting at St. Paul's Episcopal Church in the historic district of Augusta when her cell phone rang. Margaret had died.

"All her organs shut down; her brain quit telling them how to work. She slipped away in her sleep an hour ago, a peaceful look on her face," the kind doctor explained.

The emotions caused by her mother's death surprised Aurora. Her memories of Margaret when things were normal—when Aurora had felt so loved and doted on—clashed with Aurora's memories of the suffering from which her mother had just been released. She grieved now, more for herself than for her mother who was finally free of the hell she had been living for several years. And Aurora had come back to the lake for the funeral, to get Margaret's affairs in order, to mourn, and to face the memories in the house where she grew up.

A splash jolted Aurora back to the present. She watched the pair of grebes, one with a flapping fish dangling from its mouth, swim up to the dock.

"That's a nice catch you've got there. A sunfish, right? Bet you're proud of yourself."

Aurora grabbed her camera and focused it on the grebes. *Click.* She zoomed in on the grebe with the fish. *Click.* When the second grebe swam up close to its mate, Aurora lay on the dock and aimed the camera. *Click. Click.*

"What shots! Real photographic treasures. Some of these will be good enough for *Virginia Wildlife* or *National Geographic.* Thanks, guys. That reminds me. I'll take your necklace back up with me when I go. I'd forgotten about it until now."

When King put a paw on her leg, she stood up and turned around. "Yikes! Is that a dead fish you've brought me?" King dropped the bloated striper at her feet and wagged his tail. "No thanks, I prefer sticks and branches. Take the fish somewhere else. Please." King barked. "On second thought, I don't want you eating it. You stay." Aurora wrinkled her nose and kicked the fish back into the lake. "That's the second dead striper I've seen in Spawning Run since I've been here. Hope there won't be as many dead ones as there were last year."

Aurora was still thinking about the fish when she retrieved the necklace from the shed. She leaned off the dock and sloshed the necklace around in the water to wash off the scum. She sat down in the lounge chair and stared in disbelief. *Could this necklace be real?* What looked like individual diamonds set in platinum ran the entire length of the necklace. A medallion, approximately four inches in diameter and encrusted with rubies and diamonds, hung from the center.

"No way these stones are real. If they were, this necklace would be priceless. No one would be so careless as to lose a piece of jewelry this valuable in the lake. If they did, it would make the headlines in the *Smith Mountain Eagle*. No, it can't be real or it would be locked up in somebody's vault. It's still gorgeous, though, the nicest piece of costume jewelry I've ever seen. Would love to know the story behind it."

Aurora draped the necklace around her neck and wondered how it got caught on a grebe. She caressed the medallion as she stared out at the dark, blue-green water and across the wide, quiet cove at the tree line two hundred yards away. She couldn't stop thinking of her dad. Across the cove was where his boat had capsized, where he had drowned.

Unknown to Aurora, a black fishing boat hid in the shadows of the same tree line. An angry man glared at her through binoculars. "What's she doing over there?" Jimmy Ray snarled.

He spat chewing tobacco into the lake and watched as circular ripples surrounded it. A curious fish swam to the sinking wad, then darted away. Jimmy Ray wiped brown dribble from the corner of his mouth onto the sleeve of his camouflage shirt and passed the binoculars to his companion. "The boss said nobody lived in that house no more, said ain't nobody gonna care how much we use the boathouse."

"I know," said Clyde. "Damn! That looks like our necklace around her neck."

"The one Snake dropped in the lake?"

"Yeah."

"Gimme the damn glasses!" Jimmy Ray snatched the binoculars from Clyde's hands. He watched Aurora finger the necklace. "We gotta call the boss. Wonder who she is and how long she'll be here."

"I'll try to find out tomorrow."

CHAPTER THREE

In his Washington, D.C. penthouse, J. Melton Lampwerth IV adjusted his hand-painted silk tie and flicked a gray hair from the shoulder of his navy, chalk-stripe Italian suit. He snatched up his laptop, stepped into his private penthouse elevator, and pushed the button to the executive parking garage. Last night he'd loaded all the papers his accountant had thrust at him into a brown calfskin briefcase, packed a few clothes in a small suitcase, and quietly taken them to his car undetected. He'd been furious then, and even now his anger had abated only a little.

"When I'm through, somebody's head will roll," he said aloud.

Lampwerth hadn't told anyone he was going, not even Jill, his assistant. He'd only decided the night before. Well, he'd call her from the lake on Monday. She'd be wondering why he hadn't come back to the office after lunch today. This wasn't like him—he'd never done anything on the spur of the moment before. But he knew he needed solitude to think this dilemma through. Besides, Robert Reeves, Vice President of Lampwerth International, had always made the seclusion of his Smith Mountain Lake home sound inviting. Lampwerth deserved some time away from the office. He would stay at Robert's lake house for several days. The house was equipped with a fax, and he had his laptop, so he could keep in touch with the office. And when he returned to

Washington, he'd have a good idea of how to handle his problem.

Lampwerth drove into the parking lot of Executive Pet Grooming, parked, and hurried inside. Pictures of champion AKC dogs covered the walls.

"How are you, Mr. Lampwerth?" asked the receptionist. "I'll tell them in the back to get Russell for you."

"Thanks." He was glad he'd remembered to pick up his Jack Russell terrier before leaving D.C. If he hadn't, the groomer would have called his office, then his penthouse, and the search for him would have started three days too soon. Lampwerth recognized the shrill bark coming from the hall. The door opened and in burst Russell, his body wriggling with delight and his groomer in tow.

"Mr. Lampwerth, good to see you, sir." Danny was always glad to see big-tipping Mr. Lampwerth. "I bathed and trimmed Russell today, clipped his nails, the whole shebang. As usual, he was a pleasure to work with."

Lampwerth paid his bill, tipped Danny, and walked out the door with Russell.

"In all the time I've been grooming Russell, this is the first time Mr. Lampwerth didn't seem excited to see his dog," Danny said to the receptionist. They watched Russell relieve himself on the plastic fire hydrant outside the building, then eagerly leap into the front seat of the BMW.

"I know what you mean. Usually he lets Russell jump in his arms and wash his face with yucky wet kisses. Odd, isn't it?" said the receptionist.

In the car, Lampwerth looked down at Russell perched contentedly on the passenger seat. Lampwerth had never planned to love anything, much less a dog. Four years ago Marian had filed for divorce after 30 years of marriage. "You're not capable of love," she'd said. "You only married me for my money and social status." And she was right. Lampwerth's lawyer insisted he get a dog or cat or some other animal to convince the judge that he was lonely, that he indeed needed someone or something to love. So he bought Russell and the strategy worked. His lawyer estimated that

Russell saved him half a million bucks in alimony payments. Lampwerth had planned to keep Russell a while, then give him away, but in the interim the puppy squirmed his way into Lampwerth's cold heart.

The silver BMW purred along Interstate 66. Traffic wasn't nearly as heavy as it was when Lampwerth left Washington, and the heavy rain had now become a drizzle. Lampwerth reached Gainesville and turned off 66 onto 29 South. He was glad he decided to accept Robert's long-standing offer to stay at the lake house. Lampwerth had been very angry last evening when Louis Beale, the firm's accountant, had told him someone had been screwing around with the books, even hinted that some funds had been skimmed off the top. And that look on the accountant's face, almost as if he suspected Lampwerth. Ridiculous. He was President and C.E.O. of Lampwerth International. He would never do anything to hurt his own company, the company he'd built thirty-five years ago. Everyone knew that.

He slowed the BMW, turned onto 460 West, and skirted Lynchburg. The rain started again. He turned on his windshield wipers. Thirty-five minutes later he reached his turn onto 122 in Bedford and glanced down at the directions. Good, only about forty minutes left according to Robert's notes. Lampwerth pressed harder on the accelerator.

Nearing Smith Mountain Lake, Lampwerth slowed. In the dark and the rain it would be easy to miss his turn off 122, one of the last turns before he reached Spawning Run Road. Robert had assured him there were only a few houses on Spawning Run Road. Most were vacant for one reason or other, and Lampwerth would have complete privacy.

"Finally," he said to Russell as the car's headlights illuminated the address—214 Spawning Run—embedded in one of the stucco columns at the driveway's entrance. Even he was impressed when he pulled into the circular drive fronting the peach-colored Mediterranean-style stucco house. Looked like Robert Reeves certainly knew how to live. A low-hanging branch thudded hard against the passenger side of the BMW, and Lampwerth made a mental note to check in the morning for scratches on his car. He would also tell Robert to get his damn trees trimmed.

Getting out of the car, he accidentally bumped the car horn. He jumped—and noted with a shudder the lonesome sound the horn made. He let Russell out to do what dogs do after a long ride in a car, then he pulled the house key out of his pocket, picked up his luggage and laptop, and walked to the front door. He stuck the key in the lock and smiled. He knew Robert would be pleased when he returned from his cruise and discovered that Lampwerth had finally accepted the invitation to stay at the lake. He turned the doorknob and stepped inside the house.

A heavy blow from behind sent him crashing to the floor. J. Melton Lampwerth IV's last thought as he lay bleeding on the white marble tile was that Robert Reeves hadn't done him a favor after all.

Next door, Aurora dropped her book. *Were those gunshots?* Ears cocked, King jumped up and growled. "Shh, boy," she commanded. Obediently, King sat down. For two minutes, woman and dog remained motionless, then Aurora crossed the living room and kitchen and went into the utility room. King padded silently by her side. Without turning on the light, Aurora pulled the window curtain aside and peered out into the night.

Outside a faint moon played hide-and-seek in the swiftly moving clouds. The wind whistled gently around the eaves of the house. "Storm's almost over, King. I don't know if we heard gunshots, thunder, or a car backfiring, but I don't see or hear anything now. Why don't we get ready for bed? It's been a long day."

Aurora stood on a stool in her parents' bedroom closet and pulled a locked metal box down from the top shelf. Then she searched in a dresser drawer until she located a key. Unlocking the box, she removed the .38 semi-automatic, checked the safety, and made sure the gun was loaded. Her hand shook. She remembered the last time she'd seen this gun; the police had found it on the telephone table in the living room in January. They'd speculated that the presence of the gun suggested her father had planned to shoot himself but for some unknown reason had drowned himself instead.

She carried the gun back to her bedroom and placed it in the drawer of her nightstand. King curled up on his dog bed under the large window and looked at Aurora. She petted him gently on his head, then climbed into her bed and tried to sleep.

CHAPTER FOUR

Saturday, April 17

Aurora was fixing breakfast when the phone rang. "Good morning, my darling Susie-Q. Did I wake you?"

"No, Sam. I'm tired, but I got up early to see one of the gorgeous lake sunrises that I've missed so much, then King and I went for a walk." She glanced at the clock—7:45. "Actually, I've gotten up early both mornings. I'll probably fall asleep on the dock this afternoon. How are you? I surely do miss you." She squeezed orange blossom honey into her bowl of oatmeal, then stirred in dried cranberries, raisins and a little skim milk.

"I miss you, too, honey. It's no fun here without you. How much longer before you come home to Augusta?"

"I'm not sure. It'll take longer than I thought to put Mom's affairs in order. I need to meet with her lawyer this week, too." She poured herself a cup of coffee. "And I'd hate to take King away from his beloved lake so soon. Wish you could see him, he's acting like a puppy again. Keeps bringing me stuff from the lake that I don't want: dead fish, a deflated inner tube, chunks of wood, sticks, pieces of Styrofoam. You wouldn't believe how much junk is in the water."

"I'm glad King's with you."

"King's better company than a lot of people we know, Sam. Smarter, too." She spooned some cereal into her mouth.

"You're right." He chuckled.

"By the way," Sam said, "Harold Johns called me late last night from Lynchburg. He wants us to join him and his wife for dinner next Saturday night. He's flying down to Augusta on business for a few days, Melinda is coming with him. Think you can make it?"

"I don't know. I'm not ready to leave yet. Like I said before, there's still a lot for me to do here." She sipped her coffee. "I'll see what I can do, though. You know I'd love to be with you."

She'd never told Sam that Harold Johns gave her the creeps. After all, Sam had to work with the arrogant man occasionally. And Harold's wife Melinda, well! She was a snobby, rich socialite who'd probably had more facelifts than she could count. "I'll think about it and let you know tomorrow. Any excuse to talk to you."

"I really do hope you can come for the weekend, Susie-Q, but I'll understand if you can't.

"How's the weather there, Aurora? Are you staying warm enough?"

"I'm plenty warm during the day, but the water's much too cold for a swim. In the evenings, I light the gas logs, pull an afghan up over me and read." King whined and nosed Aurora. She patted his head. "Can't see any sense in turning on the heat. As for the weather, that storm that roared through here has gone. Last night I thought I heard gun shots, but I'm guessing now that it was isolated claps of thunder or a car backfiring." King whined again. Aurora opened the door and let him out.

"And Sam, don't worry about me. Even though I get teary-eyed when I think of Mother—and I do miss her terribly—I know she's much better off now." Aurora didn't want to worry Sam, so she didn't mention the undercurrent of fear that never left her.

"I'm relieved to hear that, Susie-Q.

"What are your plans for the day?"

"I'm going to finish these thank-you notes to all the nice people who sent flowers and cards. I'll save the cards they sent me; I'm sure you'd enjoy reading the sweet things they said about Mother. People have been so kind, even though Mother had suffered with Alzheimer's for several years." Aurora opened the door when King barked to come back inside.

"I'd like to read the cards. By the way, did you look at the necklace again?"

"I did. Sam, it's hard to believe, but it looks like the diamonds and rubies are real." She swallowed some orange juice. "I can hardly wait to get your opinion. If it's genuine, then I'll report it to the police. But I'd feel like a fool if I made a big deal out of a piece of costume jewelry."

"I can understand that. Where'd you put it?"

"In the junk drawer in the kitchen."

"I'm looking forward to seeing it. And seeing you, too. Guess I'd better head to the office now, though. I'll call you tomorrow, Susie-Q. Love you, 'bye."

"Goodbye, Sam. I love you, too." Aurora stood for several seconds after hanging up the receiver, her fingertips touching the phone.

By mid-afternoon, Aurora sealed and stamped the final envelope. *That's a relief. Tomorrow I'll take them to the post office and put them in the mail. Right now I need to get outside.* She pushed her chair away from the antique cherry writing desk.

"King, want to go down to the dock?"

King barked. Aurora laughed. "Let me get my bathing suit on, then we'll go." She hurried to the bedroom and put on a green and blue print suit. After picking up a thick yellow towel and her digital camera, she turned on the answering machine. She grabbed two slices of bread from the kitchen cupboard and walked down to the dock with King.

She put the camera and towel on a chair. Then standing on the edge of the dock, she broke off small pieces of bread and tossed them into the water. Small fish darted out from under the dock and gobbled up the treats. Aurora laughed. "Some things never change, King." She tossed him a piece. He caught it in midair.

After throwing the last of the bread to the fish, she walked over to the boathouse and looked up at the canoe hoisted high above the pontoon boat. She knew that with the aid of the intricate system of ropes and pulleys her dad had installed, getting the old Grumman aluminum canoe down would only take a few minutes. She wanted—no, needed—to get out on the water, to prove to herself that the lake itself wasn't her enemy. However, she still wasn't ready to go swimming.

Within fifteen minutes, Aurora was in the canoe. Her camera hung from her neck. She zipped up her life jacket and said, "Okay, King, come." He stepped carefully into the boat. Aurora dipped her paddle into the water and the canoe glided away from the dock. "We'll look for the grebes, see if we can find a nest."

Thirty minutes later, after no sign of the grebes, Aurora returned to the end of the dock so King could jump out. Not yet ready to get out of the canoe, she pushed away from the dock. She put the paddle down and dangled her hands in the deep, calm water.

Aurora looked back at the two-story home her dad had designed and built on the hillside. The house's exterior blended with the surroundings. A wide, covered porch—a veranda, her mother called it—around all four sides of the house allowed first-floor windows to stay open even during a heavy rain. An L-shaped section of screened porch on one corner provided spillover sleeping during the summer. The sunroom, Aurora's favorite spot to curl up with a good book and a cup of mint tea on a winter day, was furnished with white wicker furniture, the cushions upholstered in a bright green and white fabric.

From the canoe, she admired the nicely trimmed yard and weed-free flowerbeds. Huge azaleas in shades of pink, purple, peach and white bloomed amid the white dogwoods, crape myrtles, tulip poplars and tall pines. Purple and yellow pansies blossomed profusely in the large, green clay pot on the end of the dock. Unkempt yards meant no one was home, so Sam had arranged with Tom's Tidy Lawn & Lake Service to take care of all yard maintenance after Jack died. She smiled at the weather-beaten redwood sign still attached to the boathouse: "The House That Jack Built." The sign had been repainted several times over the years. An identical sign hanging from the rail fence welcomed guests who came up the driveway.

Her father had divided the remainder of the tract into restricted five-acre lots and, as property values jumped, he sold one or two lots every couple of years. Eventually, his architectural firm grew as people in the area recognized his extraordinary talent and integrity—two qualities respected in the building industry. Aurora looked at the other homes. She was glad her parents had kept 21 acres as a buffer.

Not only had the acreage given the family plenty of privacy, it provided space for a three-stall barn with a tack room, two small paddocks, and a nine-acre pasture. She remembered the Christmas when she was ten years old, the year her family moved to the lake. That glorious Christmas morning she ran into the living room and discovered the end of a red ribbon pinned to her Christmas stocking. As her parents watched, she followed the ribbon out the front door and up to the barn. The other end of the ribbon was tied to a stall door latch. When she opened the door she saw the most gorgeous pony in the world—at least Aurora thought so. Red ribbons were woven through the pony's mane and tail. The small mare nickered softly and nuzzled Aurora with her soft-as-velvet muzzle. Because she was a dapple-gray, Aurora named her Frosty. She had loved going on trail rides with Frosty and showing her at the local shows, especially the annual New London show. Frosty died a natural death at age 22, the year Aurora left for college.

Smiling at the memory, Aurora looked up at the blue sky dotted with billowing cumulus clouds. She thought of her dad and how he would have pointed at the deep blue sky and say, "See those clouds? They're the kind N.C. Wyeth painted." Then he would have told anyone who would listen about his favorite artist/illustrator.

She pulled her camera from its case and snapped a picture of the cloud-filled sky. "This one's for you, Dad."

Since her dad's death, Aurora had been unable to recall his face unless she looked at his photograph. Now, three months later, she could picture his twinkling blue eyes, thin gray-blonde hair, and the deep laugh lines etched in the corners of his eyes. Why, she wondered, could she see him so clearly now? Was it because she finally had accepted his drowning, had forgiven him for being careless, had let go of her anger? Soothed by the water lapping against the canoe, she put down her camera, leaned back in the canoe, and closed her eyes. *I loved you so much, Dad. And I always will.*

King's deep growl startled Aurora. Paddling back to the dock, she climbed the ladder and tied up the canoe. Less than ten yards away sat a middle-aged couple in a black fishing boat.

The heavyset man wore khaki shorts, a red knit shirt, brown leather boat shoes (no socks), sunglasses, and a tan fishing cap with "Born to Fish" scrawled across it. *Hmm. Looks like a yuppie or a cleaned-up redneck to me.*

Sprigs of bottle-blonde hair escaped from under the woman's wide-brimmed straw hat tied under her chin by a pink and green striped scarf. Aurora noted the pale pink halter-top under the unbuttoned long-sleeved green linen shirt, the liberally applied makeup, the blue sandals and fuchsia shorts. *Bet she was a knockout twenty years ago.*

In the boat, two rods rigged for striper fishing rested in holders beside an empty live well for holding their catch. Aurora could hear the bait shad flitting around in the minnow bucket.

"Hey there," drawled the woman as she adjusted her tortoise shell sunglasses. "That sure is a pretty Lab."

"Thanks," said Aurora. King continued to growl.

"What's his name?"

"King."

"May I pet him?" asked the woman, stretching out a well-manicured hand heavy with rings.

"I wouldn't if I were you. He's very protective of me."

"That big head of his is just gorgeous. He's absolute perfection."

Aurora beamed, friendlier now after hearing praise for her beloved dog. "Thanks." King continued to growl.

"Is King registered? I own a registered female Lab myself."

"Yes, he is. He's descended from an old Canadian line of champion Labradors." Aurora scratched behind King's ears.

"I've been dying to breed my dog, and when I saw King standing over here on your dock, I just had to come get a better look at him. He's the nicest I've seen in a long time. Would you consider breeding him with my female? You could have your pick of the litter."

Aurora chuckled. "Won't work. His registered name is The King of Hearts, but he won't be breaking the hearts of any female dogs. We aren't in the dog breeding business, so we had him neutered when he was a year old. However, King's sire and dam are owned by friends of ours. I could give you their name and phone number, if you wish."

"Thanks, I just might take you up on that. Will you be here all next week?"

"I'm not sure."

"Well, maybe I'll see you around."

"How's the fishin'? Anybody catching anything?" asked the man.

"I've only been here a couple of days. Haven't seen anybody catch anything, although I've seen some boats out on the water. Some at night, too."

The woman looked at her companion. "Don't reckon we'll catch a fish if we don't get moving, honey." She said to Aurora, "Nice talking to you."

Aurora nodded.

CHAPTER FIVE

Monday, April 19

Jill Hathaway, J. Melton Lampwerth IV's executive secretary, was peeved and a little worried. It was Monday, 9:00 a.m., and no sign of Mr. Lampwerth. A workaholic, he never arrived later than 6:45. Never. He couldn't be stuck in traffic—he lived in the penthouse in the same building as Lampwerth International. He'd left no message, either. She frowned, leaned over her desk, and pressed the intercom button.

"Nan, have you located Mr. Lampwerth yet?" she asked her secretary.

"No, Ms. Hathaway, but I'm calling his penthouse right now. I'll let you know as soon as I learn something."

Ten minutes later Nan buzzed Jill. "I finally reached Mr. Lampwerth's housekeeper. She just came back from the dry cleaners and the grocery store. Seems that on Thursday night Mr. Lampwerth insisted she take the whole weekend off starting Friday. He told her not to come back until this morning. She took advantage of the long weekend, left the penthouse at eight o'clock Friday morning, dropped Russell off at the groomer's at nine, and drove to Baltimore to visit her sister. Said her sister's hip was still bothering her from the operation she had a month ago, and that—"

"Nan, get to the point."

"What? Sorry, sometimes I ramble. Anyhow, Lucille returned to the penthouse at eight this morning and figured Mr. Lampwerth had already gone to his office."

"Did he leave her a note or tell her his plans for the weekend?"

"I didn't ask, Ms. Hathaway."

"Well, call her back and ask. And ask her if Russell is there."

Jill stood up and paced the floor until Nan came in the office a few minutes later.

"Lucille said Mr. Lampwerth didn't leave a note and Russell isn't there."

"Get Executive Pet Grooming on the phone, Nan. Never mind, I'll call them myself," Jill said, reaching across her desk for her Rolodex. Jill quickly punched in the number. The receptionist answered on the first ring.

"Yes, Ms. Hathaway, Mr. Lampwerth picked Russell up mid-afternoon on Friday. No, he didn't say anything about taking a trip. Let me connect you with Danny, Russell's groomer," said the receptionist.

"Hello, Ms. Hathaway. You've lost Mr. Lampwerth, I hear." Danny paused, his little attempt at humor lost on Jill. "Mr. Lampwerth deviated a little from his usual routine. Small things, but noticeable to me. After all, I've been grooming Russell for four years."

"Yes, Danny, I know." Jill struggled to keep her voice calm. "Danny, I know you're an observant person, and I would certainly like to hear what you noticed. What can you tell me?"

"Well, like I said, it's small things I noticed. Usually Mr. Lampwerth holds out his arms and Russell jumps right into them and licks him all over his face." Jill grimaced at the thought of anything kissing Lampwerth's pompous, heavily jowled face. "And, you know, I just realized there's another thing he usually does but didn't do Friday," Danny added.

"Please go on, Danny." Jill frowned and drummed her perfectly manicured dark red fingernails on her mahogany Chippendale desk.

"Mr. Lampwerth is so careful with Russell that after every grooming, and even though he's often commented on what a meticulous job I do. . . . "

Jill wanted to scream "Enough!" Instead, she said, "Yes, Danny. Please get to the point."

"Well, he always insists on sticking two fingers under Russell's collar before he takes him home. After seeing Mr. Lampwerth do this a few times, I asked why, and he said he wanted to make sure if the collar ever gets caught on anything there's enough slack for Russell to yank his head out. Mr. Lampwerth didn't do that on Friday. But you can bet I checked it before I took Russell out to him. I always do."

Jill thanked Danny and hung up. If only Robert were here instead of cruising somewhere in the South Pacific. She felt a twinge of envy for the female who had surely accompanied Lampwerth International's V.P. *So I'm jealous. I admit it. Now get over it.*

She buzzed Nan and said, "Call Mr. Reeves' secretary. Tell her to locate him and have him call me immediately. Tell her it's urgent. Then call all the hospitals in D.C., and have someone else check the dog pounds and veterinary hospitals."

Jill sipped her coffee. Then she phoned the police.

CHAPTER SIX

On the far side of Spawning Run, Jimmy Ray and Clyde faced their angry boss.

"You fools! What in the hell were you thinking?" He shut off the speedboat's engine.

"Boss, we didn't have no choice. First thing we heared wuz his car horn, then he wuz unlockin' the front door. Didn't mean to kill 'im, though. Just wuz gonna knock 'im out, tie 'im up, and wait fer you. His head weren't very hard." Jimmy Ray grinned.

"Jimmy Ray's right," said Clyde. "He had to kill the dog, too."

"What dog? You didn't say anything about a dog." The boss scowled.

"The dude had a mean little dog with 'im. Tried to bite us. Chased 'im 'round the yard for maybe ten minutes. Then when Clyde here finally got a holt of his collar, the damn fool dog slipped his head clean out of it. Had to shoot 'im then." Jimmy Ray spit a wad of tobacco into the water and grinned. "Almost hit Clyde instead of the dog."

"Where'd you bury him? And the man's body, where is it?" He flicked a dragonfly off the boat's gunwale.

"We didn't find the dog, but he's dead all right. Jimmy Ray shoots real good, and we heard the dog holler," said Clyde as he pulled a beer from the cooler.

Jimmy Ray snickered. "And that fancy-dressin' city slicker's taken care of good. We dumped his body in the deep end of the cove. Used ski rope to tie a coupla cinderblocks to 'im, pushed 'im off the side of the boat into the water, and kersplash, he was gone." Jimmy Ray reached for a beer.

The boss grabbed Jimmy Ray's wrist. "Where's the man's car?"

"We drove it way in the woods, piled brush on it. Ain't nobody gonna find it," said Jimmy Ray. *And in a coupla weeks or a month when there ain't nobody lookin' for that car, I'll slip back in them woods and git it. Strip it for parts, or sell the whole thing to a dealer I know who won't ask no questions.* He rubbed his wrist when the boss released his grip.

"We got us another problem. Some woman's staying at that house over there." Clyde pointed to 210 Spawning Run Road.

"The woman, is she a good looking, classy blonde?"

"Yeah. And she's got a big black dog with her," said Jimmy Ray.

"Ah, must be the old man's daughter. I don't think she'll be here long, but find out. We can't have any more delays." He put his hand on the ignition.

"There's more, though. She's got the necklace."

"The one you idiots dropped in the lake?"

"If you mean the necklace Snake lost, yeah." Clyde didn't appreciate being called an idiot. After all, he'd warned the boss not to hire a crazy boozer like Snake who couldn't be trusted. When on a drinking binge, Snake would blab everything he knew. Just plain couldn't hold his liquor.

"How do you know she has the necklace?"

"Boss, we wuz watching her through the glasses. We saw her wearing it," said Jimmy Ray. "She looked mighty hot in her bathin' suit with all them jewels hangin' 'round her purty little neck." He gulped his beer. "Woulda paid her a nice little gitting-to-know-you visit, but she had that big dog with her."

"We won't know for sure it's our necklace until we see it up close, though," Clyde cautioned.

"Well now, guess we've got some work to do," said their boss. "And Jimmy Ray, stay away from the woman."

When Jimmy Ray frowned, the boss said, "Hey, you better leave her alone! For the time being, anyhow. Chances are the two of you will get much better acquainted before this is all over." He turned the key and the boat's engine roared to life.

Jimmy Ray grinned and blew a kiss across the cove.

CHAPTER SEVEN

Jill Hathaway lit a Salem cigarette, took two stress-relieving puffs, then ground it out in the ashtray. The two cops sitting across the desk from her looked at each other and grinned. They were no help.

"So how long has this J. Melton Lampwerth IV been missing?" asked one of the cops.

"He was last seen Friday afternoon," answered Jill. She pulled another cigarette from the pack and lit it.

"Is he married? Have any family?" asked the other cop.

"No, he's divorced, lives alone in the penthouse on the top floor of this building." She put out her cigarette.

"You say his dog, a Jack Russell terrier I believe you said, is missing, too?"

"Yes. Both were last seen Friday afternoon at Executive Pet Grooming."

"You want to know how I see it, Ms. Hathaway? Mr. Lampwerth is an adult, rich, owns his own company. He can do anything he damn well pleases so long as it's legal. There's no evidence of a crime here. My guess is that he's with some sexy woman and has lost track of time. I bet he'll soon return a much happier and relaxed man." He winked at the other cop. "But we'll file a missing person's report just in case." He jotted something in his notebook, and said, "I'll let you know if we hear anything." Then the two men left the office.

Jill fumed. The cops had talked to her in a patronizing, you're-just-an-hysterical-woman type of voice. She didn't like them. She despised their uncaring attitude and lack of professionalism, but she hoped they were right. As irritating as Lampwerth was, the company needed him. Jill reached for another cigarette, then drew back her hand. *Why did you pick now to disappear, Mr. Lampwerth, just when I've gained the courage to quit smoking again?*

CHAPTER EIGHT

Tuesday, April 20

The phone rang. Aurora leaped out of the queen-size bed, grabbed the receiver, and plopped back down on the bed. On the nightstand, the old wind-up clock with its comforting tick-tick read 6:45.

"Hello."

"Aurora, I'm so glad I caught you!"

"Carole, is that you?" Aurora sat back up.

"It is."

"How are you?"

"I'm just fine. I figured you'd be at the lake when I saw Wednesday's newspaper. So sorry about your mother, and sorry I couldn't get to the funeral. I would've gone if the service had been at a church here at the lake instead of in Forest, but I was meeting a client, and there just wasn't enough time. I loved Margaret too, you know. She was a true Southern lady. There aren't many left like her." She paused, then said, "Sorry you lost the baby, too. And your dad."

"I know. And thank you." Aurora picked a loose thread from the bedspread, dropped it in the wastebasket.

The two women chatted for a few minutes and caught up on each other's lives. Carole and Aurora, friends who had attended elementary and high school together, lost touch when they went off to college, but renewed their friendship after graduation. In fact, Carole was one of the six bridesmaids in Aurora and Sam's wedding. Even though they didn't see each other often, they still remained close friends.

Aurora smiled. She thought she knew the reason for this phone call. "Have you and Fred set a date yet, Carole?"

"Promise me, Aurora, that after this one conversation about Fred, you'll never mention his name to me again."

"What?"

"You heard me. Promise?"

"Yes, I promise. But what happened? Weren't you two engaged?"

"We were. I'd been dating him, loving him, thinking of him for over a year and a half. Had a gorgeous engagement ring, a one-carat diamond encircled with emeralds." Carole continued in a softer voice, "It was all a lie. Everything he told me was a lie. He's married, Aurora! Can you believe that?"

"How did you find out?"

"I went to Bedford with a girlfriend of mine to see a musical production by the Little Town Players. There he was. Two rows in front of me. With his lovey-dovey wife."

"How did you know she was his wife? Maybe she was a sister or a business acquaintance." King rested his head on the bed and looked at Aurora with pleading eyes. She rubbed his head.

"Nope. I saw a wedding band and a huge diamond on her left hand when she shooed a fly off the back of her neck. Then I asked the lady sitting in front of me if she knew them. She said yeah, that this was the first time in a couple of months that she'd seen them. Said they used to be in a couple's bridge club together. After I recovered from the shock, I asked her to reach over and tap Fred on the shoulder. When he turned around and saw me, I thought he would choke on his own spit. Wish he had. Anyhow, I just stared at him, didn't smile, cocked my finger at him like a gun, and mouthed 'Gotcha!'"

Aurora struggled into her robe and asked, "When did this happen?"

"About eight months ago."

"I'm so sorry."

"Don't be. I was a big fool, but believe me—it won't happen again."

"Did you give the ring back to him?"

"Girl friend, do you think I'm daft? Of course not."

"I was hoping you'd say that.

"I'd love to see what he looks like. Do you have a picture of him?"

"I had lots of pictures, but I ripped them all up. Now I'm changing the subject. Aurora, I called to talk over an idea with you. Do you have a few minutes?"

"Certainly. What's up? Do you want me to help you murder Fred? Maybe stick matches under all his toenails, light 'em and watch him burn in agony? Or slather honey all over his body and stake him out in the broiling sun near a big ant hill?"

"I wish." Carole giggled. "Remember how much fun we had at the lake in our younger days? I'll always have fond memories of our canoe adventures, especially the time we capsized and lost our paddles. We grabbed hold of the canoe and held on for nearly an hour until your mom rescued us in the speed boat."

Aurora laughed, remembering how her mother had fussed over them and insisted they take long, hot baths. When the girls finally climbed out of the tub, Margaret fed them homemade chicken soup to ward off pneumonia. And it was summertime.

"You and your parents made me feel so welcome. Maybe that's why I've always loved Smith Mountain Lake.

"Anyhow, a small real estate agency went up for sale here and I bought it five months ago. I'm beginning to think I lost all sanity, but I needed a challenge to get my mind off Fred." Carole sighed. "I'm taking a big chance; the company was nearly bankrupt when I bought it. That's why I'm calling. I need your help. Aurora, will you produce a promo for me? Please?"

"Carole, if it were any other time. . . . "

"Aurora, please say yes."

"Darn it, Carole, I hate this, but I just can't get involved in something else right now. As much as I'd love to do it for you, I have to say no. I hate to, especially to you, but I finished a promotional piece for a town in North Carolina only days before Mother died, and I'm dog-tired. I'm trying to organize her legal affairs, and many loose ends still need tidying up. I'm not ready to tackle a new assignment. Besides, I don't have all the necessary equipment with me. I'm sure there are many other qualified people around who could do it for you."

"There's something I haven't told you, Aurora." The smile in Carole's voice disappeared.

Aurora groaned. This sounded like the Carole she knew so well, the Carole who never laid all her cards on the table at the same time. Aurora waited.

"I've invested every single cent I have in this agency. A good commercial that I could use as a promo would really help. You know, a CD or DVD, something I can send to prospective clients, a clip to put on my web site, maybe even a spot on TV. I don't want a whole travelogue; just a three-minute piece would do. Guess I was hoping that since we're good friends, you'd give me a price break. Besides, you're the best in the business. And I need it in one to two weeks."

"Carole, that's not much time for anybody to put something together." She stuck her feet in her slippers.

"You're right, but I'm desperate. I need to recoup some of my investment as soon as possible. And that means contracting rentals and sales for this year if I can. I know it's pretty late for this summer, but I need to try. And a promo might get me some business for the fall season." Carole continued. "If anyone can do it, you can. You'd have complete control, and I'd help you get your resources together. I'd even drive to Roanoke and rent whatever equipment you need. Won't you do this for me? Please?"

"Carole, I'm exhausted mentally and physically. It's not a good time for me. I'm so sorry." Aurora paused. She felt so guilty. "Can we get together for dinner some night, though?" she asked.

"I'm disappointed, Aurora, but I guess I understand. And yes, we can get together for dinner. We're still friends. I just hoped we could be business associates, too," she said as she hung up.

Relieved when Aurora finally opened the kitchen door, King dashed outside.

An hour after her conversation with Carole, Aurora phoned Sam. She heard voices in the background when he answered. "Sounds like you're in the middle of a meeting, but I really needed to talk to you," she blurted.

"Sam, I'm not returning to Augusta this week. I'm worn out and emotionally drained. The lake can heal me if I give it a chance. Tell Harold Johns that I won't be there for dinner Saturday night. Okay?" Then she told him about Carole and the job offer.

"That sounds like a job made for you, Susie-Q. When do you start?"

"I don't." She could almost feel Sam's disappointment. "I turned her down. Sam, I'm just not ready for more responsibility in my life right now. Besides, the promo needs to be completed in one or two weeks. And it would mean I couldn't go back to Augusta soon." She stared out the window at the lake.

"You'll regret it if you don't do this for Carole. Aurora, you love Smith Mountain Lake. You've always said you'd like to produce a lake travelogue. And a promo piece wouldn't take nearly the time a travelogue would require. You could do this. You told me once that when you're agonizing over a decision, you ask yourself if you will be sorry if you don't do it. You need to ask yourself that question now."

"My laptop with all the necessary software is in Augusta."

"I can send your laptop and any other equipment you need by overnight delivery."

Aurora didn't reply. She needed time to rest, to mourn, to heal, to gain control. She liked Carole a lot, but darn her, why had she called now?

Sam continued, "And it would be a good distraction for you. Sure, you'll have some down times while you're working on it, but you'll miss your mother for the rest of your life. Just like you do your dad." *Just like we both miss our unborn child.* Then he added in the low, sexy voice she loved so much, the voice that never failed to send goose bumps racing over her entire body, "And I'll come for visits every weekend if you want me to."

"Sam, I'm too tired to argue any longer. Maybe you're right. That's probably the advice I would offer someone else. I'll call Carole right now. She offered to drive to Roanoke to rent what I need, but I'd rather use my own stuff. I'll work up a list of everything I want you to send me and e-mail it to you." She opened the drawer and pulled out a pencil and note pad. "I know you're having a business dinner with Harold and Melinda on Saturday, but would you please come to the lake the following weekend?"

The doorbell rang before Sam could respond. Over the din of King's barking, Aurora said goodbye and opened the door. A man wearing tan overalls with "Tom's Tidy Lawn & Lake Service" and "Biff" stitched in yellow on a dark green patch stood on the porch.

"Good morning, ma'am. Are you Ms. Harris?" He kept a wary eye on King who stood between them.

"Yes, I am. Are you here to cut the grass?"

"Yes, ma'am. I came to work on the yard and noticed your car. Didn't want to startle you none, so I figured I'd just better let you know I was here. Actually, I was surprised to see your car; the Service thought y'all would be away longer."

"I came back Thursday for my Mother's funeral. I don't know how long I'll be staying. Could you continue doing the yard work? It would be a big help to my husband and me."

"Yes, ma'am, the Service will be happy for the business." Biff walked off to start the push mower.

"By the way, the pot of pansies on the dock is a really nice touch!" Aurora hollered after him. Then she closed the door and phoned Carole.

"I'll do it. That is, if you still want me," Aurora said. Carole shrieked with delight.

"I think videotape will be fine for what you want. Then, if you wish, I can transfer the tape to CD and DVD. If I use 16mm motion picture film, the price will jump considerably. Is that agreeable with you?"

"Videotape will be perfect," said Carole.

After discussing Aurora's requirements, Carole agreed to have a boat with guide Luke Stancill at Aurora's dock by 2:00 that afternoon. Even though the day had started out dreary and rainy, the sky was now clear. Carole and Aurora both knew good weather was iffy this time of year. With such a tight time schedule, they couldn't waste a minute.

Pad and pencil in hand, Aurora listed items she needed to take with her on the boat: video camera, 35mm camera, digital camera, tripods, lenses, map of the lake with locations of marinas and other points of interest marked, binoculars, water bottle. She admitted to herself that Sam was right. She could feel her creative juices beginning to flow.

Her stomach growled so she stopped and made lunch. King whined and scratched on the front door. Aurora let him out while she chewed on a peanut butter and peach jam sandwich. "Okay, King, go. Just don't be gone too long."

Years ago Aurora had been familiar with much of the shoreline; she'd explored many of the coves by canoe or kayak from above Hales Ford Bridge all the way to the dam. But new businesses and residential communities had cropped up since she and Sam had moved to Augusta, and the shoreline had changed. Taking advantage of the time remaining before the guide arrived, she opened the phone book to the yellow pages and jotted down names and addresses of waterfront locations unfamiliar to her. She would ask the guide about these.

Deep in thought, she opened the door at the sound of King's "Here-I-am-let-me-in" bark. In he trotted, followed by a bedraggled dog hobbling on three legs. The small dog's short coat was matted with burrs and mud, and his ribs were plainly visible.

"King, what in the world have you brought home?"

Aurora knelt down to get a closer look at the dog and King licked Aurora's face with his big, sloppy tongue. Then he whined and nudged the filthy dog.

Gently she ran her hands along the dog's body. He shook, and several times he whimpered and winced when she touched a sensitive spot, but never once did he growl or snap. "Hey, little guy, what happened to you?" She decided to call him Little Guy.

"Time for a bath, Little Guy." Aurora carefully picked him up and carried him to the laundry tub. He shuddered when she cleaned the dried blood and mud from the large wound running along the left side of his body. She dried him gently with a thick towel, poured peroxide on a cotton ball, and dabbed at the inflamed and oozing cuts.

Aurora studied Little Guy as he sprawled on the bed of clean towels she'd piled up for him. He was mostly white with brown ears and brown around his dark, almond-shaped eyes. He had a large irregular tan spot on his right side. He had no collar or any visible identification tattoos. Little Guy ate a piece of dry dog food from Aurora's hand and wagged his stubby tail.

Aurora smiled as she gently stroked Little Guy's head. She'd always liked Jack Russell terriers.

CHAPTER NINE

Hallelujah! At last arrangements to fly Robert Reeves back to Washington were complete. Ten days ago he'd left on a cruise and wasn't due back for another week. Jill had a devil of a time locating him; he'd neglected to leave the name of the cruise line. Not like it used to be. Six years ago she would have had no trouble knowing his whereabouts. In fact, she probably would have been with him. Only late last night had she been able to reach his sister-in-law and find out how to get in touch with him.

By age eight, Jill knew she wanted to go to college right after high school, but that wasn't an option. She would still break into sweats when she remembered the sweltering summer day her Poppa came home with the precious, newborn baby girl. Jill and her brothers and sisters had kept watch all day, each hoping to be the one to yell, "Momma's home!" Jill, sitting astride a limb high up in a maple tree, was the first to see their dusty old farm truck turn onto the dirt drive, and she scrambled down and hollered to the other children. But when Poppa drove up and got out of the car, Momma wasn't there—only the baby. In tears, her father had knelt down on the ground, hugged his children close to him, and told them they'd have to be strong, that mother had gone to heaven and wouldn't be coming home.

So at ten, Jill was forced to help raise seven younger siblings. She cooked, cleaned, washed and ironed clothes, bandaged the physical hurts and soothed the emotional ones.

But she never complained. Instead she planned. When the last child graduated from high school, Jill, age twenty-eight, put herself through a community college near her home in upstate New York. After getting an associate's degree in business, she worked as a secretary while attending night school. By the time she'd earned a B.A. in business management, she'd moved up the professional ladder. Then she left New York and joined Lampwerth International.

And met Robert Reeves.

She and Robert were attracted to each other the first day they met. Soon they spent every spare minute with each other, even took vacations together. Jill, age thirty-two, and Robert, eight years older, fell madly and passionately in love. Then J. Melton Lampwerth IV enforced his company's no-dating policy. Robert, already vice-president of the firm, begged Jill to resign her position and marry him. They didn't need the money, he'd said. But she said no. She'd dreamed too long and sacrificed too much to throw it all away. She vowed to put her hard-earned education to use. After only two years with the company, Jill earned Lampwerth's trust and respect. She soon became executive secretary/assistant to the president, number one employee. She remained single and lonely, while Robert became one of D.C.'s most eligible bachelors.

When she finally talked with Robert early this morning, he hadn't seemed the least bit worried about Mr. Lampwerth. "He'll either call you soon or walk through the door any minute," he said. He assured her that Mr. Lampwerth was taking some much needed R&R. Two hours later he called back and instructed Jill to arrange his transportation home to Washington ASAP.

"Why did you change your mind, Robert?"

"I'll tell you when I see you at the airport."

A private helicopter would pluck him from the cruise ship on Wednesday and fly him to a little airport on the Australian coast. From there he'd take a puddle jumper to Sydney, and then catch a commercial flight to D.C., arriving at Reagan National Airport at 7:39 p.m. Thursday. None too soon for Jill.

Nan tapped on the door, then entered Jill's office. She hesitated in front of Jill's desk and fidgeted with her jacket sleeve. "Miss Hathaway, there's something you should know." Jill waited. "Mary Ellen Bagby from accounting said there's a rumor going around that Lampwerth International is broke. She said Mr. Lampwerth and Mr. Reeves have taken all the money and have fled the country together."

"That's absurd. I've talked with Mr. Reeves twice today, will pick him up at the airport Thursday night. So you can tell Mary Ellen Bagby to go to—uh, well, that she is incorrect."

"But what about Mr. Lampwerth, Miss Hathaway? Have you heard from him yet?"

"Nan, I'll be honest with you. I haven't talked with him, and I'm worried. So is Mr. Reeves. But I can tell you this much; Mr. Lampwerth loves Lampwerth International. It's his baby, and he would never steal from the company he started. I'm sure there's an explanation. When Mr. Reeves arrives, we'll get to the bottom of this.

"And now, Nan, I have a stack of work to do and phone calls to make. Please shut the door on your way out."

Jill hoped Robert's presence would squelch the rumors before they spread. She and Robert would consult with the accountant first thing Friday morning. She reached for a cigarette.

CHAPTER TEN

Three short barks from King announced a boat's arrival. Aurora glanced at the waterproof watch Sam had given her two years ago for her birthday—1:50. Good, Luke was punctual, even early, and she liked that. Grabbing her water bottle and slipping her arms into a red, white and green plaid windbreaker, she rushed out the door, onto the deck and down the steps. On ground level, Aurora paused to give King a quick pat, then grabbed the video camera and other equipment. She looped the 35mm and digital cameras over her neck and shoulders. Then she hurried on down the winding path to the dock.

"Hi, I'm Luke Stancill. You must be Aurora." He was young, thirtyish, good-looking with curly brown hair. His big, dark eyes crinkled in the corners when he smiled. He wore faded Levi's, a white turtleneck shirt, and an unzipped red, white and green plaid windbreaker. Both burst out laughing as they realized they wore matching jackets.

"Yes, I'm Aurora, and we both have excellent taste in clothes." She took his steadying hand and stepped into the boat. "Do you mind if King comes? He loves riding in a boat."

"Love to have 'im. He'll add some class." Luke held onto the dock and asked, "Carole told me to drive you around so you could videotape the lake, but what specifically do you want?"

"Good footage of several residential areas like Mountain View Shores, Cedar Key, Mariners Landing, Waverly and Waters Edge, marinas, the State Park, and Hales Ford Bridge would all be great. I'd welcome any ideas you have, too." Aurora handed him her list. "Also some shots of the mountain and dam, the cliffs, wide-water views, and quiet coves. And shooting from Saunders Parkway Marina is an absolute must. Maybe we could even photograph a fisherman reeling in a bass or a striper. I'd really love to get a shot of a bald eagle gliding just above the water and an osprey diving for his dinner. And it would be great if we could find a great blue heron waiting patiently for a fish to swim by."

He laughed. "You don't want much, do you?"

"Well, you asked me, didn't you?"

"Yeah, guess I did. We'd better get moving if we're going to film all that," Luke said, grinning.

Aurora buckled on her life vest and draped one arm over King's neck. The big dog licked her face and the two settled back to enjoy the ride.

"Want a towel?" Luke asked. Aurora laughed.

"How about videotaping the Virginia Dare? She's a paddle wheeler made out-of-state and trucked to Virginia over ten years ago," Luke said.

"Great idea. I'm sure locals know about her, but those unfamiliar with the area could use this information. Do they still run dinner cruises?"

"Yeah. I think they have lunch cruises, too, as well as non-meal related ones. Carole and I took a dinner cruise a few months ago. We both enjoyed it."

Aurora enjoyed working with Luke. He supplied tidbits of local lore about the lake that she either had forgotten or didn't know. She knew the thick forests bordering parts of the lake were home to deer, black bears and bobcats. She hadn't heard that coyotes had moved into the area or that the population of bald eagles had increased in the last ten years.

"I've heard a few reports of mountain lion sightings over near the dam, but I've never seen one," Luke said. He pointed out the vacation homes of a couple of best-selling authors and a former actress, and showed Aurora the area where a record-breaking striper was hooked. "My friend Jim caught it. I think the smile is still on his face."

The afternoon seemed to fly by. At 5:30, Luke suggested they anchor at the mouth of a large cove and wait for the sunset. The wait proved worthwhile. A spectacular bright orange sun shot vivid streaks of red, gold, yellow and gray into the sky. Aurora stretched out across the boat's bow and photographed a sailboat sailing through the sun's reflection in the water.

"Wow! That's what I call a million-dollar shot," she said. Luke agreed.

A ring-ring-ring from Aurora's tote bag interrupted the sunset magic.

"I can't believe you brought a cell phone with you," Luke exclaimed, shaking his head. Grinning sheepishly, Aurora dug in her bag for her phone.

"Hello."

"Aurora, Doc Eggleston here. I've finished checking out Little Guy. He was in pretty bad shape, but he'll make it. He's a feisty one."

Aurora sighed with relief. Little Guy would be okay. Doc said so.

"When can I pick him up?"

"I need to keep him here a couple of days. I think the wound on his side was made by a bullet."

"Somebody shot Little Guy? Are you serious?"

"Yeah, I am. He's a lucky dog; any deeper and the bullet would've done major internal damage. The wound's infected and he's running a fever. I'll call you if there's any change for the worse."

Aurora thanked Doc and told him she'd check on Little Guy in the morning. She hung up and promptly burst into tears. She struggled to regain her composure, then looked sheepishly at Luke.

"Sorry for that. I'm fine now."

"What happened?"

"Around lunch time today, King barked to come in the house. I opened the door and in he trotted with a dirty little dog close behind him. The dog was limping badly. I examined him, then gave him a bath. I could tell he had some nasty wounds on him, so I bundled him in a beach towel and rushed him to Doc Eggleston. I left him there. Didn't want to miss our two o'clock appointment."

"I would've understood, Aurora. I like dogs. What kind is he?"

"A Jack Russell terrier. I call him Little Guy."

On the ride back to Aurora's house, Luke watched Aurora drape her arm around King's neck. The compassion she had for a stray, injured little dog didn't surprise him.

Back at the dock, Aurora and King stepped out of the boat. "Luke, thank you so much for a wonderful and productive afternoon. Thanks to you, I got some great shots."

Luke smiled. "Glad I could help. Do you think you'll need me again?"

"Since you asked, yes. Would you be available to photograph the sunrise tomorrow morning?"

Luke groaned, knowing they'd have to be on the water early, but he liked Aurora and wanted her to get the pictures she needed. Besides, it would help Carole, too, and that's why he became involved in the first place. *Gratis,* of course. Somehow Carole usually managed to involve her friends in all her ventures.

"If you insist. Just don't make a habit of asking me to get up that early. Can you meet me here at 4:30 tomorrow morning?"

"I'll be here. Thanks, Luke." He waved goodbye and pushed off from the dock.

Aurora and King ran up the path to the house—she, energized by creative thoughts of this project; he, by visions of his dinner. Inside, Aurora poured dry, chunky dog food into King's blue and white dog bowl and set it on the floor. *It's really bad when even a dog bowl makes me cry.* She wiped a tear from one eye. Her mother had bought the bowl at Emerson Creek Pottery for Duke, the family's Lab, when

Aurora was fifteen. She shoved thoughts of her mother aside and put the lake tape into the VCR. Too excited to fix a from-scratch meal, she popped a frozen dinner into the microwave and turned on the TV.

As she watched the footage and ate her meal, Aurora paused the tape often to admire several new residential communities. She knew she'd use some of the incredible wide-water mountain-view shots from Saunders Parkway Marina in the promo, as well as shots of the sunset from the same location.

I'll start the piece with a sunrise, then end with a sunset, she decided, but first I need to make an outline. As Aurora watched the video, she paused the tape often to make notes. She knew much editing would be necessary, and she still wanted good footage of a brave soul parasailing 500 feet above the water. Three hours later she stood and stretched, then fixed popcorn dripping with melted butter just the way she liked it. She poured herself a glass of Chablis and thought how glad she was that Sam wasn't here to lecture her about eating all that butter. Aurora continued reviewing the tape and taking notes until bedtime.

She showered and went to bed, but nightmares of calm water suddenly turning into huge waves with dead bodies floating in the lake kept waking her. *Are these dreams premonitions of what will come?* In desperation, she inserted a classical music CD into the player on her nightstand and finally drifted off to sleep.

A gentle nudge and soft growl from King awakened Aurora. Immediately alert, she crept out of bed in the pitch-black room and padded barefoot to the open window overlooking the water. She flicked a switch, and light flooded the entire exterior of the house, boathouse, and dock. A man cursed and a boat roared out of the boathouse.

Exhausted, Aurora went back to bed, but she couldn't sleep. Why had a strange boat entered her boathouse for the second time in a week? She knew that in mid-April the stripers were fair game and fishermen were out en masse, often all night long. But if someone were just fishing, why the profanity when the light came on? And why speed away?

She reached for the telephone to call Sam, then stopped. *Don't be ridiculous, Aurora. It's two-thirty in the morning, Sam is in Augusta, there's nothing he can do. Besides, he doesn't have a suspicious bone in his body, trusts everyone. He'd probably tell me to rein in that big imagination, say there's nothing to worry about.*

"It was probably just a fisherman, King. Let's try to get some sleep."

At 4:25, Aurora and King walked to the lighted dock to wait for Luke. "The water looks different this morning," she said to King.

Sploosh. Splat. Beside the dock and just inside the boathouse, large fish broke the water's surface.

They must be feeding on something to be that active. King growled and the hair stood up on the back of his neck.

"It's okay, King," she laughed. "It's just some carp or stripers. You're not accustomed to being on the dock this early. Me either, thank goodness." She patted her dog, then turned when she heard a boat approaching. Luke waved and pulled up to the dock.

Quickly Aurora passed her cameras and tripods to Luke and stepped into the boat. King, still growling, followed reluctantly.

"What's with him? Did he get up on the wrong side of his dog bed?" Luke asked.

"Looks that way, doesn't it? Actually, neither King nor I slept well last night—a boat paid a quick visit to my boathouse in the middle of the night. I think King's a little miffed that he couldn't go chase them away himself. And when we came down to the dock a few minutes ago, lots of fish were rolling. I guess they were feeding on something or spawning, but King didn't like it. I think he thought that if he showed his displeasure by growling, the fish would leave." Luke and Aurora both laughed.

"You know, don't you, that stripers don't spawn in Smith Mountain Lake," Luke said. "The lake is stocked annually with striped bass fingerlings."

"I know few stripers are able to reproduce here. But they still spawn."

"No, they don't. Aurora, they can't reproduce in this lake."

"But the stripers don't know that, so they go through the *act* of spawning. I've seen it happen many times."

"Aurora, you're a hopeless romantic."

"I know. And I like being that way."

As they motored away from the dock, Aurora opened up her camera bag and removed the video camera, 35mm camera, digital camera and two tripods.

"Don't know if these will help any," said Luke, "but last night I threw together a couple of wooden frames for your tripods." He pointed to the frames already attached to swivel seats.

"How thoughtful, Luke. Thank you. But I'm sure you didn't just 'throw them together.' They look much too sturdy for that." Luke smiled.

Slowly they motored out of the cove and cruised out to the main channel. Luke dropped anchor about 30 feet from shore and offered Aurora a cup of steaming, black coffee from his thermos.

"Thanks. Coffee will taste great right now." She wrapped her chilly hands around the hot cup.

Luke volunteered to shoot with the 35mm camera so Aurora could concentrate on getting pictures with the digital and video cameras. They bolted the video camera onto one of the wooden frames and turned on the cameras. Then they settled back to wait for the sun.

"So, Luke, do you have any other ideas for the promo? I realized last night that I still need a shot of someone parasailing, but can you think of anything else we've missed?" She finished her coffee and set the mug down.

"How about somebody wake boarding?"

"Great idea. Maybe—"

"Look out, Aurora! They're gonna ram us!"

Out of the darkness, a speedboat zoomed straight toward them. At the last second, the speeding boat veered sharply to starboard, missing them by inches. The turbulence created by the boat's wake nearly capsized Luke's smaller craft. Aurora grabbed hold of the seat with one hand and the gunwale with the other. Luke did the same. King, who'd been dozing on the bow, fell overboard. As the surprised dog swam to the side of the boat, Luke reached out, grabbed his collar, and hauled him back in. After examining King for injuries and making sure all equipment was still intact, Luke picked up the two bailers he always kept on board, tossed one to Aurora, and they bailed water from the boat. Both seethed with anger.

"We could've been killed! Why he didn't hit us, I don't know!" cried Aurora as she continued to bail. "He must be crazy. Or drunk. We even had our running lights on. You know he saw us."

"He saw us, all right. And he had no running lights." His thoughts racing, Luke frowned. "Aurora, have you noticed anything strange since you've been here?"

"Well, a few things had been moved around in the house sometime before I arrived last Thursday. One night I thought I heard gun shots, but decided it was a car backfiring or thunder. Oh, I almost forgot—you were with me when Doc Eggleston told me that Little Guy had a gunshot wound. And a boat went in my boathouse a couple of nights ago, and King's been antsy a lot. Last night he woke me, and when I turned on the outside lights I heard cursing, and then a boat shot out of the boathouse. Probably just some fishermen netting stripers illegally, don't you think?"

"You're probably right, but please be extra cautious from now on. And keep King with you at all times, okay?" His concern for Aurora surprised him; he'd just met her yesterday.

Aurora laughed. "I can barely take two steps without King beside me."

"Good." Then he pointed. "Look over there. The sun's rising." Aurora quickly swiveled the video camera into position and started taping.

They returned to Aurora's dock a little after 7:00.

"Luke, would you like to come up to the house? I'll fix us some breakfast."

He grinned. "I'd be an idiot to refuse. Can't resist good home cookin'."

"I'm glad."

Once they were in the house, Aurora said, "Why don't you review the video footage we shot this morning while I fix breakfast. The VCR is over there," Aurora said, pointing in its direction.

"Good idea." Luke removed the tape from the camera, put the tape in the machine, then settled back on the sofa.

Aurora hurried into the kitchen and turned her attention to preparing scrambled eggs, bacon, toast and, her favorite, grits—with puddles of butter, of course.

"Aurora, this is incredible!" Luke cried. "You've gotta come see this now!"

She turned off the gas burner and hurried over to view the TV screen just as Luke finished rewinding the tape. He hit "Play," and they saw the speedboat heading straight for them. Unable to recognize the people on board in the early morning light, they did, however, get a good look at the boat.

"I hadn't turned off the camera!" Aurora exclaimed. "They came so fast that all I thought about was staying in the boat."

"You know, I think those two fools were looking directly at us. Aurora, I don't think this encounter was an accident."

"But why in the world would they want to harm you, Luke?"

"I don't believe I'm their target. I don't want to scare you, but I think they're after you, Aurora. Have you noticed anything else unusual since you've been at the lake?"

Aurora frowned and shrugged her shoulders. "Only what I told you earlier."

"Tell you what. I'll go do the dishes after we eat if you'll think about what I just asked. See if you can remember anything that would cause someone to want to scare you. Make a list of everything that's happened since you arrived on Thursday. And I mean everything. Okay?"

"Okay."

When they finished breakfast, Luke took the dirty dishes to the kitchen and Aurora picked up a pencil and note pad. She thought back to the day she arrived after her mother's funeral, and started writing.

Thursday:
Afternoon- arrived, rescued grebe, found necklace;
Late afternoon- read on dock, watched grebes;
Early evening- back up to house, fed King, retrieved book from dock, saw boat go in/out of boathouse, Sam called;
Evening- read book.
Friday:
Morning- faced memories and "ghosts" in basement, saw picture frames Dad made, wrote thank-you notes;
Afternoon- wrote thank-you notes;
Evening- read book, heard noise that sounded like gun shots or car backfiring.
Saturday:
Morning- call from Sam, wrote thank-you notes;
Afternoon- stayed inside, read novel;
Sunday:
Morning- went to church, St. Stephen's, Forest;
Afternoon- ate lunch with old friends from church, went Jefferson Choral Society concert in Lynchburg;
Evening- played with King, talked to Sam, looked at old photo albums, cried a little.
Monday:
Morning- call from Sam, wrote thank-you notes;
Afternoon- canoed, boat with woman and man came to dock (woman wants to breed female with King).
Tuesday:

61

*Morning- call from Carole about promo, called Sam,
Biff came, Little Guy appeared, took Little Guy to vet;
Afternoon- went with Luke to shoot scenes of lake,
made plans for shooting sunrise Wed. a.m. early;
Night- awakened by King, saw boat leave boathouse.*
<u>Wednesday</u>:
*Morning- met Luke at dock, nearly rammed by boat,
videotaped sunrise, reviewed tape.*

Aurora twisted a strand of her hair as she contemplated what she'd written. She had talked with Sam every day; canoed once; twice she'd been with Luke.

"Except for boats being in my boathouse a couple of nights, there isn't anything on this list that would warrant an attack on me." Aurora paused, then added in a teasing tone, "Although you and I have 'been together' twice. Do you have a jealous significant other, perhaps?" she called into the kitchen where Luke was finishing the breakfast dishes.

"Actually, I do. I'm almost engaged to a great gal, but she isn't the jealous type." Then he said, brown eyes twinkling, "But she's never seen you, either."

Aurora blushed. But she said only, "Thank you for doing the dishes. It wasn't necessary."

"I do 'em at my place all the time. Kind of a habit, I guess.

"Aurora, is this your husband in the picture with you?"

"The one on the wall by the kitchen door?"

"Yeah."

"Yes, that's Sam."

"Who's the couple in the photograph on the kitchen counter?"

"My parents. Both died within the last three months."

"I'm sorry. What was your dad's name?"

"Jack Anderson. Mother's name was Margaret. Why do you ask? Did you know them?"

Luke dried his hands on the kitchen towel and stepped into the living room. He dropped down onto the chair across from Aurora and stared into her eyes. "I met your dad once."

"You knew him?"

"Not exactly." He swallowed. "I'm the diver who recovered his body."

Aurora gasped. Luke moved over to the sofa beside her and put his arm around her shoulder.

"I'm so sorry. I shouldn't have told you." He stroked her hair.

"No, I'm glad you were the one who found him. He would have liked you, Luke."

Pulling a tissue from her pocket, she dabbed at her eyes and looked at him. "What do you think happened to Dad? Do you think he killed himself?"

"Is that what the authorities said?"

"At first, yes. Then they said 'accidental death by drowning' when they couldn't conclusively prove suicide. I'm positive he didn't kill himself. It took a while, but a few days ago I finally accepted that Dad's death was accidental. I had a hard time coming to that decision because Dad was always so careful in a boat. What do you think?"

Luke frowned. How could he explain to this still-grieving lady the feelings he had when he saw her dad's body suspended from the anchor rope? Would it do her any good to hear that he thought Jack's death was neither a suicide nor an accident?

"Aurora, I don't know what to think. I've got to go. Please think hard about what could have caused this morning's attack. Keep your doors locked and King with you. I'll report the incident to the cops. Call me if you need me. I've gotta go, Aurora."

"But you must have noticed—"

Luke smiled and waved goodbye as he hurried down the path to the dock.

A few minutes later Aurora heard his boat start as he motored out of the cove. *Wonder what his girl looks like? Probably a real knock-out.*

King whined at the kitchen door. "Okay, boy, go on out. I need to relax, too. I'll join you in a minute."

Aurora put on a black two-piece bathing suit and picked up a big green beach towel. *Don't know why I keep taking a towel to the dock. Dad drowned in the lake. There's no way I'm going swimming in that water.* She tossed the towel on the bed and walked out on the deck. When she saw King swimming near the boathouse, she smiled. *Bet he's trying to catch the fish we saw earlier this morning, just like he did when he was a puppy.*

After navigating the path to the dock, she unlocked the storage shed and pulled out a life jacket and paddle. *An hour in the canoe is just what I need to unwind. And maybe this time I'll be lucky and find the grebes' nest.*

Aurora stepped carefully into the canoe, tossed the life jacket on the floor, and shoved off with the paddle.

"Darn, I forgot my camera," she said aloud. She looked up at the house and groaned. "Well, I'm not trudging back up that hill. If I find the grebes, I'll come back and get the camera."

"King, want to go for a canoe ride?" King turned his head to look at her, then resumed dog-paddling near the shore. "Guess that's a no. I'll be back in a little while. Don't get into trouble."

Aurora dug her paddle deep in the water and pulled hard. Her spirits rose as she skimmed across the blue-green water. *There's nothing in this lake to be afraid of. Dad's death was accidental; the lake didn't kill him.* She swerved to avoid a floating log. *Whew, that was close. I'd hate to hit a log that big with a canoe. I'd capsize for sure, and the water is still too cold for a swim. I need to pay more attention to my surroundings.* She slowed down, shortened her strokes.

Something white bobbed in the water ahead of her. She paddled up beside it and pulled up a large piece of Styrofoam. An empty plastic bottle floated near the shoreline and she scooped that up, too. Picking up litter when she could, Aurora continued paddling close to shore in hopes of spotting the grebes' nest. After forty-five minutes, a dented plastic cooler, three McDonald's drink cups, cigarette wrappers, more plastic bottles, short pieces of lumber, and a couple of small logs littered the floor of the canoe.

"What's wrong with people? Don't they care about the lake or the wildlife around here?" she said when she saw a plastic six-pack soft drink holder, its holes still intact. "A bird could get stuck in that. Some people make me so mad!"

Aurora jerked her head up when she heard a squawk from the bank. Standing on one leg, a great blue heron watched her. Aurora smiled. "Hey, there. I think you agree with me." The heron flapped his wings. "I'll go. Sorry to disturb you."

Aurora paddled across the cove to her dock. "King, where are you?" King answered with a high-pitched bark.

"King?" She paddled around to the other side of the boathouse. King swam near the shore, his back to her.

"King, come!" The Lab barked, but refused to obey.

"I don't know what you've found, but leave it. Come! Now!" King ignored her.

"If you're eating another dead fish, you're going to be in big trouble!"

Aurora was puzzled. It wasn't like King to ignore a command from her. She maneuvered the canoe closer to him. On the shore, branches, logs and other debris were piled on top of each other for several feet up the bank. Tangled clumps of pine and cedar branches dangled in the lake.

A lot of this mess probably washed up during heavy rains. I think Carole said the lake's had more rainfall than usual this year.

She watched as King continued to tug on something in the water. Aurora couldn't see what interested him, but since he wanted it so badly. . . . She leaned over as far as she dared. Sticking one arm through the brush and into the water, she grabbed hold of King's prize and pulled. The canoe rocked wildly.

"What in the world have you found? It feels like. . . ."

The great blue heron wading the shallow water across the cove flapped his huge wings and took flight as a high-pitched scream from Aurora shattered the stillness. The canoe capsized and she screamed again.

Is this how Dad died? Will I die, too?

Fighting to the water's surface, she struggled to free herself from the human body floating face up inches from her face. The nostril-searing stench enveloped her as she tried to shove it away.

CHAPTER ELEVEN

"Ms. Hathaway, Mr. Beale's on his way up. That okay with you? He says it's urgent."

Jill adjusted the cuffs of her butter-colored silk blouse and smoothed down her straight, knee-length navy skirt. "That's fine, Nan. Tell Louis to come on in when he arrives." Picking up the papers she'd been working on, she tapped the ends on the desktop to straighten them and laid the stack aside.

Closing the door softly behind him, Louis Beale entered the office. "Good morning, Ms. Hathaway. How are you today?"

"Hi, Louis. I'm well, thank you. Hope you are, too. Please sit down. I was planning to phone you later today. There's a rumor circulating that funds are missing. Is it true?"

He sat down in one of the tapestry-covered antique chairs and pulled a thick folder from his black leather briefcase. "I'm afraid so. These records show that someone's been embezzling funds for several years, Ms. Hathaway. The person was quite clever, but the proof's here. Hate to report it now when Mr. Lampwerth's missing and all, but couldn't sit on it any longer."

Jill studied the young accountant while he showed her the records. At first glance he looked like an average recent college graduate. Black wavy hair barely tickled his shirt collar, silver wire-framed glasses sat just a little too low on his nose, and his khaki suit bagged fashionably away from his lean, hard body. Passion shone in his violet-blue, intelligent eyes. Elizabeth Taylor eyes, she thought, as she sat across the desk from him. Shame to waste them on a man.

She'd hired him seven months ago after old Mr. Tinsley, who came on board way back when Mr. Lampwerth started the company, had a fatal heart attack. Louis graduated from Harvard just four years ago and had already earned a sterling reputation. Lampwerth International was lucky to get him. Jill hoped he'd stay. She knew that most of the young, single female employees, and even some of the married ones, hoped he'd stay, too.

If I were ten years younger. . . .

"In fact, I discussed it with him last Thursday."

Jill snapped back to the present. "You talked with him when?"

"On Thursday evening, last week, oh, I'd say around six-thirty. Let me tell you, he was not thrilled with what I had to say. Turned red in the face, and his eyes got that cold-steel look that makes most people around here tremble. But not I. I was sure of myself; had the facts right there in front of me."

"So what happened?"

"He took all the papers from me, said he'd study them overnight. Told me to leave and not mention this to anyone or—and his eyes narrowed even more when he said it—he'd fire me. I think he would have, too." He hesitated, then admitted, "Maybe I shouldn't have done it, but I believe in covering my backside. Before I went to his office, I made copies of everything." He tapped the folder in his lap. "Got them right here."

"Do you think Mr. Lampwerth's the embezzler?"

"No, no, not at all. Wasn't sure who it was when he and I talked. But I can tell you this: it certainly made Mr. Lampwerth angry. Don't know if it was because he couldn't believe anyone would steal from his company, or if he thought I was accusing him. Anyway, he told me to leave, then stormed out of his office with all the papers, and that's the last time I saw him."

Beale kept quiet for a minute, weighing the pros and cons of telling her more. Then he said, "I believe the embezzler is Mr. Reeves."

"Mr. Reeves is the embezzler?" He nodded. "Then show me what you have, Louis," she said. She thought she might throw up. *I can't be hearing this. It can't be true. Not Robert.*

CHAPTER TWELVE

Aurora kicked again. Her left foot caught in the tattered shirt. She pushed the bloated body hard with her right hand. The body brushed her leg and she screamed again.

She struggled in the cold, deep water. Land wasn't far away, but she was so cold. She wished she'd put the life jacket on instead of tossing it in the canoe. *Lord, help me!*

She made it to shore and struggled over riprap. Fighting nausea, Aurora stumbled up the path toward the house. Only when she reached the top of the hill did she pause to catch her breath and turn for one quick look down at the lake.

"No, King!" she yelled. Still in the water, King towed the body toward the dock.

"Leave it!" King stopped swimming and looked at her.

"Come! Now!" He looked once at his treasure, then swam to shore and trotted to Aurora.

"You're drenched. I don't want you in the house, but right now I have no choice. I can't have you down there with that—that thing."

Inside, Aurora grabbed the phone and dialed 911. *Lord, I'm so cold. That towel I didn't expect to need would feel good right now.* She wrapped her mother's afghan around her and shouted into the phone's mouthpiece.

"Hurry! There's a dead body floating in the lake!"

"Did you say there's a body in the lake?" asked the dispatcher.

"Yes! Please send someone immediately."

"Is your address 210 Spawning Run Road?"

"Yes!"

"Someone from the sheriff's office will arrive soon. Please stay. . . . "

"Hurry!" Aurora slammed down the phone.

She dialed Sam's office in Augusta as she hurried to the kitchen for a drink. She tried to sip water, but her hand shook. *Why doesn't he answer?* Visions of the body sent her running to the bathroom, her hand covering her mouth.

The nausea over, she brushed her teeth and took off her wet bathing suit. After dressing in gray sweat pants and sweat shirt, she tried Sam again—still no answer. Will I ever be warm again? she wondered as she dialed Carole.

"Hey, Aurora. I just talked to Luke. He told me about the near boat collision early this morning. Are you. . . . ?"

"Carole, there's a dead body in the lake! I pulled on something that King found in the water. It was a body! Oh, God! It was horrible! And then the canoe capsized and I fell on top of the body. And my foot got caught in the shirt. It was horrible. I can't get the sight and smell out of my head!"

"I'm coming over right now. Have you called the police?"

"Yes, they're on their way. Luke doesn't know about this. Would you call him for me?"

"Of course."

Aurora paced as she waited for the police and Carole to arrive, then remembered she hadn't checked the answering machine. The machine signaled three new messages.

Praying Sam had phoned, she pushed the "play" button and heard a dial tone. The caller hadn't left a message.

The second message, from Doc Eggleston, asked her to phone him. *Little Guy, please be okay.* Hoping for good news, she dialed Doc.

"This is Aurora Harris. I'm returning Doc's call," Aurora said when the receptionist answered the phone.

"Oh, Ms. Harris. Um, yes, Dr. Eggleston's tried to reach you."

"Do you know how Little Guy's doing?"

"Um, I'm afraid I really can't say. You'd have to talk to the doctor."

"Well, may I talk to him then?"

"He was in surgery a little while ago—an emergency with one of our patients—and I don't know if he's finished."

"Can you check?"

"It could be a while. Might be better if the doctor calls you when he gets chance."

"Is Little Guy the patient he's operating on?"

"I'm sorry. I really can't say."

Aurora felt the fear rising, fear that Little Guy wouldn't make it. *I don't think I could stand it if he died.* In a small voice, she said to the receptionist, "Will you please go see if Doc's out of surgery? I'll stay on the line." She chewed on her bottom lip. "Please."

"Well, okay, but it could be a few minutes."

Three minutes passed. Aurora sat down, then stood back up. She paced the floor and watched the clock. Five minutes now. *Why's it taking so long just to see if Doc's still in surgery?*

"Aurora." Doc Eggleston's voice on the phone caused her to jump. "I'm glad you called. Little Guy's improving fast, you can pick him up tomorrow afternoon."

"Thank goodness!" Relief filled her voice. "That's great news, Doc."

"I thought you'd be happy." Doc paused, then said, "And guess what I found. He's such a nice dog, obviously has excellent bloodlines, and someone cared enough to neuter him. So I checked him with my microchip scanner. And *voila!* There's a microchip imbedded in his neck. We're tracking down his owner right now."

"Thanks, Doc. I appreciate all you've done for him. I'll pick Little Guy up tomorrow afternoon," and she hung up the phone.

Emotions ran through Aurora. *Didn't take me long to get attached.* She glanced over at King snoring softly as he slept on the well-worn Oriental rug in front of the fireplace. His legs twitched. *Probably dreaming of chasing a rabbit. Or pulling on a body.* She felt the nausea rising again and forced herself to think of Little Guy and the people who'd lost him. She knew how distraught she'd be if she lost King.

She heard tires crunch on the gravel drive. Moments later Carole, stylishly dressed in a tan linen pants suit and lime-green silk sweater, burst into the house. King rushed to greet her.

"King, down. You're wet. Don't jump on Carole." Aurora grabbed his collar.

"Are you okay, Aurora?" Carole asked as she leaned over and patted King's head. "I came as fast as I could."

"I'm okay, Carole. Thanks for coming."

"Are you hungry? I'll fix us some lunch," Carole said, hurrying toward the kitchen.

"You must be joking. Right now I don't even want to think about food, much less eat anything," Aurora said. She could feel her stomach churning again.

"How about a soothing cup of hot tea, then? It'll settle your stomach and your nerves."

"That would be nice, Carole. Thank you. The tea's in the cabinet over the stove."

Outside, brakes squealed as two vehicles overshot the driveway entrance. Aurora peered out the window in time to see a police car back up, then turn into her drive. Two uniformed men stepped onto the front porch as Aurora opened the door.

"Good morning, ma'am. I'm Field Lieutenant Conner, Ian Conner. This is Sergeant Joe Johnson."

"Hey, ma'am. Pleased to meetcha." Sergeant Johnson tipped his hat.

"You called a little while ago about a dead body in the lake?" asked Lieutenant Conner.

Aurora ushered the two deputies inside and, looking at her watch, replied, "Yes, I called ages ago, at least it seems like it. There's a dead man floating in the water. I fell on top of him."

"Have you called the game warden?"

"No. Should I have?"

"It depends on whether or not the body is from a boat. Are you familiar with Smith Mountain Lake?"

"Yes, I lived in this house for years. Before I married and moved away."

"Then you're probably well aware of the unusual law enforcement arrangements here. On the water itself, any one of the three counties' law enforcement agencies or the game wardens can be involved."

"Yes, I heard that years ago, but I forgot about it. I've never needed the police before this."

"Tell you what, Ms. Harris. Just tell us what happened and we'll take it from there."

"Okay." She sat on the sofa and, with shaking hand, took a sip of the peppermint tea Carole handed her. She pointed to King. "My dog was trying to get something that was caught under piles of brush at the water's edge. When I leaned over to help, my canoe capsized." She swallowed. "I fell on top of a dead body."

The deputies looked at each other. "Where 'bouts was the body?" asked Sergeant Johnson.

"About a hundred feet to the left of my boathouse and dock. Nestled against the shore."

"We'll go check it out," said Conner. "You try to relax. Come on, Johnson. Let's find us a body."

"Did you hear him? 'Try to relax,' he said. Is he kidding?" Aurora said to Carole after the deputies left the house. Still queasy, she dialed Sam again. No answer. She sat back down and sipped more of the tea. "Thanks again for the tea, Carole. And for being here."

"You're welcome. Ready for a second cup?"

"Not yet, maybe in a few minutes." She set the cup down on the coffee table and walked to a window that overlooked the waterfront. "How can the lake be so clear and calm when there's a dead man floating in it, Carole? I feel like this isn't real, like I'm watching a horror movie. And what's taking the deputies so long?"

Carole joined her friend at the window and took her by the arm. "Come sit back down, Aurora, and tell me about the dog you found. Luke told me a little about him. A Jack Russell terrier, I think he said."

Aurora sat on the sofa beside her friend. "Yes, a Jack Russell terrier. I call him Little Guy."

"That's a cute name. Tell me about him."

"You're trying to distract me, Carole. It won't work. I'm going outside to find the deputies." Aurora stood up and headed to the door.

"No need, Aurora. They're coming now."

"About time," Aurora said when Conner and Johnson entered the house.

"We looked thoroughly, Ms. Harris. Searched the bank and under the dock. Saw your overturned canoe, an orange life jacket, and lots of trash floating, but no body. Nothing's there, ma'am," Lieutenant Conner announced. "Maybe you saw a large fish or snapping turtle or garbage or something. With all the rain we've had this spring, there's lots of debris in the lake, some big logs, too."

"Lieutenant Conner, I saw it. I felt it. I smelled it. It was grotesque. I fell on top of it. It was horrible. And the smell— oh Lord, the smell."

"Ma'am, there ain't no body under the dock, in the boat-house, or near the shore. There's no dead man in the water," Johnson said.

"If you see it again, give us a shout," said Conner. The officers turned to leave.

"Wait, there's something we haven't discussed yet."

Lieutenant Conner turned to Aurora and asked politely, "And what would that be, ma'am?"

"A big speedboat nearly rammed our smaller boat this morning. Luke Stancill reported it. It was almost daylight, although still dark enough for a boat to have its running lights on. But that speedboat wasn't using running lights. Our lights were on, though, so they had to see us. Their wake nearly swamped us, and King here fell into the lake. Not only that, but the two guys on board looked straight at us."

Conner and Johnson looked at each other, then Conner said, "We didn't receive a report. Maybe he notified the game warden." He pulled out a cell phone, called the game warden, and hung up after a brief conversation. "They didn't receive a report about a boat attack. Ma'am, how do you know the folks in the boat looked straight at you?"

"I've got it on videotape," Aurora announced, then explained why she was on the lake with a video camera so early in the morning.

"Guess we need to have a look at the videotape," Conner said.

Aurora readied the VCR. "Understand that I haven't edited this yet. The final version will be much better, but I guess you don't care about that."

"Okay if I watch, too?" asked Carole.

Aurora nodded. Carole joined Aurora on the loveseat.

The deputies sat on the sofa and watched as the tape rolled. Practice shots filled the screen as Aurora and Luke checked the video camera's settings. Luke's shouted warning was clearly audible when a speeding boat popped out of the faint shafts of early morning light and headed straight toward Luke's boat.

"You're lucky, ma'am. That looked deliberate to me, too." Conner's earlier impression of Aurora changed for one of respect. *Had she been right about a dead person, too?* He made a mental note to further investigate the missing body. "I'll take the tape to headquarters for Sheriff Rogers to see, ma'am. You'll get it back in a few days."

"Lieutenant, besides the boat attack, that tape also has excellent footage of the sunrise for the promo I'm producing, and I need it. I'm on a tight time schedule."

"Tell you what, ma'am. We'll just make a copy for you, and I'll run it back over here tomorrow morning," said Sergeant Johnson. "At the office, we can enlarge the shot of the guys in the boat. That'll assist us in identifying them.

"By the way, Ms. Harris, I almost forgot to ask. Have you ever seen this car in your neighborhood?" He pulled a rumpled photograph out of his shirt pocket.

Aurora studied the picture he thrust at her. "No, I can't remember seeing a car like that around here, but I didn't arrive until Thursday. How about you, Carole?"

"Nope, 'fraid not. What kind is it?" Carole asked as she handed the picture back to Sergeant Johnson.

"It's a BMW, ma'am. Bird watchers discovered it less than a mile from here, so I thought maybe y'all had seen it, what with the body Ms. Harris said she saw, and all. Guess we'll check with your neighbors while we're here."

"You probably won't have any luck. The house on the left is a rental. The one on the right is owned by a man in D.C., only comes a few times a year. I think he drives an S.U.V. Green one, I believe. Those homes closer to the main road are used only in the summer."

"Do you happen to have their names?"

"I do, at least my folks did. And I can give you their addresses and telephone numbers, too, if you'd like."

"We'd appreciate it."

While Aurora flipped through the address file box, she said, "Since I've been here, boats have entered my boathouse twice at night. Doesn't that sound suspicious to you?"

"Maybe a little. But then this is prime fishin' time at Smith Mountain Lake. Striper fishin' is pretty good in this part of the lake. I wouldn't worry about it if I were you."

"But. . . ."

Johnson finished copying the information from the index cards and handed the originals back to Aurora.

"Thanks, Ms. Harris," he said as he and Conner walked out the door.

"It's Mrs.," Aurora called after him.

"Pity," said Conner to Johnson as they walked to their cars.

"Carole, they don't believe I found a body." She looked at her friend. "You believe me, don't you?"

"I think you *believe* you saw a body. But like the cops said, there's lots of debris in the water this spring. Conner and Johnson said there was trash floating near the canoe.

And I've even heard of animal carcasses washing into the lake occasionally. Maybe that's what you saw."

Aurora stared at Carole. "I saw a body. I fell on top of it. And the trash is junk I picked up while I was canoeing, before I capsized and landed on the body."

"But, Aurora, where is the body now? How could it have disappeared so fast?"

"I don't know where the body is now. But I do know that a dead person was floating near my dock."

I want Sam. I need to talk to Sam. He'd believe me, Aurora thought.

"Let's go to Homestead Creamery for an ice cream cone," Carole said, changing the subject. "You need to get away from here for a while. The three of us will go—you, me, and King. My treat."

"You're probably right. I could use a change of scenery. But King's not quite dry."

Carole reached over and touched the damp dog. "That's okay. He's dry enough."

"Well, if you're sure. But let me try Sam one more time first."

Two minutes later, Aurora came back in the living room. "He still doesn't answer. I'll try again when we get back." She called King and the three walked out the door.

"Susie-Q" by Dale Hawkins had been playing in Sam's mind all day. Anything could set a song off in his head—a name, a word, a picture—and there the song would reside until another came along. Car windows down and sunroof open, Sam sang as the red Mitsubishi Eclipse sped up Interstate 20, then 77 to Charlotte. He smiled. If Aurora were with him, she would chime in with her slightly off-key voice that he adored. In three more hours he'd see his Susie-Q, the nickname he gave to Aurora Sue Anderson on their first date.

Sam stopped in Greensboro for gas and a down-home North Carolina pork barbecue sandwich with coleslaw on a sesame seed bun. Harold Johns had made Sam's day when he'd called early that morning to say he wouldn't be going to

Augusta after all. Something had come up. Now Sam wouldn't have to meet Harold and Melinda for dinner Saturday night. He checked his calendar. He could reschedule a few appointments, take some work with him, and enjoy an extra-long weekend. He hadn't seen Aurora for over three weeks, and he longed to hold her in his arms. By 10:00 he'd wrapped up a couple of loose ends, packed his bag and briefcase, and was on the road. He'd tried to call Aurora, but didn't get an answer. Rather than leave a message on her machine, he decided to surprise her this afternoon. Maybe he'd take her out to dinner, or perhaps a romantic tête-à-tête at the lake house. He'd cross over that mountain when he reached it.

Smith Mountain loomed on the horizon as Sam sang the song "Over the Mountain, Across the Sea . . ." Soon he'd see his girl, his Aurora, his Susie-Q.

"King, want to go for a ride in the car?" Aurora asked. King barked and ran to Aurora's Jeep.

"Not that car, King," Carole said, laughing. "Today you ride in an older vehicle." She opened the back door and he jumped in. He leaned over the front seat between Carole and Aurora.

"If you put the back windows down about ten inches, he won't hang over your shoulder," Aurora said. "He'll be too busy sniffing the scents outside."

Carole laughed and lowered the windows.

Hidden by a weeping willow's overhanging branches, a speedboat nestled against the shore. With binoculars trained on the house, a man watched Carole drive off with Aurora and King.

"Let's go," he said to his three cronies. They scrambled from the boat, ran up the hill, and pushed through the thin stand of pines, oaks and maples to the house.

"I've got a key. Remember, all we're looking for is the necklace and the pictures the old man took. Understand?"

The woman and two men nodded.

*

Sam turned onto Spawning Run Road. *Six hours and twelve minutes. Not bad.* Stopping for the barbecue sandwich in Greensboro hadn't cost him much time. He smiled. Aurora would be thrilled that he'd brought a small cooler from Augusta for the sole purpose of bringing his Susie-Q some barbecue or, as he called it, North Carolina Gold. What they didn't eat over the weekend, she could freeze.

Sam pulled into the driveway. Good, Aurora's Jeep was in the carport. He rang the doorbell, unlocked the utility room door, and called for Aurora. He wanted to surprise her, not scare her out of her wits.

"Susie-Q, it's me," he called as he walked into the kitchen. As he rounded the corner to the living room, a blow to his chest slammed him backward. Sam collapsed in a heap, his head whacking hard against the floor. Before he passed out, he glimpsed feet with bright red toenails in blue leather sandals.

"Let's get the hell out of here!" a voice yelled.

"Sam's here!" Aurora shrieked, and she jumped out of Carole's car before it came to a complete stop. King bounded to the red car, sniffed, then, nose to the ground, dashed ahead of Aurora and Carole to the utility room door. Earlier, the two women had laughed over King's introduction to a vanilla ice cream cone, and Aurora could hardly wait to see Sam's reaction when she described it. And his strong, warm arms around her again would feel so good. She hoped Carole wouldn't prolong her visit.

"Sam, honey, I'm home! Where are you?" Turning the corner, Aurora nearly tripped over Sam lying on the living room floor. Luke towered over Sam. A baseball bat dangled from Luke's left hand.

"No!" Aurora yelled.

CHAPTER THIRTEEN

Two hours later, Aurora waited in the emergency room at Lynchburg General. *Don't die, Sam. Please don't die. Lord, I lost my baby, my dad, my mom. Please don't let me lose Sam, too. Please!*

Aurora remembered the moment she and Sam met—the summer after her sophomore year at Virginia Tech. She was dozing on the dock when a deep, male voice had awakened her. Startled, she'd sat up quickly to see a speedboat idling in the water.

"Ahoy the dock. We need help," said the skipper.

She noticed his twinkling blue eyes, his lean, muscular frame, and the sheepish grin that spread across his face. Despite the summer temperature of 94 degrees, she broke out in goose bumps.

"We're lost," he said, indicating the two girls and the other guy on board. "Could you please direct me?" He unfolded a map and passed it to Aurora.

As she studied the map, she could feel him staring at her. She blushed and said, "You're here. Where do you wish to go?"

He produced an address and buoy marker number, and then, with the pencil he handed her, Aurora traced the route they should take. "You shouldn't have any trouble now." Their fingers brushed as she handed the map and pencil back to him, and she trembled slightly.

"Thanks a lot. Uh, what's your name?"

"Aurora."

"Thanks, Aurora. You've been a huge help. Amazing we could get so turned around."

"It's because we were having so much fun skiin' and swimmin', Sam darlin'," drawled the bikini-clad brunette as she leaned her perfect body against him.

"Whatever," he said. "Again, thanks a lot."

Aurora watched as he navigated away from the dock and into the main channel. He turned, waved goodbye, and Aurora's life changed forever.

The next afternoon, Aurora's dad said, "A young man stopped by today. He was looking for you, said he met you on the dock yesterday. Came by boat, a sleek vintage Chris-Craft. Told him you'd gone to town, didn't know when you'd be back."

"What did he look like, Dad? Did he tell you his name?"

"Blonde hair, blue eyes. Think he said his name was Sam. Wasn't it Sam, Margaret?" Aurora's mother nodded. "Your mother and I were eating lunch by the water. He seemed like a nice, clean-cut young man. You know your mother; she invited him to join us."

"He graduated a year ago from North Carolina State University with a Master's degree in engineering. Your father was impressed." Aurora's mother smiled fondly at her husband and patted his hand. "You know how your father likes to 'talk technical.' They discussed new innovations in engineering design and architecture."

Aurora's heart pounded. "Did he say anything else?"

"Oh, yes, he did mention that he'd be back to take you to dinner tonight. When I told him you might have plans, he said he'd stop by anyway around six-thirty, that if you couldn't join him, he'd catch up with you some other time. I gave him directions to the house by car." Margaret hadn't missed the effect this news had on her daughter.

Aurora remembered everything about that storybook evening. She had agonized for an hour over what to wear, finally settling on a red and white cotton pique print dress with short sleeves, scoop neck and flared skirt. White, daisy-shaped earrings, pearl necklace, and low-heeled white open-toed sandals completed her ensemble. Never would she forget how handsome Sam looked in his khaki suit and blue cotton shirt that matched his eyes exactly. He even surprised her with one perfect long-stemmed red rose. When he helped her slip into her white cashmere cardigan, the air seemed to crackle from the sparks flying between them.

They drove to the Peaks of Otter for dinner, then headed home via the Blue Ridge Parkway. When they stopped at a scenic overlook, Sam turned up the car radio and asked, "Care to dance?"

"I'd love to."

With a full moon providing the lighting, they shagged to beach music and slow-danced to songs for lovers. An hour later, Sam said in a husky voice, "We'd better go."

When Sam delivered her to her door at 2:00 a.m., she invited him in for coffee. They ended up talking on the dock until dawn. Aurora learned later that her dad saw them at six in the morning sitting side by side on the dock, with their blonde heads close together, shoulders touching, and their feet dangling in the water. Occasionally the sound of Aurora's infectious laugh floated up to the house. Jack woke Margaret, pointed to Aurora and Sam, and Margaret smiled, aware that something very special was happening to her daughter.

Sam and Aurora married three years later at historic St. Stephen's Episcopal Church in Forest. The hazy Blue Ridge Mountains in the distance provided the perfect backdrop for freshly mown fields of hay and the herd of black angus cattle that grazed in the pasture adjoining the church yard. Black-eyed Susans, daisies, and sweet-scented orange butterfly weed swayed in the breeze along the fence line. As the six bridesmaids, dressed in pale blue, ankle-length organza gowns began their ceremonial walk down the aisle to the altar steps, Aurora waited at the church entrance with her dad and thought there could not have been a more perfect day for a wedding.

But then the music stopped and the organist screamed when a squirrel jumped from the top of the organ to the first pew, ducked around old Mr. Bendall who was seated in the fourth row on the bride's side, ran to the groom's side of the church, and shattered a vase of fresh flowers as it leaped up on a window sill.

Thirty minutes later, after the groomsmen and some wedding guests had chased the squirrel out of the church, the wedding party re-grouped. Her mother, still laughing, assured Aurora that the event would give everybody something to talk about for years to come at dinner parties and bridge tables when the conversation lagged. Her mother was still giggling when Aurora, her arm entwined in her father's, walked down the aisle to the altar and a lifetime as Mrs. Samuel Ross Harris. Aurora smiled at the memory. Her mother had been right, as usual.

Aurora had long ago decided that fate caused their first meeting. If Sam hadn't gotten lost at the lake, they probably never would have met. Their worlds had been so different. When Sam was twelve, his father, then a professor in the Genetics Department at North Carolina State University in Raleigh, accepted a prestigious job in London. His mother adored England, had relatives in Cornwall, and looked forward to experiencing the opportunity of a lifetime.

Sam had loved England, still did. But when it was time to go to college, he said goodbye to his British friends and enrolled at N.C. State. After graduation, he landed an engineering design job at Designs Plus in Roanoke, Virginia, one thing led to another, he got lost at the lake, met Aurora, and fell madly in love.

Doctor Cameron's soft voice interrupted her memories. "Mrs. Harris, your husband has a concussion and three cracked ribs. He'll hurt for a while, and should have bed rest for a few days, but he'll be okay. As a precaution, I'll keep him here overnight, but I think he'll be able to go home tomorrow. He's in his room now; you may go see him if you wish."

"Hey, Sam. I'm here," Aurora whispered as she bent over her husband's bed and kissed him tenderly on the forehead.

"Hey, Susie-Q. I brought you some barbecue," Sam muttered. "Did you find it? And what hit me?"

"Shhh, don't talk. Yes, Carole found the barbecue and put it in the refrigerator. And I think you were hit with a baseball bat.

"Darling, I called your parents in London after I talked with Dr. Cameron. They send you their love, said to tell you to behave and obey me. Your mom wanted to catch a flight over right that minute, but I told her that wasn't necessary."

"It was thoughtful of you to call them."

"I'm looking forward to their visit with us in August."

Sam's bedside phone rang. Aurora answered it. "Hello."

"Your house was crawling with cops, King kept poking his nose into everything—literally—so I brought him home with me," Carole said. "I hope that's okay with you."

Aurora thanked her for taking King and updated Carole on Sam's condition.

"Don't worry at all about King. I'll keep him as long as necessary," Carole said before she hung up.

Even though Dr. Cameron and the nurses promised they would take excellent care of her husband, Aurora kept watch by Sam's bed throughout the night. Eventually her thoughts turned from the past to the present. She thought about the list she made yesterday with Luke. She pulled a pad from her purse and wrote:

What's going on at the lake?
Why were fishermen / boaters in our boathouse?
Fishing?
Carrying on a clandestine affair?
Drugs? Drinking?
Was that a gunshot I heard?
Little Guy—where did he come from?

Who shot him? Why?

Why did the speedboat nearly ram us?

Didn't see us? No way!

To kill us? To scare us? Why?

Why was body in the water? And where is it now?

Accidental drowning? Murder?

Luke—why was he standing over Sam with a bat?

Did he hit Sam? What was he doing in our house?

Who attacked Sam? Why?

While she kept watch over Sam, Aurora rehashed each incident. She wondered what she'd missed. There were so many unanswered questions. Then she realized what was bothering her. *Someone had ransacked the house!* She squeezed her eyes shut and pictured the scene when she rounded the corner to the living room and discovered Sam and Luke. Books and tapes strewn across the floor, the VCR and TV knocked off their shelves. Papers from the desktop tossed around the room. Chair and sofa cushions, ripped open, piled askew on the floor.

Sam had surprised intruders! Was Luke one of them?

Thursday, April 22

The next day, Aurora pushed Sam's wheelchair out the hospital exit door to her Jeep. She'd been delighted when Dr. Cameron had discharged him, but apprehensive at the same time. Sensing Sam's independent personality, the doctor had wagged a finger at him and insisted Sam stay in bed and rest when he returned to the lake house; under no circumstances was he to go up and down stairs. Aurora knew that keeping Sam quiet would be nearly impossible. She prayed there would be a ball game or a classic shoot-'em-up western on TV to keep him occupied.

Aurora kept glancing at Sam dozing in the shotgun seat. She knew he needed rest, but she wanted to poke him with her finger to satisfy herself he was alive. *If anything ever happened to him. . . .* The doctor had assured her he'd recover completely, but Sam was so quiet, so still. Was he really all right? When he snorted and shifted in the seat, Aurora relaxed and concentrated on the road. The familiar sight of the Blue Ridge Mountains and the Peaks of Otter soothed her, reminding her of fun hikes, trail rides and picnics on Sharp Top and Flat Top.

But Sam no longer slept. He sneaked a look at Aurora through half-shut eyes. *She's so beautiful, so smart, so sweet, so much more than any other woman could ever be.* He loved the way strands of her blonde hair curled over her right ear and the expression on her face as she concentrated on driving.

He thought about the unborn baby they had lost. When they discovered Aurora was pregnant, Sam had nearly burst with joy, certain that if the baby was a girl she would look exactly like Aurora. Losing the baby had been hard on both of them, but he still felt blessed that he had his Susie-Q. *If anything ever happened to her. . . .*

"How did your Jeep get to the hospital?" His voice startled Aurora.

She glanced at him. "I followed the ambulance from the house. One of the EMTs pointed out that having my car at the hospital would make things less complicated. I'm glad he suggested it, otherwise I wouldn't have been able to drive home early this morning and get the bedroom ready for you."

"Why don't we swing by the vet's and pick up that little dog you told me about? Didn't Dr. Eggleston say he'd release Little Guy today?" Sam asked.

"Are you sure you feel up to that?"

"Certainly. We pass right by the vet's. It wouldn't make sense for you to go back later. I promise I'll stay in the car. Besides, I'm looking forward to meeting him. I've always liked Jack Russell terriers."

Aurora looked at Sam, called Dr. Eggleston on the cell phone, and turned into the vet's parking lot fifteen minutes later.

"He's ready for you, Aurora. Just try to keep him quiet. Don't want him to split his sutures," the vet said.

"I'll put him in the room with Sam. They can keep each other company." She knelt on the floor to greet Little Guy and stroked him gently as he licked her face. She scratched him behind his ears and said, "Guess I'm a little surprised he's so happy to see me. He was with me only a short time before I brought him to you."

"He definitely remembers you. Didn't I tell you he was a smart dog?"

Both Dr. Eggleston and Aurora laughed when she opened the car door and Little Guy sat down on the pavement in front of Sam and offered Sam a paw. Despite the pain in his ribs, Sam leaned over and shook Little Guy's paw.

The bond between man and dog was sealed.

CHAPTER FOURTEEN

"Aurora, I think Little Guy needs to go out," Sam called.

Aurora stopped loading the dishwasher and hurried to the bedroom. "I figured you'd sleep the rest of the day, Sam. How do you feel?"

"Not too bad, but I'm pretty sore. I feel like an old, battered man. Go with Aurora, Little Guy."

Aurora didn't want Little Guy to open up any of his wounds, so she lifted him off the bed and set him on the floor.

"While you're waiting for Little Guy to relieve himself, would you mind fetching my guitar at the same time? I left it in my car. In the back seat."

"Here you are," she said several minutes later when she handed the guitar to Sam. "It's a gorgeous day. Lots of fishermen are out on the water."

"Wish I were one of 'em." Sam sighed.

"You will be soon."

"I noticed you brought the equipment I need to put Carole's promo together. Thanks."

"You're welcome."

Little Guy, alias Russell, jumped back up on the four-poster bed before Aurora could stop him, circled a spot next to Sam several times until the covers were scrunched and bunched to his satisfaction, then dropped down beside Sam. Last night Aurora had made Little Guy a soft, warm, comfortable spot on the floor, the kind no pampered, self-respecting dog could pass up. He stayed on the makeshift bed all night, but the minute Aurora left the bedroom, he leaped up on the bed and stretched out beside Sam. Now Aurora almost ordered him off, but her instincts told her he'd just jump back up when she left the room. Close to Sam he stayed, a contented, smug look on his face.

"How do you like the collar I bought him at the vet's today? Do you think the metal studs on the brown leather are too tacky?"

"No, I kind of like the studs. Makes him look the way he feels—tough, macho." Sam fingered the collar, then said, "Seems a little thick to me."

"It should. There's a little zipper hidden on the inside. I asked Doc Eggleston why on earth anyone would need a dog collar with a zipper. He told me that some people like to keep emergency or medical info about their pets right in the collar; some folks even hide a house key there, especially joggers who take their dogs running with them. And, according to him, some pet owners keep cash hidden in the collar, sort of doubles as a money belt. I would have preferred one without the zipper, but this was the only studded one that fit him, so I bought it.

"I'll leave you two tough guys alone and go fix you something to eat. Any requests?"

"I'd love some fried eggs, bacon and grits. Is that too much trouble?"

"Nope. I'll be back in a little while."

"Would you please close the door on your way out?" He noticed Aurora's raised eyebrow and grinned. "Don't ask, it's a surprise." He picked up the guitar and strummed a few chords as Aurora pulled the bedroom door shut.

She returned to the bedroom carrying a white wicker tray loaded with a mug of steaming coffee, a tall glass of orange juice, two fried eggs done over easy, a side order of grits, two slices of bacon, and two pieces of whole wheat toast with butter and strawberry jam. Little Guy sniffed and whined.

"I like you, little buddy, but I'm not going to share my vittles with you," Sam said to the terrier. When Sam unfolded his napkin, a piece of paper fluttered onto the tray.

"What's this?" He picked it up, turned it over and read it. He smiled at his wife. "I've missed your sweet notes in my lunches, Aurora. Thank you for this one. I love you, too."

Aurora leaned over and kissed him on the cheek. "Call me if you need me." On her way out of the room, she looked back and saw Sam feed Little Guy a small bite of his toast. She smiled and closed the bedroom door.

Now that Sam was fed and the dishes done, Aurora took time to inspect the damage caused by the vandals. The police had left the house worse than they had found it. Traces of fingerprinting powder lightly blanketed tables, shelves, and the door. Should she touch anything? She wondered where to start. The doorbell rang. She jumped.

Conner and Johnson stood on the front porch. "Sorry to leave your house such a mess, Mrs. Harris," said Conner.

"Guess it couldn't be helped," she said. "I drove back here early this morning and cleaned the bedroom. Didn't want my husband to wait while I put the room in order. Haven't had the opportunity to clean the rest of the house yet." She put her hand to her mouth and asked, "Was that all right? I hope I didn't disturb any clues."

"It's okay; don't worry about it. May we talk with you?"

"Of course." Aurora ushered them into the kitchen. "Guess we'll have to sit here." She pointed to the barstools pushed half way under the counter top. From there she could see the destruction in the living room. She wondered if the upholstered sofa and chairs would ever come clean, then remembered they'd need to be reupholstered anyhow since most of the cushions had been slashed numerous times. She swiveled her stool around and faced the two deputies. "What do you want to talk about?"

"Has your husband remembered anything else, Mrs. Harris?"

"Only what I told you last night when you came to the hospital. He remembers driving up to the house yesterday, seeing my Jeep in the carport, unlocking the door, turning the corner into the living room, and being bashed across the chest and falling. Nothing else. He didn't see his attacker." Aurora thought for a second. "Maybe Carole can add something, but I doubt it."

"We spoke with her after you and Mr. Harris left for the hospital. She gave us permission to search the house. Said it would be okay with you. Anyhow, she told us everything she could.

"That big, black dog of yours—I think he'd planned to solve this himself—sniffed every inch of the floor, even the furniture. None of us could control him, and we were afraid he'd destroy evidence. Glad your girlfriend took him home with her."

"She's a good person, never minds pitching in to help."

"What can you tell us about your friend Luke?" asked Conner. "How long have you known him?"

Aurora cocked her head and listened to the faint sounds of guitar music coming from the bedroom and grinned. She recognized the song—"How Much Is That Doggie In The Window." She giggled when Little Guy barked "arf arf" in the appropriate spot. She decided that must be the surprise Sam had in mind when he sent her to get his guitar earlier.

"Mrs. Harris?"

"I'm sorry. What did you say?"

"I asked how long you've known Luke Stancill."

"Only three days. I needed film footage for the promo I'm doing about the lake, so Carole hired him to squire me around in his boat. I know he has his own business, he's almost engaged, and," she smiled at the memory, "he has great taste in clothes."

"Great taste in clothes?"

"It's an inside joke; don't worry about it."

"I understand Mr. Stancill was standing over your husband with a baseball bat in his hand when you walked in the room," Conner said as he glanced at the note pad in his hand.

"That's true, he was. I'm puzzled, though. I don't know him well, but I can't believe he'd attack Sam. Even though he and Sam had never met, Luke has seen several pictures of Sam and me together. I would think he'd recognize my husband right away." She stopped speaking and frowned. "How did he get in my house, and why? Did you ask him?"

"Yes. He said Carole left a message on his answering machine saying you found a body in the lake, so he hurried to your house by boat—quickest route, he said. When he rounded the point and headed into Spawning Run, he saw a speedboat leaving your dock full throttle. And he thought the boat looked like the one that nearly rammed y'all. He wasn't close enough to recognize anybody, but thinks there were three, possibly four, people on board.

"He says he tied up his boat, rushed up the hill, and entered the house through an unlocked door. He feared for your safety. Said it liked to have scared him to death when he saw your husband crumpled on the floor. He'd never met Mr. Harris, but thought it was him. He admits he never should have picked up the bat. He was trying to figure out what to do when you came in and found them."

"Is he a suspect?"

"Well, yeah. His prints were on the bat, of course. But there were other prints as well. The lab's trying to identify them now."

"Something else that's interesting about that bat," said Lieutenant Conner as he bent down and tied his shoelace.

"What's that?" asked Aurora.

"There were faint blood stains on it. Human blood."

"But my husband had no open wounds."

"Exactly. So where did the blood come from?"

CHAPTER FIFTEEN

In Washington, cherry trees, their blossoms now fading, lined the avenues. Thousands of cars and buses jammed the streets. Squealing brakes and honking horns added to the chaos. Jill Hathaway, oblivious to the cherry blossoms, maneuvered her burgundy Chrysler sedan through traffic snarls and jaywalking sightseers. The car picked up speed as she left the hubbub of the city.

When her alarm clock woke her at 6:30 that morning, Jill had considered rolling over and going back to sleep. She didn't want to face what she knew would be waiting when she arrived at the office. And she was right—her day had been absolutely crazy. Reporters from all major networks and *The Washington Post* had swarmed on her at nine.

"Is it true that J. Melton Lampwerth IV embezzled millions of dollars?"

"Now that Lampwerth International is bankrupt, what will happen to the three hundred employees?"

"How could you and the Vice President not know what Lampwerth was doing? Or are you both in it with him?"

"Interesting, isn't it, that both the President and Vice President of Lampwerth International are missing. Is it true they're gay and have run off together?"

Jill had wanted to scream. Instead, she answered all the media's questions as indirectly as possible, ending with, "And now, ladies and gentlemen, I have a lot of work waiting for me. I'll let you know when I have more information. Nan will see you to the door."

Knowing that she and the accountant must confront Robert with Louis' suspicions as soon as possible, she buzzed Louis Beale's office as soon as the media left. He was home sick. "Severe nausea, diarrhea, chills and a fever," his assistant said. "Doctor says it's most likely the flu. Probably won't be back at work until Monday. Sure hope I don't catch it."

Then late that afternoon, Mr. Lampwerth's housekeeper called. "Ms. Hathaway, this is Lucille. I think I've found Russell."

"Wonderful! How did you find him?"

"I never listen to the messages on Mr. Lampwerth's answering machine. To me it's like rummaging through somebody's purse. But a little while ago I noticed there were twenty-three calls on it. I don't know how many it will hold, and besides, some could be important. So I listened." She paused, wanting assurance from Jill that she hadn't violated Mr. Lampwerth's privacy.

"You did the right thing, Lucille. Please go on."

"Several messages were from you. But the last one—it came in several hours ago while I was at the market—was from a national dog registry. Evidently, someone in Virginia has Russell. Seems a woman found him and took him to a vet. He was identified through the microchip in his neck. Thought you'd want to know."

"Lucille, that's good news. Where in Virginia is he?" Jill picked up a pen and reached for her notepad.

"Oh, let me see. I wrote it down on a piece of paper . . . now where did I put that? I had it just a minute ago." Jill waited while Lucille rummaged through papers stacked on the telephone table in the penthouse. "Here it is. Let me see, it says Smith Mountain Lake, Virginia, and gives a phone number to call for directions and information. A Dr. Eggleston reported Russell to the registry, then the registry called Mr. Lampwerth and left the message I just told you about."

Jill jotted down the information, thanked Lucille, and dialed the veterinarian.

"Ms. Hathaway, I'm relieved the registry found you. Yes, the dog will recover. Mrs. Aurora Harris found him—he'd been injured—and she brought him to me. I had him for a couple of days. Aurora picked him up late yesterday. You can probably catch her at home." He added, "Good thing you had a microchip implanted."

Jill didn't tell Dr. Eggleston she wasn't Russell's owner. She poured herself a cup of coffee and called the number the vet gave her.

"Hello."

"May I speak with Aurora Harris?"

"This is she. What may I do for you?"

"Mrs. Harris, my name is Jill Hathaway. I'm calling from Washington, D.C. A veterinarian, Dr. Eggleston, gave me your telephone number, said you had my dog. Actually, Russell belongs to my boss J. Melton Lampwerth, who hasn't been seen since Friday afternoon. Maybe you've seen him. He's in his sixties, short and heavy, has gray hair but going bald, wears expensive clothes, suits mostly."

"Afraid I've seen only a dog. What does your missing dog Russell look like?"

"He's a Jack Russell terrier, white with brown spots. He's incredibly smart."

"The dog I found sounds like Russell. I've been calling him Little Guy. Afraid I haven't seen anyone that matches Mr. Lampwerth's description, though." Aurora added, "Did Doc Eggleston tell you that Little Guy, sorry, I mean Russell, had been shot?"

Jill gasped. *Shot! Why? And how did Russell get to Smith Mountain Lake, and where was Lampwerth?* Jill told Aurora she would make arrangements to have Russell picked up in a couple of days, and hung up.

Aurora wondered if the body in the lake could be Lampwerth, but she hadn't mentioned it to Jill. After all, there wasn't a body for Jill to identify. She decided to tell Lieutenant Conner about Russell and Mr. Lampwerth.

*

Jill waited impatiently at Reagan National Airport for Robert Reeves. She glanced at the clock on the terminal wall. Ten-thirty p.m. She was irritated and starving. If she'd known his flight would be so late, she would have eaten a decent dinner instead of a burger, fries and shake. She checked the arrival board. Robert's flight should land any minute. *This will be the first time in over five years that Robert and I have been alone together. Why am I so nervous?* To her surprise, her heart fluttered when he walked into the terminal.

"Fill me in, Jill," he said as she rushed to keep pace with his long stride. She told him everything except that he was a suspected embezzler. That could wait.

"Where at Smith Mountain Lake did the woman find Russell?" Robert asked.

"Mrs. Harris said 210 Spawning Run Road."

"I own a house on Spawning Run Road," he said. "I built it five years ago. To take my mind off you." Robert stopped walking and looked straight at her.

She turned her head away from his piercing eyes. *Don't do this to me, Robert.*

Man and woman walked in silence for a moment. Then he explained that he had often encouraged Lampwerth to spend some quiet time at Smith Mountain Lake, but that Lampwerth never had. "He has a key; I gave him one a couple of years ago. When you first tracked me down and told me he was missing, I assumed he'd finally accepted my offer. But no one answered when I called. That's why I returned." He glanced at her. "Sorry if I was curt on the phone."

"That's okay. I understand."

Robert retrieved his luggage, loaded it into the trunk of Jill's car, told her he'd drive, and sped away from the airport. He stopped at Wal-Mart.

"Jill, I want you to buy yourself a change or two of clothes, a nightgown, and any toiletries you might need." He looked down at her feet. "And get out of those heels. Buy some comfortable shoes. Here, use my Visa." He pulled the credit card from his wallet.

"I can pay my own way. And besides, why should I buy those things?"

"Because we're not going back to D.C. We're driving straight to Smith Mountain Lake. Now."

CHAPTER SIXTEEN

Friday, April 23

"What the hell . . . ? " Robert Reeves stood speechless in the large foyer of his Smith Mountain Lake home. Once expensively appointed, the house now contained only a few large pieces of furniture and some room-size rugs. Smaller paintings, sculptures and art objects were missing. Small oriental rugs were gone, too.

"I've been robbed! Stay where you are, Jill. Don't touch anything. I'll get the cell phone from the car and call the police."

"Robert, what if someone is still in the house?" Jill whispered. "I'll be damned if I'll stay in here by myself."

"Of course you won't. Come with me. We can both wait in the car until the police arrive."

Jill figured it would be hours before she could get some sleep. She looked at her watch—3:57 a.m. The drive from Reagan National had been long, awkward, and quiet. She had wanted to say something, but somehow idle chitchat didn't seem appropriate. And now she had a splitting headache.

Two cars drove into the cobblestone drive, their flashing blue lights bouncing from window to window.

"Really glad to see you fellows," Robert said to the two deputies when they climbed from their vehicles. "I haven't walked through the house yet; don't know if someone could still be inside, although I doubt it."

The lieutenant instructed the other deputy to search the house, then he turned to Robert. "Can you tell me exactly what's missing?"

"No, I haven't done an inventory yet; I thought I should wait until you checked out the house. When I realized I'd been robbed, Jill and I came straight outside and called from the car phone. Like I told you a minute ago, I haven't walked through the house yet."

"That's fine. We'll dust for prints, Mr. Reeves, then when we're finished you can work up a list of the stolen items."

Three hours later, Jill sat at the kitchen counter and feasted on warm apple cinnamon buns and strong coffee—black, just the way she liked it. Robert had remembered. Had food ever tasted so good? She silently thanked Robert and his resourcefulness. While she had bought clothes and toiletries in Wal-Mart, he had stocked a newly purchased cooler with a small bag of ice, the buns, a loaf of whole wheat bread, orange juice, butter, cream, bacon, and a dozen eggs. The French-roasted coffee beans came from the freezer in the house. She'd watched while he measured out the correct amount, ground it, and started the coffeepot before joining the policemen fifteen minutes ago. She was glad the cops had said she could use the toaster oven to warm the buns.

Jill looked around for an ashtray, settled for a Styrofoam cup, and plucked a pack of Virginia Slims and an initialed gold lighter from her purse. This definitely isn't the day to quit smoking, she thought.

Robert and the lieutenant pored over the inventory list that Robert retrieved from his desk drawer. Now he was glad he'd followed his insurance agent's advice and listed everything in the house, even though it had been a pain at the time.

"It seems that the larger valuables were spared," Robert said, glancing at the Picasso still hanging on the wall.

"Smaller original paintings—a Reubens, another Picasso, a Perigal—are gone. All the Repoussé sterling flatware, the antique silver service, a Ming vase, and a framed, original letter signed by Patrick Henry are all missing, as are five Persian rugs." Suddenly, he hurried to the hall closet. He groaned. "They took my autographed Babe Ruth baseball bat, too." Robert slumped into a chair.

"Does anyone check the house periodically?" asked a deputy.

"Good thought. Yes, the housekeeping service cleans monthly. I'll call them, they should be opening any time now." He glanced over at Jill, still in her suit. He wondered how anyone could be that tired and still look so gorgeous. "Is it okay for Jill to change her clothes in the bedroom now?"

"Sure."

Jill flashed Robert an appreciative smile, picked up her bag with the newly purchased items, and hurried to the bedroom Robert had assigned to her. She dressed quickly in dark blue gabardine slacks, plaid navy and teal cotton blouse, and a white crew neck long-sleeved cotton sweater, socks, and sensible walking shoes. She ran a comb through her hair, touched her lips with a medium wine lipstick, took a deep breath, and walked out to join Robert.

He hung up the phone as she entered the kitchen, turned back to the lieutenant, and said, "Ella Mae last cleaned the house two weeks ago. Everything was in order then."

"You'd better come here." The other deputy poked his head in the doorway and motioned to the lieutenant.

"I'll be back in a minute," the lieutenant said.

"Jill, you said Russell is at 210 Spawning Run Road? That's the house over there." Robert pointed in the direction of the rambling stone and wood house on the hillside. "You can't get a good look at it right now because it's still too dark out. I tried to buy that house, said he could name his price, but the owner, Jack Anderson, wouldn't part with it for any amount of money. Said there really were some things money just couldn't buy. I didn't like his answer, but I admired the man for his integrity. So he sold me this five-acre piece of property and I hired a contractor from Moneta to build this house. Does it look familiar to you, anything like the villa we visited on the French Riviera?"

Jill knew she'd never forget those romantic weekends, the perfect days and nights in *Villefranche sur Mer*, but she bit her lip, looked down at the floor, and remained silent.

"Sad thing happened a few months ago, though," Robert continued. "Jack drowned. He'd gone fishing early one morning, and when he didn't show up at a friend's house for supper and couldn't be reached the next day, the friend called the authorities. They found his overturned rowboat, then discovered his body. Somehow he'd gotten his foot tangled in the anchor rope. When the boat overturned, the anchor sank to the lake bottom. And, of course, so did Jack."

"How awful."

"Nearly broke his daughter's heart. His wife never missed him, though. She'd been in a nursing home in Lynchburg for a while by then and never even realized he'd died. She had Alzheimer's. Horrible disease, horrible."

The lieutenant hurried into the kitchen. "I need to get the lab guys here," he said as he reached for the phone. "There's a faint trace of blood on the foyer floor."

CHAPTER SEVENTEEN

Later on Friday morning, Sergeant Johnson stopped by Aurora's house to return the video. "It's okay for you to give the house a good cleaning now."

"Good. Don't think I could put up with this mess much longer." Then she asked, "What do you think caused all this vandalism?"

"We're guessing the vandals wanted the videotape. When they couldn't find it, they went ballistic."

"They're crazy."

Johnson shrugged. "We'll check back with you later. Put the video in a safe place, lock your doors, and call us if you suspect anything unusual. And if you think of anything else, call one of us immediately. You still have our number?"

"Yes."

"Has the body surfaced again?" he asked.

"No." She shuddered at the thought.

"By the way, Ms. Harris, there was a burglary in your neighborhood. Lieutenant Graham investigated it early this morning. A lot of expensive items were stolen. You should be extra cautious, keep your doors locked."

"Thank you. I will."

"I'll check in with you later," Johnson said as he left the house.

Aurora's mind raced. Who knew about the tape? Other than herself, she could think of only four people: Carole, investigators Lieutenant Conner and Sergeant Johnson—and

Luke. She eliminated Carole, of course. Aurora didn't suspect Conner and Johnson. And she didn't want to think Luke capable of such a violent act.

But what do I really know about him? He's told me nothing about his background. And Johnson and Conner hadn't heard of the boat attack, even though Luke promised me he'd call the police.

Frowning at the mess around her, Aurora bent over and picked sofa cushions up from the floor. *Those responsible for this must have enjoyed creating it.*

The corner of a gold leaf picture frame poked out from under the bottom cushion, and Aurora froze. *Not the N.C. Wyeth painting. Surely even maniacs wouldn't destroy such a treasure.* She carefully extricated her dad's favorite painting from under the pile and breathed a sigh of relief. The frame was chipped, but that could be fixed. The only damage other than to the frame was a neat slice approximately six inches long on the brown paper backing. That would be easy to fix later. She blew off traces of fingerprinting powder, hung the painting back in its place of honor over the massive stone fireplace, and resumed cleaning.

An hour later, with little to show for her work, she thumbed through the telephone book in search of a cleaning service. The ringing phone interrupted her.

"I just heard about Sam, Aurora. That's terrible. How is he? He will recover, I hope." She recognized Harold Johns' voice.

"It isn't as bad as we first thought, Harold. He's home, but needs to stay calm for a few days."

"I'm glad to hear he's recuperating nicely. I imagine your house is a wreck, so I've arranged for a cleaning crew to come over today. They're professionals and will do a good job."

"Why, Harold, that's very kind of you." Aurora thanked him and hung up. She didn't like Harold, but she knew she could certainly use the help. And, she admitted to herself, it really was a thoughtful thing for him to do. *I'll go tell Sam. He'll be pleased.*

Hearing faint singing, she stood outside the bedroom door and listened. She would've entered the room, but didn't want to interrupt Sam's performance.

When the singing and strumming stopped, Aurora, laughing, pushed opened the bedroom door. "You must be feeling better. But whatever possessed you to start singing a Carl Perkins / Elvis Presley song? I haven't heard you sing 'Blue Suede Shoes' in years."

"I've no idea, but it's been playing in my head for the last half hour, and it finally just popped out." He put his hand on her shoulder as Aurora bent over him to plump the pillows behind his back. "Come sit with me a while. I'm lonesome."

"You have Little Guy for company. What could you possibly want with me?" Aurora teased. She smiled at the mischievous expression on his face. "Later, dear heart. You heard Dr. Cameron say you shouldn't exert yourself.

"Seriously, Sam, how do you think Little Guy got here from D.C.? No one that I know of has seen his owner. Ms. Hathaway told me when she called Thursday that the owner's name is Lampwerth, or something like that, said he owns his own company. Sounds like some big-shot businessman."

Sam took a good, long look at the woman he loved more than life itself. Worry lines replaced her usual *joie de vivre* attitude. *I've been so wrapped up in myself and my injuries that I hadn't noticed the subtle changes in Aurora. What's she keeping from me?*

"We really haven't talked about you, Aurora—it's all been about me. I haven't been much help to you. I was in Japan for three weeks, then someone beat up on me. So what's been going on?"

He listened as Aurora, sitting beside him on the bed, her legs stretched out on the white *matelassé* coverlet, reminded him about that first evening after her mother's funeral when she saw a boat enter the boathouse. "And remember, King woke me one night, and when I turned on the boathouse light a boat sped away. I told you about that. I'm sure someone had been in the house, too. And King and I heard what sounded like gunshots one evening, but then I figured it was either a car backfiring or thunder." Sam nodded. "You know about Carole's telephone call—you convinced me to do the promo for her. And I told you about King bringing Little Guy home, and the afternoon fact-gathering tour of the lake with Luke."

"Yes, I know all that. But something else is weighing on you, Aurora. What is it?"

"Where do I start?" She thought for a minute, then said, "Okay, here goes. You remember the day Carole called and asked me to produce a promo for her?"

"Yeah."

"The next morning—Wednesday, the same day you were bonked hard on the head—I met Luke on our dock at 4:30 to film the sunrise." Aurora smoothed a wrinkle in the bedspread. "We were anchored, waiting for the sun to pop up, when suddenly a speedboat nearly rammed Luke's boat. King fell overboard."

"King fell overboard?"

"Yes. He wasn't hurt, thank heavens. Luke pulled him back on board. Anyhow, when we returned to the house, I invited Luke in, told him to check out the videotape while I fixed breakfast. It's amazing, but we had captured a clear shot of the attacking boat. It appeared that the two men on board were looking straight at us, so it couldn't have been an accident."

He squeezed her hand. "Go on."

"After breakfast, Luke left. He said he'd report the boat attack to the cops. I needed to clear my head and relax a bit, so I launched the canoe to see if I could find the grebes' nest. King was swimming near the dock and didn't want to go with me."

Now came the hard part, the part she didn't want to recall. "Sam, when I returned in the canoe, King was pulling on something in the water. Whatever he wanted was hung up in some branches, so I leaned over and pulled, too." She trembled. "It was a body, Sam."

Sam stared. "A dead body?"

"Yes. And then the canoe capsized, and Sam—oh this is horrible—I fell on top of the body! I can still smell it and see it."

"Good heavens, Aurora! Why didn't you call me?"

"I tried, but you were already on your way here, remember?"

"Yeah, you're right. Where's the videotape? I want to see it."

"You don't suppose, do you, Sam, that the body is Mr. Lampwerth? After all, his dog Russell is here. And he was shot."

At the sound of his name, Russell lifted his head from Sam's leg, whined, then dropped back off to sleep.

Sam kissed his wife's cheek and said, "I doubt it. Did you give Lampwerth's name to the police when they were here this morning?"

"No, I was busy and just forgot. So much was going on. I'll tell them the next time I talk to them."

Aurora retrieved the tape from the living room and took it to the bedroom. She pushed it into the bedroom VCR and hoped the vandals hadn't damaged the VCR when they knocked it on the floor. Miraculously, it still worked. Now she needed Sam's comforting and analytical mind. He could watch the tape while she was busy doing something else. Besides, the tape would help keep him occupied. And maybe he'd come up with some answers.

"Whom should we trust? I have a tendency to trust everyone, you know." She handed him the remote.

"Well, the police for starters. And you've known Carole nearly all your life, so I guess she's okay. That leaves Luke, and my gut feeling is that we need to be careful how much we tell him. I know you think he's nice, but you really know nothing about him. Let's take it slow with Luke. Do you agree?"

"I guess so."

Aurora hurried to the front door when the doorbell chimed. Maybe the cleaning service had arrived. She hoped so. But standing on her front porch were Robert Reeves and a woman she'd never seen before.

"Hello, Aurora. This is Jill Hathaway; you spoke with her yesterday about Russell."

"Yes, I remember talking with you," Aurora said to Jill as the two women shook hands. "Nice to meet you, Ms. Hathaway. I didn't expect to see you. As I remember from our phone conversation, you said you'd send someone from Washington to pick up Little Guy—sorry, Russell—in a few days.

"And, Robert, seeing you is both a surprise and a treat. Haven't seen you in eons. I didn't expect you today, either. Do you two know each other?" Aurora quizzed, looking from one to the other.

"Please call me Jill. And yes, we do know each other. In fact, both of us work for the same company, Lampwerth International. J. Melton Lampwerth IV is president and also Russell's owner." Jill explained why she'd come herself rather than sending someone else. "Hope you don't mind."

"Of course not. Little Guy—sorry, I did it again—is stretched out on the bed with my husband. Sam had an accident day before yesterday, and, uh, Russell, if he's the dog you're looking for, is keeping him company."

"Did someone break in here, too?" Robert asked, gazing at the destruction around him.

"Yes, and someone attacked Sam, but . . . What do you mean, 'Break in here, too?'"

"I've been robbed. Lost most of the smaller valuables, including some paintings, even that Perigal you liked so much. You remember it? The one painted in 1865?" Aurora nodded. "Some Persian rugs are missing, too. And the police found a trace of dried blood on the foyer floor."

"Whoa!" Aurora exclaimed. "Sam needs to hear this."

As Aurora led them toward the bedroom, Little Guy barked ecstatically. Jill called, "Russell, is that you?" The dog whined and howled, and jumped repeatedly against the closed bedroom door.

"Aurora, you'd better get this dog before he hurts himself in here," hollered Sam. "I'm afraid he's gonna rip out some stitches."

Aurora, Jill and Robert entered the bedroom, and after a three-minute wiggling, jumping and licking spree, Russell calmed down and again rested on the bed, his head nestled against Sam's thigh.

"Tell him, Robert," Aurora said.

"Maybe I'd better start from the beginning," Robert said. "When Jill told me Melton Lampwerth was missing, I assumed Melton had acted on my long-standing offer to use my house. Evidently I was correct, only Melton is still missing, and Russell has turned up injured. Jill and I arrived around four o'clock this morning and discovered I'd been robbed." Robert repeated everything he'd told Aurora earlier.

"That's incredible," Sam said. "I wonder if the two break-ins are related. Did they vandalize your house, too?"

"That's the strange thing. The only damage in the house is the missing property. The house was neat, just a whole lot emptier."

"But there's blood on your floor, and blood on the bat that hit me," Sam added.

"You were hit by a bat?"

"That's what I'm told."

"My prize baseball bat, autographed by Babe Ruth himself, is missing. Do you suppose my bat is the one that hit you?"

"Good point. I'll call Lieutenant Conner. Maybe the bat and the blood are links the police have overlooked," Aurora said.

Something occurred to Aurora. She asked, "What kind of car does Lampwerth drive?"

Jill replied, "A silver BMW."

Aurora excused herself, went in the living room, picked up the phone, and dialed the number Lieutenant Conner had left with her.

"He's not here, ma'am, but I'll leave a message for him to call you as soon as he and Sergeant Johnson return."

109

"I'll just call back later. Thanks, anyhow."

Aurora returned to the bedroom and sat quietly in the chair beside Sam's bed as he, Robert and Jill discussed the two break-ins. The two incidents were not the same, and yet she had a gnawing feeling they were related. She excused herself again, walked back into the living room, and picked up the phone. *Unfortunately, it always seems to boil down to whom you know.*

CHAPTER EIGHTEEN

"Judge Charlie Anderson here," answered the gruff voice.

"Uncle Charlie, this is Aurora."

"Aurora, dear, how are you?"

"I'm okay, Uncle Charlie, but I do have a problem. Do you have a minute?"

"Anything for my favorite niece." Actually, Aurora was Charlie Anderson's only niece, his brother Jack's daughter, but he knew she'd still be his favorite even if he had a hundred nieces. She was fun, inquisitive, loving. Always had been. He remembered the excitement in her voice a year ago when she called from Augusta and told him she was pregnant. Sam was thrilled, she'd told him, and had dashed out of the doctor's office to buy his unborn son a football—NFL size. The next day Sam came home from work with a doll baby, one whose eyes opened and shut, tucked under his arm. Just in case, he'd said.

Then tragedy struck. Four months into the pregnancy, Aurora miscarried. Aurora, Sam and Jack were devastated. Margaret, in a nursing home by then, was unaware of the loss. And five months after the miscarriage, Jack drowned. Some folks called it suicide, said the unborn baby's death, coupled with the guilt of no longer being able to care for his wife, drove him to end his life. Others said that the spark in him had died, that he no longer paid attention to details, and that simple carelessness caused him to get his foot tangled in the anchor rope that dragged him to his death.

Aurora had taken her father's death hard. Her inability to accept his death as either a suicide or an accident had kept her feelings in turmoil, but a few days ago when he was out of town, she'd left him a message saying she had finally accepted the official verdict of accidental drowning. He was glad. Suspicion and anger could eat your insides up. He'd seen it happen to too many good people.

And then, as if the card game of life hadn't dealt her a bad enough hand, last week her mother died. A blessing? Charlie didn't know. He knew that his wife Annie's death five years ago from colon cancer was a blessing for her. People told him it was a blessing for him, too, that he no longer had to watch Annie suffer in agony. Theoretically they were probably right, but the long days and sleepless nights without her. . . . Lord, he missed her so much, missed caring for her, fixing her meals, rubbing her back, hearing the sweet sound of her voice.

"I always have a minute for you, Aurora, dear. More, if you need it," he said. "What's on your mind?"

"Someone broke into Mom and Dad's house. Unfortunately, Sam surprised the intruders and received a concussion and cracked ribs."

"And you didn't call me?"

"You were out of town. You left from the cemetery immediately after Mother's funeral. Some convention or something in Acapulco. I called your office and left a message. Your secretary said you were due to return very late last night, that you'd be back in the office today."

Then Aurora told him about the theft at Robert's house. "Uncle Charlie, instinct tells me the vandalism of my house and the robbery of Robert Reeves' house are tied together."

Silence. Or was that a soft groan she heard coming from her uncle?

"But Aurora, dear, from what you just told me, the crime scenes weren't at all alike. The M.O. isn't the same."

"But different policemen investigated the two crimes. Investigators Conner and Johnson are on this case; I don't know the names of the deputies who are looking into Robert's burglary. And listen to this. Someone tried to ram the boat I was in. A hotshot businessman from Washington, D.C.—his name is J. Melton Lampwerth—has disappeared and his dog Russell showed up at this house, and he'd been shot. I fell on top of a body floating in the water, but it was gone when Conner and Johnson searched for it. There's a bloodstain on the foyer floor where Lampwerth was probably staying, 214 Spawning Run Road, and the house had been robbed. My house was ransacked. Sam was hit with a baseball bat. There was blood on the bat, even though there were no open wounds on Sam. And I would bet anything that the bat is the one stolen from Robert Reeves' house."

"Aurora . . ."

"I'm not through. The abandoned car discovered less than a mile from my house was a BMW. I just learned a few minutes ago from Jill Hathaway—she works for Lampwerth—that Mr. Lampwerth drives a BMW."

"Aurora, I haven't been a District Attorney for nearly fifteen years. I'm a judge. Besides, Smith Mountain Lake isn't in my jurisdiction. You know that."

"Uncle Charlie, please won't you check into it? At least find out if the blood on the bat and the blood in the foyer match. You've got lots of contacts; you can pull strings and make people listen to you. Aren't you and Sheriff Rogers good friends, golf buddies? Won't you please help me?"

"I guess I could make a few phone calls. What you say makes sense. I'll suggest they run a check on the blood samples if they haven't done so already. Now what's this about a boat nearly ramming you, and a body in the lake?"

Aurora felt the tension drain out of her. Uncle Charlie would look into the two cases. Then she told him about the videotape of the boat. By the time she hung up the phone, she felt much better. At least now someone was paying attention to her. And that someone had lots of clout.

She returned to the bedroom to join Sam, Jill and Robert.

CHAPTER NINETEEN

When Aurora opened the front door for Jill and Robert to leave, a woman was standing on the porch. The woman, her finger poised to push the doorbell, looked startled.

`"I know you!" exclaimed Aurora. "You wanted to breed your female Lab to King."

"You have a good memory for faces, honey. I'm surprised you recognized me in this ugly old uniform." She smoothed down her tight pale-pink slacks and adjusted the collar on the matching blouse. "I'm Sheila."

"Did you come for our friends' address and phone number? You know, the folks who bred King?"

"Actually, no. I'm from the cleaning service. Mr. Johns sent me. The rest of the team will be here any minute. I'm the advance guard, you might say." She smiled at Aurora.

"Please come in. You can see we're desperate for help."

Aurora waved goodbye to Robert and Jill, promising to see them later. For now, Little Guy would stay with Aurora. Besides, Sam could use the company.

Sheila turned slowly as she looked around the living room. "What happened? Did a tornado roar through here?"

"Not unless a tornado's capable of slicing cushions."

"You're kidding! A person did all this? Whatever for?"

"Beats me. The police are working on that as we speak."

"Did they take anything?"

"Nope. Only my sense of security."

"Aren't you scared to stay here alone?"

"I hadn't thought about it." *She has a point. If the intruder were after the videotape, he may come back. And somebody robbed Robert, and the police found blood on his foyer floor.*

But she said to Sheila, "I don't think there's a thing to worry about. And I'm not alone; my husband's here with me."

"Oh, that's good. Where's King? I was hoping I'd get a chance to see him again."

"King is staying with a friend right now. He thought he should be in charge of the investigation." Both women laughed. "The police told me King wanted to solve the attack on my husband and the vandalism here all by himself."

"It wouldn't surprise me at all if King could do that," said Sheila. "After all, he's a Labrador retriever."

They discussed the break-in, then Sheila said, "I'll just take a walk-through to see what needs to be done, then when the rest of the team gets here we'll be ready to work. Don't you fret yourself one little bit, Mrs. Harris, honey; we'll soon have you neat and tidy." She gave Aurora a little pat on her shoulder.

"Let me get out of your way, then. I'll be in the bedroom if you need me. And please call me Aurora."

Aurora picked up her cross-stitch bag, walked in the bedroom, and shut the door. Sam slept peacefully, his chest rising and falling in rhythm with his light snoring. Little Guy opened one eye to see who had come in, then dropped back off to sleep. Smiling at the recuperating pair, Aurora moved Sam's guitar off the bed and turned off the television. Sam must have fallen asleep as the tape played. For him, watching TV was more effective than a sleeping pill. She wondered how much of the videotape he saw before zoning out.

Not again, she thought as the vivid memories of the bloated body reappeared in her head. The feel, the sight, the smell enveloped her as if she were back in the lake. She shuddered.

Determined to put all depressing thoughts out of her head until she talked with the police, Aurora settled down on the floral-covered *chaise longue* between the bed and the wide, water-view window. She looked around at the comforting room, her bedroom when she was growing up. Her parents' bedroom, actually a suite, was much larger, but she couldn't bring herself to claim it. In her room, with its antique cherry four-poster bed, armoire, the old cherry chest of drawers, and the cottage pine dressing table, Aurora felt comfortable, at home. And safe.

She pulled the latest cross-stitch project from the tote bag. Cross-stitching always relaxed her, and she hoped it wouldn't fail her now. This particular project depicted the shoreline of Washington, North Carolina—known to locals there as "Little Washington" or "the Original Washington." She had used a picture she'd taken of Washington Park from the river to design the cross-stitch. The town enchanted her. Old stately homes peeked through moss-laden trees and weather-beaten piers reached out into the Pamlico River. Aurora smiled. What stories those piers could tell.

Computers now simplified the design of a cross-stitch kit. Before leaving Augusta, she had scanned the picture she wished to use from the travelogue onto the computer, then loaded the image into the cross-stitch program. Next she chose the colors of the threads, and the computer did the work. Occasionally, however, the program could not produce the exact shades she desired. That was the case with this project. Aurora sorted through her well-stocked bag and pulled out a board containing skeins of floss in varying shades of gray. Settling on a dull gray with a slight hint of green, she threaded her needle and began stitching a facsimile of the Spanish moss onto the cream-colored 18-count Aida fabric. Good, the moss was easy; this shade would work perfectly. Selecting the colors for the piers hadn't been this simple. She mingled several different grays and silvers to obtain the exact look she wanted for them.

Aurora usually worked on a new travelogue as she created a cross-stitch work of art from an old one. Friends didn't understand how she could do both at the same time, but she had perfected a system that worked well for her. She would thread her needle, then turn on the tiny dictating machine she always carried in her tote bag, thereby freeing her hands for needlework. Sometimes she would have scrawled notes beside her, but not today. She began dictating, confident Sam wouldn't be awakened by her voice.

First she would paint a word picture of Smith Mountain Lake at sunrise. A brief history of the Lake's origin would come next, then a view of the dam and the numerous recreational opportunities the lake provided. She would weave in the shops, restaurants, the different types of housing, some local churches, night spots, and the small towns that helped give the lake its charm. She'd end the promo with the spectacular sunset she and Luke had recorded. The completed brochure and videotape would pair well together or separately, depending on what Carole wanted to send to prospective clients.

Jill and Robert sat across from each other on the redwood deck overlooking the water. Both were surprised at Aurora's reaction when told that Lampwerth drove a BMW. Then when Aurora explained about the abandoned car article that appeared in *The Smith Mountain Eagle* and the picture the police had shown her, an undercurrent of doom had engulfed all of them. Jill had felt faint and had to sit down. Aurora had quickly brewed them each a cup of green tea, and the color gradually crept back in Jill's face.

"Do you think we'll find Mr. Lampwerth alive, Robert?" Jill asked now.

"It doesn't look good. Aurora said the BMW had been stripped of all tags, the serial number scratched off, glove compartment emptied. The windshield was broken and the vehicle identification number removed. Someone went to a lot of trouble to dispose of all identification. And don't forget the blood in the foyer. I'm afraid he's dead."

"But there's no motive, Robert. Why would anybody want to kill Mr. Lampwerth?"

"Even though they respected him, not too many people really liked him, Jill, not even you or me. You know that."

"But that's no reason to kill him. Maybe he's being held for ransom," she said. "After all, he's an extremely wealthy man."

"I suppose that's possible, but not very probable. If he were being held for ransom, one of us would have received a ransom note by now. My guess is that he simply surprised a burglar. I think he was just in the wrong place at the wrong time."

"I suppose you're right." She reached for a cigarette, then changed her mind.

"Jill, tell me anything—no detail is too small—that you suspect could have upset Melton, something that prompted him to finally come to the lake. There has to be something. Think."

Jill groaned, knowing she could no longer shield Robert from the accountant's suspicions. He had to know. She shifted in her seat and stared down at the floor.

"Louis Beale told me in strict confidence on Tuesday that someone's been embezzling funds from Lampwerth International. He hit Lampwerth with this news the Thursday evening before he disappeared." She paused and glanced at Robert.

"Go on."

Jill looked deep into Robert's eyes. "Robert, I didn't want to tell you this until we were back in D.C., but Louis believes you're the embezzler."

He sat quietly in the chair with his eyes closed and hands clasped together before responding.

"Guess I knew it would come out sometime. But it's not what you or Louis Beale think, Jill. There's an explanation, although rather far-fetched. You probably won't believe me."

Puzzled, she stared at Robert. She'd expected him to deny vehemently any knowledge of embezzlement.

"Try me, Robert," she said.

CHAPTER TWENTY

*Smith Mountain Lake, created primarily to pro-
duce electricity and completed in 1966, is a haven for
fishing, boating and just plain relaxing. Northern
folks have discovered that, dollar for dollar, selling
their homes in New Jersey, Pennsylvania, or New
York and retiring to this Virginia lake, is a smart
investment. If you motor slowly along the breathtak-
ing, 500 miles of squiggly shoreline, you will see
weekend cottages and permanent homes often side by
side. Manicured lawns, some with masses of flowers
cascading to the water's edge, contrast spectacularly
with unspoiled wooded areas dotted with blooming
dogwoods, red bud trees, and mountain laurel. During the spring and summer months, colorful pots
overflowing with a variety of blossoms stand like
welcoming sentinels on many large and small docks.
You might even glimpse a great blue heron fishing at
the water's edge, a bald eagle dipping, gliding and
soaring in a cloud-free sky, or a red-tailed hawk
searching for prey."*

Aurora turned off the tape recorder. Something nagged at
her. Flowerpots, colorful flowerpots. She glanced out the
window, then looked again. A bright, red pot rested at the
end of the dock; gone was the green one she had admired
soon after her arrival. She looked across the cove at Robert

119

Reeves' boathouse, and saw a man replacing an orange flowerpot with a red one. There had been a green pot on Robert's dock and her dock the day she arrived at the lake. She picked up her binoculars and read "Tom's Tidy Lawn & Lake Service" on the back of the man's tan coveralls. *Interesting. Two color changes on my dock, three changes on Robert's dock. And all in less than a week. Why would any lawn service put different colored pots on adjacent docks? And why change them so often? Oh, well, if that's how they want to spend their time. . . .*

Having lived at the lake for years, she recognized most of the landscapers' signature trademarks. For instance, Tom's Tidy Lawn & Lake Service maintained this yard and dock. His "thing" for docks consisted mainly of large clay pots in colors of orange, green, or red. Depending on the season, the pots were planted with pansies, petunias or geraniums. She picked up the binoculars again and recognized Biff, the same man who came to the house last week. She decided that the next time she saw him she'd give him some unsolicited advice on time management, even though she doubted he'd appreciate it.

A faint snort from Little Guy brought her back to the present, and she put down the binoculars and turned on the recorder that rested in her lap.

Luke paced his office floor. He couldn't concentrate on his work. Usually getting out on the water soothed him, which is why he had started his scuba diving business and his sight-seeing / water-taxi service three years ago. An hour earlier he had grabbed his tackle box and casting rod, and gone fishing. When he missed a couple of good strikes, he realized that his attention was on Aurora and Sam, that there was no point in trying to fish. He had reeled in his line and returned to the office.

Luke knew the cops suspected him of breaking into Aurora's house and clobbering Sam. He didn't know what Aurora thought. Surely she didn't believe he could do such a thing. Then again, they'd only known each other a few days.

If only he had called the police himself to report the boating incident. And how could he have been so stupid as to pick up that baseball bat? He walked over to the phone and dialed Aurora.

"Hey, Aurora," he said when she answered.

"Hello, Luke," she said in an icy voice.

"How's Sam? And how are you?"

"We're okay. The doctor ordered Sam to bed for a few days, but he won't have any lasting ill effects." She kept her voice low so she wouldn't wake her husband. He needed all the sleep he could get.

"You don't believe I did what the cops are saying, do you?" Aurora didn't answer. Luke repeated his question.

"I don't know what to think. You were in my house. The bat was in your hand. And you didn't report the boat attack to the police as you said you would."

"I had an influential client waiting when I returned to the office, so I told my secretary to call the police. She assured me she'd take care of it right away."

"Don't you think she would've reported it if you asked her to? That wasn't a casual request you made. Or was it?" Aurora was so angry her voice shook.

"She swears she called them immediately."

Aurora forced herself to keep her voice down. "Why didn't you call from your boat phone as soon as you left my house?"

"I tried. The battery was dead."

"Oh, Luke. Do you expect me to believe that? You don't honestly think I'm that gullible, do you?"

Luke knew their relationship had changed. He was sorry. He and Aurora had clicked immediately; he already considered her a good friend. The phone conversation wasn't going well; he needed to talk to her in person.

"It's no good trying to talk to you over the telephone. I'm coming over some time today, Aurora. See you in a while. 'Bye."

Aurora hung up. She didn't want to see Luke. She remembered Sam's recent warning about him.

She looked over at Sam still sleeping peacefully on the bed, quietly closed the bedroom door behind her, and walked through the house. She was impressed with the cleaning service. In only a few hours, the three workers had vacuumed, dusted, picked up the slashed cushions and other items from the floor, and scrubbed fingerprinting powder off walls.

"Ms. Harris, we're 'bout done except for cleaning the bathrooms and hanging a few pictures. Don't know which ones go where. And we still need to do the room across the hall over there."

"I'll hang the pictures myself, Sheila. And don't worry about cleaning my bedroom. I cleaned it thoroughly before bringing my husband home from the hospital. Just didn't have time to do anything with the rest of the house."

"Are you sure? It wouldn't be any trouble for us."

"It's nice of you to offer, but I'm sure. And my husband needs to rest.

"How much longer before you're ready to leave? I'll get a check ready."

"We'll be here for about another hour. And don't worry 'bout writing us a check; Mr. Johns took care of it already."

CHAPTER TWENTY-ONE

Aurora quit stuffing darks in the washing machine when the telephone rang. Sam had brought all his dirty laundry with him from Augusta, and she'd not had time to wash but one load since he'd arrived. Until now, that is. Frowning, she left the laundry and hurried to the telephone.

"Mrs. Harris, a body has surfaced!" Lieutenant Conner exclaimed. "Could possibly be the one you discovered on Wednesday."

"Where?" Aurora asked, as the familiar undercurrent of fear burned in her stomach. She sat down next to the phone, squeezed her eyes shut, and willed the fear to go away.

"One cove over from Spawning Run. I'll explain it all to you when I see you. Can you come down to the station right away?"

"I can be there in about forty-five minutes," she said. "But I'm not looking forward to this."

"I understand, but I'm glad you can come. Our office is on the third floor. See you then."

Aurora cradled the receiver and headed to the bedroom to leave a note for Sam. She didn't want to wake him if he was still sleeping, but she couldn't leave without letting him know where she was going.

In the bedroom, Sam had heard the phone ring. He sat up, flung back the covers, swung his legs over the side of the bed, and stood up. He waited, expecting a slightly off-balance feeling to hit him. Pleased, and a little surprised when it didn't happen, he hobbled over to the dresser, pulled out underwear, jeans, and a faded black sweatshirt. He dressed, then sat down to put on his socks and walking shoes. Little Guy, sensing a change, barked.

"And just what is going on in here?" demanded Aurora as she entered the bedroom. "Hush, Little Guy. Sam, you get right back in that bed."

"Nope. Not gonna do it. I'm sick of being cooped up. Little Guy's tired of it, too. Just look at him."

Aurora stood there, hands on her hips. "You know you need one more day of bed rest. You heard Dr. Cameron."

"Susie-Q, I'm okay. Honest. I'm also bored beyond belief. Bet you didn't know there are 309 dogwood blossoms on that tree just outside the window."

"I don't believe you." She grinned in spite of herself.

"Fine, count them for yourself. But Little Guy and I are going for a short walk." He turned and sauntered out of the room.

Aurora glanced at the large dogwood tree on the other side of the window. There was no way she was going to count all the white blossoms, but Sam had piqued her curiosity. She hurried to catch up with him and Little Guy.

"Want to walk with us?"

"I'd love to, but Lieutenant Conner just called. He wants me at the police station as soon as I can get there. They found a body."

"I'll ride with you."

"No, someone needs to be close by in case the cleaning service has any last minute questions. Besides, I'm ready for King to come home. It's incredible how much I've missed him. I'll call Carole from the car phone later, see if I can go pick him up. She's probably had just about enough of The King of Hearts. If it suits Carole, I'll swing by her place after I leave the police station, probably visit with her for a few minutes, too."

Chirp. Chirp.

"The battery in one of the smoke detectors must be weak. I'll go change it," Sam said.

Chirp. Chirp.

"No, you shouldn't be going up and down stairs. I'll go. It'll only take me a minute."

She gave Sam a quick kiss as he walked out the front door, implored him to walk slowly, and followed the chirp-chirp to the basement. She looked around, amazed as always at what a neat shop her dad had kept. She reached over a workbench and pulled a box marked "Smoke Detector Batteries" off the well-organized shelf.

Setting the box on the workbench, she saw again the completed picture frame waiting for the craftsman who would never return. Fighting back tears, she picked up the frame and turned it over.

Puzzled, Aurora stared at the inscription her father had written on a portion of the frame. It didn't surprise her that he had written something; that was his custom. But this was the first time the message had been handwritten with a black marker instead of routed. And usually her dad inscribed a short line from a favorite poem or hymn, one that the two of them both loved. This one, however, read simply "Ask Wyeth."

Ask Wyeth? I have absolutely no clue what that means, Dad.

She shook her head, returned the frame to its place on the bench, and replaced the battery in the smoke detector. Back upstairs, Aurora snatched up her car keys and headed to the police station. She blew Sam a kiss as she passed him in the driveway.

"Drive carefully," he called after her.

Aurora pulled into a parking spot in front of the three-story red brick building. She entered the police station through wide double doors and bypassed the elevator to walk the two flights of stairs instead. As she came out of the stairwell on the third floor, she nearly collided with Sergeant Johnson.

He grinned. "I thought I'd meet you in the lobby. Almost perfect timing, don't you think? Our office is just down the hall." He ushered her into a large room equipped with four desks, computers and several file cabinets. Stacks of papers and file folders were piled around the room.

"Ms. Harris, we need you to look at the body we fished out of the lake today. Hope you're up to that. I have to warn you, though. It's a gruesome sight. Are you ready?"

"Once was enough for me. Do you have a picture I could see instead? I honestly think I'd throw up if I smelled that body again."

"We wear masks; we'll get one for you. We think it's important that you view the actual corpse."

"Okay, I'll try." She donned the mask Lieutenant Conner handed her and followed the men into the morgue.

The thump, thump, thump of her heart blocked out all other sounds. The blood in her head drummed against her temples. Every single detail of the floating mass—the smell, the feel, the hanging flesh—flashed through her brain. She knew she was close to losing it. She shut her eyes, clutched the doorjamb, and waited until the room stopped spinning before she opened her eyes and walked over to view the corpse laid out on the gurney.

"It's the same one." She wheeled and fled from the room.

Once seated in the office, Aurora silently congratulated herself. She hadn't thrown up. She hadn't passed out. She had faced her demon and won. She felt a surge of strength she hadn't possessed since her dad died. She sipped on the bottle of ice-cold Coca-Cola Sergeant Johnson handed her.

Conner said, "Forensics compared the blood stains in the foyer of the 214 residence to the stained bat at your house. They matched perfectly. We suspect that the dead man is J. Melton Lampwerth IV, but we haven't received the final word from the lab yet." He paused, then added, "And by the way, why didn't you tell us Judge Anderson is your uncle?

Aurora shrugged her shoulders, grinned sheepishly, then said, "Sorry. Does that cause a problem?"

"Nope."

"Good. Now there's one thing I must say before I leave. That mask you gave me didn't hide the stench at all."

"We know," said Johnson, chuckling. "But would you have gone in the morgue without it?"

Back in the car, Aurora stuck a beach music CD in the CD player. She loved the sound of the Tams, the Catalinas, the Embers, the Drifters. She made a mental note to take Sam shagging at a local dance club when he recovered. Her fingers tapped the steering wheel in rhythm to "I Love Beach Music" as she headed home. The fear that had plagued her was gone. She felt rejuvenated, alive, capable of tackling anything.

Happiness swelled inside her. For the first time in many months, life was good again. Sam was healing fast, she now accepted her father's death as an accident, her mother no longer suffered, and soon King would be with her. And the house was clean. Yes, life was good.

CHAPTER TWENTY-TWO

Jimmy Ray crouched in the thick woods across Spawning Run and sighted down the cold, gray rifle barrel. His finger twitched in anticipation as he touched the trigger. He aimed at the young water skiier struggling to cross the boat's wake. "Pow! You're dead!" Jimmy Ray lowered the rifle and grinned. "At least you coulda been. Jimmy Ray don't miss."

"How many times do I hafta tell you to stop pointing that gun at people, Jimmy Ray?"

"Whatsa matter, Clyde? Do I make you nervous? You a little scairt of ol' Jimmy Ray, huh?"

"You don't scare me none. But the boss don't want you shootin' people for fun. We're supposed to lay low. That rifle of yours got a hair trigger, don't it? It could go off if you sneeze or even burp." *And yes, you scare the hell out of me, but I won't give you the satisfaction of knowing it.*

Jimmy Ray glared at Clyde. "How long we gonna sit in these here woods? I'm gittin' downright bored. Ain't no action goin' on 'cross the cove. I say we git in the boat, sneak over there and make somethin' happen. That little gal what's been staying in that house is a real looker." He pointed to the house at 210 Spawning Run Road. "And we ain't seen her big dog for a coupla days. I'll give her a real good time. And when I finish, you can have her. Probably just what you need."

Clyde forced a laugh. "You know my old lady would kill me if I messed around with another woman. Might be fun, though."

He didn't know how much longer he could control Jimmy Ray. Clyde had warned the boss several times about Jimmy Ray, told him Jimmy Ray was sick in the head, crazy even, a killer, ten times meaner than Snake. But the boss said that a cold-blooded killer who loved his work comes in handy sometimes.

Jimmy Ray was five the first time he watched his daddy Rufus kick a cat to death, then toss the body in the air to see how many times he could shoot it before it hit the ground. Jimmy Ray was four when Rufus took him way back up in the mountains to his first dog fight in old man Potts' barn. When the cops raided the place, they dropped Jimmy Ray off at his family's shack, then hauled Rufus and the other men to jail. The beating Jimmy Ray got from Opal, his mama, after the deputies left hurt bad. "That's for gitting caught!" she'd screamed as the razor strap cut into his back.

Jimmy Ray kind of liked it the times Rufus was in jail. Most of the uncles who visited his mama would hand him money to "go somewhere else fer a spell." Sometimes he took the money and left, but most times he stayed and peeped. Once when Jimmy Ray was 12, his daddy caught Opal with an uncle. Rufus beat Opal half to death, knocked out some teeth, cut her with a whisky bottle, and split open her head with a piece of kindling.

"Daddy, stop! You're gonna kill her!" This beating was the worst yet. "She won't cook for us no more if you don't stop."

His daddy just laughed. "Wise up, Jimmy Ray. She likes it. She aggravates me on purpose so I'll beat her. Why else would she stay? Listen good, kid. Ain't nothin' gonna respect you iffen they ain't scairt of you. Remember that."

Two days after his daddy's last release from jail, Jimmy Ray, age fourteen, stabbed his daddy to death for attacking mama with an axe. Jimmy Ray bragged to Clyde recently how he'd enjoyed the killing, said he wouldn't have cared if

129

his old man had chopped his mama into a hundred pieces. After all, she was only a slut, a whore. He laughed, said that protecting her had just been the excuse he needed to kill. The judge called it justifiable homicide.

Clyde recognized in Jimmy Ray the same sick traits that were evident in Jimmy Ray's old man.

"Speaking of my old lady, have you ever tasted her cold meatball sandwiches? Ain't nothing better on God's green earth. I swear it, Jimmy Ray. The meatballs are somethin' else. She packed me an extra sandwich today. You want it, Jimmy Ray?"

Clyde breathed a sigh of relief when his companion leaned his rifle against a tall pine tree and reached for the sandwich. Food was usually a good distraction for Jimmy Ray.

Ring. Ring. Jimmy Ray pulled his cell phone out of its case and answered. "Yeah, I understand. 'Bout time she called you."

"That the boss?" Clyde asked.

"Yeah. Your old lady just called him. Said to git on with our plans." Jimmy Ray and Clyde climbed in the boat and motored out of Spawning Run.

"Dammit." Judge Anderson hung up the phone. He swiveled around in his chair and bellowed for Conner and Johnson.

"Guess what?" he said as the two men hurried into the makeshift office Sheriff Rogers had set up for Judge Anderson. The judge liked the effect he had on the police force, the mayor, everyone. When he said jump, they jumped. That was the way it should be. Judges should be respected. He'd been a police officer, then district attorney before becoming a judge, and he knew he had a lot of influence. Normally, he didn't use his connections, hadn't even used them when his brother Jack drowned since it was obviously an accident. But now his beloved niece needed him, and he'd stop at nothing to help her. He knew the cooperation from Conner and Johnson was due to orders from Sheriff Rogers, one of his best friends for over thirty years. Overworked and understaffed, the sheriff welcomed the judge's help.

Anderson said to the deputies, "You know the blood on the baseball bat at 210 Spawning Run Road and the blood on the floor at 214 match. Unfortunately, neither matches your floater. And get this. Your John Doe died from a gunshot wound to the head, not a baseball bat. Not only that, but Lampwerth's dental records don't match the victim's. I was positive you'd found Lampwerth. Positive. But according to the medical examiner, the body in the morgue had been in the water about two months. Lampwerth was last seen on Friday of last week."

"So where's Lampwerth, and who's in the morgue?" asked Sergeant Johnson between puffs on his cigar.

"I wish I knew. Let me think, let me think." Anderson leaned back in his chair, locked fingers from both hands together on the top of his shiny, bald head, and frowned.

"Okay, here's what you'll do. I suggest, mind you I can only suggest, that Conner here start checking missing persons reports. In the meantime, Johnson can notify all Virginia police departments that a John Doe floated up today. Fax them pictures of the body and his vitals. Johnson, you take the blow-ups you made from Aurora's videotape to her. Maybe she'll recognize one of the people in the boat."

He paused, then said, "If Sheriff Rogers approves, that is."

CHAPTER TWENTY-THREE

"Thank you for calling Your Real Estate Agency. This is Carole. How may I help you?"

"Carole, have you had enough of my big black dog?" asked Aurora into the phone. "You sound tense to me. Could that have anything to do with King?"

"I sound tense? How could you possibly think I'm tense?"

Aurora grinned. "Is King getting to you?"

"If you mean is his constant floor-pacing wearing a rut in my carpet, or his unraveling my silk sweater that matched my teal linen pants suit, or his refusal to eat, or his whining every time he hears a car drive up bothering me, then the answer to your question is 'Yes!' But enough of me. When are you coming to get this gem of a dog?"

Aurora covered her mouth with her hand. She couldn't answer for fear she'd break out laughing. And Carole would not appreciate that.

"Are you snickering, Aurora? I don't recall hearing anyone say anything funny."

Aurora swallowed her laughter and willed her brain to conjure up horrid images of the body she had just identified in the morgue. Seconds later, her laughter under control, she said to her friend, "I know you'll miss King terribly when he's gone, but would you mind if I come get him?"

"How soon can you be here?"

"I'm calling from my car, so I can probably be there in ten minutes, maybe a little longer."

"That long. Oh well, it will give me ten extra minutes with this gem of a dog. We'll both be waiting. And waiting."

Aurora, tears running down her cheeks, laughed all the way to the real estate office. Carole and King met her when the car pulled into the parking lot. Barking ecstatically, King jumped into the car's front seat and Aurora's lap the instant she opened the door. After a long hug and some petting from Aurora, King backed out of the car and the three walked inside the agency.

"This is the calmest he's been in three days," said Carole. Aurora sat on the office sofa. King spilled out of her lap. The Lab gazed adoringly up at his mistress as his tail wagged a language that only Aurora and he understood. "He never crawled up in *my* lap like that, although I invited him on numerous occasions."

Aurora stroked King's head and back. He looked lovingly at her. "Carole, how well do you know Luke Stancill?"

"Luke? He grew up in Union Hall in Franklin County, went to Virginia Tech for two years, played basketball there. Then his father dropped dead from a massive heart attack. Luke quit school to help support his mom and three younger sisters. He's since taken several night courses at Ferrum College. He's working on a degree; I think it's in business. He opened his own business two or three years ago.

"Just between the two of us, I don't know him as well as I would like. He's a really nice guy, good looking, smart, honest, hard working. Did I mention good looking? A good dancer, too. He's the only man I've been the least bit interested in since Fred. Luke and I dated a few times, and I thought he was getting as interested in me as I was in him. Then wham! Little Miss Sexpot Vanessa strolls into his office asking for a part-time job, and that's the end of my romantic dream. Why do you ask?"

"Is Vanessa the secretary who didn't report the attempted ramming of Luke's boat to the police?"

"Yep, same person. Has to be." Carole fetched a bowl and set it on the floor. "I know it sounds like I'm a jealous woman, but something's not right with Vanessa. My feeling is that she's using Luke, but he evidently doesn't see it that way. And, of course, I can't tell him."

Carole poured dry dog food into the bowl. King jumped off Aurora's lap and began wolfing down his meal. "Look at him! You'd think I hadn't offered him food the whole time he's been here. Aurora, I tried everything I could think of, even pretended to chew on a morsel or two myself. No luck; he'd never take more than a few bites at a time."

"Don't worry about it. He does the same thing with Sam when I'm out of town." She scratched his neck. "Guess I'd better go. I need to stop off at Diamond Hill General Store before I go home, and I don't want to be too late. No telling what kind of trouble Sam and Little Guy will get into if I'm away very long."

The two friends hugged good-bye as the Lab tugged at his leash. "Thank you so much for looking after King, Carole. I missed him, but I didn't worry about him."

Knowing King wouldn't jump out of the car, Aurora rolled the windows all the way down after parking in Diamond Hill's parking lot. Quickly putting tuna fish, pasta, milk, orange juice, eggs, and two bottles of local wine from Hickory Hill Vineyards in her cart, she paid for her items and loaded them into the Jeep. "King, let's go home."

Home. That sounded strange. She hadn't called the house on Spawning Run Road home since her marriage to Sam. She reminded herself that home was their house in Augusta, but she knew in her heart that Smith Mountain Lake was really home, always would be. But now her parents, the people who gave the house its warmth, would never return.

A wave of sympathy hit her when she passed Robert's house. He and Jill deserved to hear what had transpired at the police station. Maybe she could break the bad news about Lampwerth's body floating up, kind of soften the blow before the proof came back from the lab. She backed up, drove in Robert's drive, and rang the doorbell.

Jill greeted her with a limp hug. "Would you like to join Robert and me in the kitchen for a cup of coffee?" Jill didn't wait for a reply, but led the way into the gourmet kitchen.

"Hi," Robert said to Aurora. She had the feeling she'd interrupted something, that she should have called instead. She made up her mind to stay only a few minutes.

Jill handed Aurora a cup of coffee and moved over to stand beside Robert. They stared at Aurora. "What's up?" Robert asked, his arms folded across his chest.

Aurora wanted to melt into the floor, to be anywhere but in that room with these two obviously upset people. But she said, "I've just come from police headquarters. They fished a body out of the lake this morning. Asked me to identify it." Aurora paused, stared at her feet, and said, "It was the one I saw two days ago."

Robert unfolded his arms and rested his hands on Jill's shoulders. In a soft voice he asked, "Man or woman? The body, I mean."

"A man." Aurora looked down at her cup and watched the rich, brown coffee swirl around as she stirred it.

"Do they think it's Lampwerth?" Robert asked bluntly, his hands tightening protectively on Jill's shoulders.

"I'm afraid they suspect that, but the lab results haven't come in yet." She hated this. She wished she hadn't come. "I'm so sorry. I wouldn't have told you, but I thought you'd want to know."

"You're right, we do."

"Was the body clothed?" Jill whispered.

"Yes."

"What was it wearing?" asked Jill.

"Looked like the remnants of a plaid flannel shirt and jeans." She wished she'd minded her own business.

In a low voice, Jill Hathaway said, "Then it's not Mr. Lampwerth. I'm sure of it. He's never in his life worn blue jeans. Or a plaid shirt. At least not since he was a child. Every shirt he's ever owned was either white or light blue. Casual dress for him means no tie. No pun intended, but he once told me he wouldn't be caught dead in plaid."

Back at her parents' home, Aurora parked beside Sam's car, opened the car door for King, and stepped back out of his way. Happy to be back at Spawning Run Road, he raced around the yard, nose to the ground as he tracked every enticing new and familiar scent. Even though Carole had allowed him to keep her company at the agency and even permitted him to sleep in her bedroom, King had been in mourning most of the time. Until he saw Aurora, that is.

Aurora retrieved the groceries from the Jeep and entered the house. The cleaning service had finished and left; the house was immaculate. But something important was missing. She'd anticipated a loving greeting from Sam and Little Guy. Where were they? She looked at her watch. She'd been gone over two hours. Surely Sam had returned from his walk by now. She stepped out on the deck and eyed the dock and shoreline. No sign of Sam or the terrier.

When the doorbell rang, she jerked open the door and frowned. Luke stood on the porch.

"I'm in the middle of something right now, Luke." She started to shut the door.

"Aurora, we have to talk."

She wasn't afraid of Luke. King obviously liked him. Despite Sam's words of caution, she relented and let him in.

Within a few minutes, the two were talking as freely with each other as they had before the attack on Sam.

"Why didn't you report the boat assault to the cops?"

"The battery in the boat phone was dead. I already told you that. By the time I arrived at my office, an upset and extremely influential client was waiting for me. Actually, he was getting in his car to leave when I ran up from the dock. I coaxed him back inside and told my secretary to call the police. Gave her your name and phone number to pass on to them. Because I trusted Vanessa to relay the message and because the client could make or break me, I made the wrong decision. I'll never forgive myself, Aurora, but I'd like you to forgive me."

"You're forgiven, Luke, but I still don't understand why the police didn't get the message."

"I asked Vanessa the same question. She swears she called them, said the problem must have been at the police station."

"I don't buy that. How long has she worked for you? What do you know about her?" King whined. Aurora rose from the sofa and put him outside.

Luke's shoulders stiffened. "She's worked part time for me for four months, two or three days a week. I can't afford to have her full time, so she works another part-time job, too. Her parents live at the lake, and she lives with them. She's very good with my clients. They all adore her.

"Once you asked if I had a 'significant other'. Well, Vanessa's the one I told you about. The relationship isn't as significant to her as I'd like it to be, but I'm working on it. I trust her completely, and I know you'd like her."

I doubt it. But Aurora said only, "Let's look at the tape one more time. I'll get it."

As Aurora went to the bedroom to fetch the tape, she wondered again where Sam could have gone. She pushed the eject button on the VCR. No responding whir. No tape. Nothing. *That's strange. It was here when I left.* She looked on the nightstand, on the bed, under the bed, then rummaged through her cross-stitch bag. Still no tape. She picked up her tape recorder and turned off the switch. She'd left it running.

Then she realized that Sam must have returned to the house, turned on the VCR, and discovered something important on the videotape. A clue, perhaps? He must have contacted the police, and they came by and picked up Sam and the tape. And, of course, Sam wouldn't leave Little Guy here alone. *Sam is surely safe. No use to worry. But he should have left me a note.*

Empty-handed, she returned to the living room and to Luke.

CHAPTER TWENTY-FOUR

Hoping it was Sam calling, Aurora dashed to the phone and picked it up on the second ring. Her uncle's raspy voice greeted her.

"I'm on my way over, honey. Got a couple of things to talk over with you and Sam. Some interesting facts have surfaced."

"Sam's not here, Uncle Charlie. I think he must be with Lieutenant Conner and Sergeant Johnson. He and Little Guy were gone when I arrived home a little while ago."

"Be there in under ten minutes," he barked into the phone before hanging up.

"I'm leaving," Luke said when Aurora told him Uncle Charlie was on his way. "I've got a scary feeling I'm about to be arrested."

"My uncle can't arrest you; he's a judge, not a cop. But you'd be wise to tell him everything you just told me. If he believes you, he just might go to bat for you with the police. He has considerable influence, you know." King barked at the door and Aurora let him in.

"I believe you're innocent, but there are some problems with your story. For instance, why didn't Vanessa call the police? No, don't tell me the fault lies with the police department. Something strange is going on here, Luke. The police need to talk to Vanessa."

"I don't want them talking to Vanessa. She hasn't done anything wrong. I'm leaving."

"Too late." She pointed out the window as a police car and a black Lincoln pulled in beside Luke's car. The judge and deputies Conner and Johnson walked up to the house. Aurora let them in.

"Well, well, well," remarked Conner as he fended off an exuberant King. "I didn't expect to find you here, Mr. Stancill." He scratched King behind the ears.

"I didn't expect you to find me here, either. So am I under arrest?"

"Not yet, but I will want to talk with you."

Aurora looked at Conner and Johnson. "Where are Sam and Little Guy?"

"I have no idea," Conner answered, puzzled.

"But I thought he was with you."

"Aurora, why did you think Sam and Little Guy were with these fellows?" asked the judge.

"Well, the tape was missing from the VCR, and Sam and Little Guy are gone, and I figured that Sam had found a clue on the tape and. . . ." She sank into a chair. King whined and put his head on her knee.

"Sam and Little Guy left for a walk over two hours ago. I drove to the police station to identify a body, then went to Carole's to pick up King. After that, I made a quick stop at the store for milk and a few other things, stopped off at the Reeves house for only a minute, and when I returned home Sam and Little Guy still weren't back from their walk. And when I discovered the tape was missing. . . ." She thought for a moment. "Where could he be? Do you think he's in trouble, Uncle Charlie?"

Her uncle scowled. "Probably not."

"Don't look at me, Judge Anderson," said Luke. "I'm innocent."

"Yeah, right," said Sergeant Johnson.

"The cleaning service was still here when I left," Aurora said. "Maybe they know something." She rushed to the desk, looked up the number for the cleaning service, and dialed.

Sheila finally answered. "Hello."

"Is this Sheila?" asked Aurora.

"Yes, this is Sheila."

"This is Aurora Harris. You cleaned my house today?"

"Yes, ma'am. I remember." She paused, then asked, "Is something wrong with our work?"

"Oh, no. You and your crew did an excellent job. I just wanted to know if my husband returned to the house before you left."

"No, ma'am, Mr. Harris didn't come back while we were still there. Sorry I cain't help you."

"Did you see him walking on the road anywhere when you drove out?"

"No, ma'am."

Aurora thanked Sheila and hung up. *This isn't like Sam.*

"Has she seen him?" asked Uncle Charlie.

Aurora looked at her uncle. "No."

"We need to talk with you privately, Mrs. Harris," said Lieutenant Conner as he eyed Luke.

"Luke," Aurora said.

"I can take a hint, Aurora, although that was more like an ultimatum from your illustrious law enforcement officer here."

"There's no need to talk like that, Luke," Aurora said. "Don't make things worse."

"Sorry, you're right." Clicking his heels together, he saluted Conner, Johnson, and Anderson before he left.

"Is he always like that?" Uncle Charlie asked. Aurora shrugged.

"Thought he'd never leave. I didn't want him to hear it, but I don't believe he's guilty of anything except bad judgment. Lieutenant Conner, however, is almost ready to make an arrest," said Uncle Charlie.

"For what? Who is he planning to arrest?"

"Your neighbor Robert Reeves is not as squeaky clean as you think," said Uncle Charlie. "Seems the accountant at Lampwerth International was ready to spill the beans to Lampwerth. The accountant warned him the day before he disappeared that someone in the company was embezzling funds. At the time, the accountant didn't know for sure who it was, but when he mentioned this, Lampwerth became furious—and disappeared. The accountant, a Mr. Louis Beale, told Lieutenant Conner less than an hour ago on the phone that he believes Robert Reeves is the embezzler."

"I don't buy that. Robert's too nice a guy."

"And why wouldn't he be a nice guy? He's rolling in money. And you must admit that house of his is very expensive, probably worth at least a couple million. And it's only his weekend retreat. The Babe Ruth bat that clobbered Sam belonged to Reeves. And in the foyer of Reeves' house the police found bloodstains that match Lampwerth's. Just haven't found the correct body yet." Uncle Charlie paused to light his pipe. "But they will. You can count on that."

"We've gotta go, judge," said Conner.

"I do, too," said the judge. "I'll call you later, Aurora." He kissed her cheek.

Aurora walked them to the door and waved goodbye. "Drive carefully," she said.

CHAPTER TWENTY-FIVE

His hands jammed in the pockets of his brown gabardine pants, Robert Reeves stood in the Florida room of his house and stared out at the lake. A few minutes ago the water's surface was calm with reflections of clouds and trees so clear that if he'd taken a picture and turned it upside down, he'd be hard pressed to say which were the actual trees and sky. And up until a few days ago, his life had been that calm, too. Now a soft breeze stirred the water, spoiling the perfect surface. And Reeves knew that before it was finished the lake would get rough and choppy. And so would his life.

He looked over at Jill asleep on the white wicker sofa and spread a lightweight red and white quilt over her legs. He longed to touch her, caress her, kiss her, hold her so close she could never leave him. Part of him wished she'd never come back into his life with such a force; the other part treasured each moment he had with her.

That first day in Lampwerth's office, when Jill's innocent brown eyes looked into his searching gray ones, he knew he was in love, not lust, for the first time in his life. Both of them understood Lampwerth International's no-dating policy among employees, but they couldn't help themselves. Destined to be together, they ignored the policy. And fell deeper and deeper in love.

The day their world crashed started out like any other normal day. Robert phoned Jill with his customary wake-up call to her apartment, they met at the Morning Glory Diner for breakfast, ate sweet rolls, talked sweet talk, and left—separately—for the office and a routine pretend-you-don't-mean-anything-to-me day.

That day a jealous secretary, one who had her eye on Robert during his pre-Jill days, decided to enlighten J. Melton Lampwerth IV. Lampwerth had known about the affair between his two valuable employees and pretended not to notice. But when the woman came running to him with the information, he had no choice but to adhere to his own rules. And Lampwerth had issued an ultimatum to Robert and Jill.

That day five years ago, when Jill Hathaway refused his marriage proposal and picked her career at Lampwerth International over a lifetime career as Mrs. Robert Reeves, nearly destroyed him.

"Jill, I love you. With all my heart and soul I love you. Marry me; give up your job. We don't need the money," he'd pleaded. He didn't tell her he had inherited millions of old Delaware money, owned half a dozen steeplechasers that raced in France and England. He donated most of his Lampwerth salary to charitable causes. He never told Jill about his fortune. Old-money folks didn't flaunt their wealth; only the social climbers and *nouveaux-riches* paraded their assets for all to see.

But she had refused his proposal. "I love you, too, Robert. But I'm the Executive Secretary / Assistant to the President," she'd said, pride apparent in her voice. "I've worked too many years, endured too many hardships. I can't give it up for a life of cooking, cleaning, socializing at the country club, and playing bridge every day. Robert," she said softly, "I'm not the type to spend my life waiting for you to come home."

"I'll hire a cook and a housekeeper if you want me to. And I'll love you more than any woman on this earth has ever been loved."

"No, Robert."

He watched her change from a warm, life-loving person to a cold, driven woman. She had pushed her chair away from the table, walked out of the restaurant and, except when he saw her at Lampwerth International, out of his life.

Because of that, a part of him despised J. Melton Lampwerth IV.

He thinks I'm still asleep, thought Jill. Through half-closed eyes she watched Robert as he stood peering out at the lake. She wished she could go back to that night when he'd asked her to marry him, had promised he'd love her forever. *How could I have been so stupid? My life's been empty without him. He can't still love me. If he did, he'd wrap his arms around me, whisper in my ear, ask me again to be Mrs. Robert Reeves.*

Instead of placing the blame on herself, Jill had blamed Lampwerth. After all, it was his policy that split the two lovers apart. But now reality hit her, and she knew that her ambition had destroyed the most perfect relationship any two people could experience. And silently she cried.

Jill hated herself. And she hated J. Melton Lampwerth IV.

CHAPTER TWENTY-SIX

Aurora looked down at her trembling hands. *Get a grip on yourself, Aurora.* She walked over to the large window and looked out at the lake. *Sam should have been back hours ago. He's in danger. I can feel it.*

Think, Aurora. You can't help Sam if you panic. Find something to do and wait for either Uncle Charlie or Sam to call you.

She wandered into the bedroom and looked around. "I need something to keep busy," she said. Aurora dug in her tote bag for her cross-stitching, picked up the tape recorder from her bag, re-wound it, and settled back to cross-stitch and review what she'd dictated earlier in the day. King stretched out at her feet.

She stopped the tape occasionally to jot new ideas and changes onto a yellow legal pad. She heard a vaguely familiar voice on the tape just as she reached to shut off the recorder. *Who was that? And how did it get on the recorder? Oh yeah, I accidentally left the recorder running this morning.*

Aurora quickly pressed "rewind," then "stop," then "play."

She heard a female voice exclaim, "I found it! The tape was right there in the VCR. I don't know how we missed it when Jimmy Ray and Clyde searched the room earlier. But then we were looking for pictures and the necklace; we didn't know nothing 'bout a tape." Pause. "Yeah, it's the one you're looking for." The voice stopped for a few seconds, then continued. "How do I know it's the right tape? Dammit, contrary to what you've always believed, I'm sure as hell not stupid. I watched it."

Aurora picked up the recorder and kissed it. If she had purchased the cheap recorder she'd originally planned to buy, the tape would have run out before the voice could be recorded. At Sam's insistence, she bought a more expensive model, a voice-activated one. *Who are Jimmy Ray and Clyde?* And the voice on the tape, she knew she'd heard it before. *But where?*

She played the tape again, but the identity of the voice continued to elude her. Over and over she listened to the tape, then dialed Uncle Charlie. *Pictures. What pictures?* She slammed down the receiver, just missing Uncle Charlie's "Hello."

The voice mentioned pictures. And the necklace. At first Aurora had been so intent on placing the voice that she hadn't paid attention to the words.

She ran to the kitchen and pulled open the junk drawer. She saw the necklace still in the back of the drawer where she'd left it. Relieved, she quickly searched all the places in the house where pictures were stored, even flipped through photograph albums. *There are no pictures here that would interest anyone except family and close friends. Besides, most of the albums were dumped on the floor the day Sam surprised the intruders.*

Questions she couldn't answer bombarded her. *Were Sam's attackers looking for pictures and the diamond and ruby necklace? If so, they didn't find the necklace. But did they find the pictures? Or were his attackers random burglars who panicked when Sam surprised them? Whose voice is on the recorder, where have I heard it before, and how did the voice get in my house? Who was the voice talking to on the phone? Who are Jimmy Ray and Clyde? And most important, where are Sam and Little Guy?*

Aurora nearly tripped over her mother's needlepoint footstool in her haste to answer the telephone when it rang. *Please let it be Sam.*

"Hi, Aurora. This is Jill Hathaway."

"Oh, hey." She slumped down in the chair.

"Are you okay, Aurora? Your voice sounds funny, not like you."

"I thought you might be Sam. I'm worried about him. He left the house with Little Guy around nine o'clock for a short walk and hasn't returned. Hasn't called, either. No one I've talked to knows where he is. I can't shake the feeling something's wrong. Have either you or Robert seen him today?"

"I haven't. Hold on a sec and I'll ask Robert." Aurora held her breath as she waited.

"Sorry, Robert hasn't seen him, either. Sam probably stopped at a neighbor's house and forgot to call. You know how men are. Every male from age nine on believes he's invincible and figures the woman in his life knows this. At least that's what my grandmother always told me."

Jill glanced at the clock beside the telephone, snapped her suitcase shut, and motioned to Robert that she was ready to leave.

"Aurora, I called to ask you a favor and to tell you I'm flying back to Washington, leaving in just a few minutes. Robert and I wondered if you would keep Russell a while longer. I won't be here, and Robert's too distraught right now to be a good caretaker, wouldn't do as good a job taking care of Russell as you and Sam will do. Could you keep him for a few more days?"

"We'd be happy to keep Russell for as long as you wish, but right now I don't even know where he is."

"I'm sure Sam and Russell will come marching home any minute now. I must go, Aurora. Robert's hired a private plane at the Smith Mountain Lake Airport to fly me back to D.C. Robert will drive me to the airport. He can't go with me to Washington; the local police strongly advised him to stay here a while longer. Something about making himself available in case more questions surface. It was nice meeting you. I wouldn't worry about your husband if I were you; I'm sure he will turn up soon. Goodbye."

Aurora stared at the telephone receiver still in her hand. Was Jill's voice the one on the tape? She wished she'd paid closer attention.

CHAPTER TWENTY-SEVEN

Clyde jammed the cell phone back in the case that hung from his black leather belt. He had dreaded calling Jimmy Ray. The guy was just plain nuts. He'd unleashed a stream of cuss words on Clyde before slamming the phone down. Why hadn't Clyde told the boss to call Jimmy Ray himself? But Clyde knew the answer: he plain didn't have the guts. If he bucked the boss, refused to do as instructed, the big money would stop rolling in, and his wife's supply of drugs would cease. Clyde knew too much, and if he didn't follow orders, his life wouldn't be worth a damn. He'd seen it happen too often to poor suckers who crossed the boss. If the boss didn't kill him, Clyde's wife would destroy everything when he couldn't supply her with the meth she craved. She said they were just diet pills, but he was no idiot. He knew she was addicted to them, as well as to crack.

The sound of squealing brakes startled him. Jimmy Ray, dressed in faded jeans and a black tee shirt printed with buxom topless women astride motorcycles, pulled himself out of the black four-wheel drive pickup truck, slammed the door shut, and leaned against it. He stuck his hand in through the open window and pulled out a beer, popped open the can, and took a long swig.

"Clyde, Clyde, Clyde. Why'd ya do it, man? Do you have the foggiest idea how good it wuz gonna git? That chick was hot. Real hot. Not a good time for a phone call, man."

Jimmy Ray's angry red face scared Clyde, but the look in those cold, squinty eyes frightened him the most. Moving a drowned man from the bottom of the lake didn't appeal to Jimmy Ray, and Clyde knew he had to think smart and fast to prevent Jimmy Ray from blowing out of control.

"The boss needs you to help with this big-deal job for one reason only—he knows you'll get it done right. He says to me, he says 'Git Jimmy Ray. He won't screw up. I can depend on the man. There ain't a better team anywhere than Jimmy Ray Thompson and Clyde Perkins.'" Clyde hesitated, afraid to push his luck, but finally added, "So you ready to get to work?"

Jimmy Ray gnawed off a hangnail, pulled a cigarette from his shirt pocket. He lit it, took three long drags, and tossed it to the ground. "Think I'll just check in with the boss myself," he said, yanking a cell phone identical to Clyde's from its holder.

"What'd he say?" asked Clyde as Jimmy Ray finished talking to the boss. He wiped at the sweat trickling down his face. Jimmy Ray and the boss had talked for several minutes, although all Jimmy Ray had said was an occasional "Yep," "Okay," and "Will do."

Jimmy Ray shrugged his shoulders and said only, "Let's do it."

Aurora lowered the binoculars. Hoping to glimpse Sam and Little Guy, she had scanned the shoreline on both sides of Spawning Run. Dejected, she walked away from the window just as King growled. Aurora whirled around to see a boat slowly motoring to the opposite side of the cove. "It's *Bad Boat,* the boat that almost rammed Luke's boat!" she said. She watched through the binoculars as the two men maneuvered the craft beyond her line of vision. Trying to spot the boat from a different angle, she stepped out on the deck. *Good, I can see better now.* The boat bobbed gently in the water. She panned the binoculars to the registration number on the side of the boat, but couldn't read it. Her hands trembled too much.

She focused on the boat's occupants. The larger man unbuttoned his shirt, folded it, and placed it neatly on the seat. He removed his shoes, then stuffed each with a brown sock. Aurora sucked in her breath when he unzipped his pants. Relieved when she saw a yellow and black bathing suit, she studied the man's face through the binoculars.

Where have I seen him before? They're up to something. She quickly ducked back inside the house and returned with the video camera and her digital camera. *Whatever it is, I'm not going to miss it.*

Aurora filmed as the man in the swimming trunks pulled on a diver's wet suit. Next came the scuba unit—the buoyancy control device, scuba tank and regulator.

Aurora shivered as she remembered a long-ago dive. Several years back, Sam had treated both of them to scuba diving lessons in Augusta and, after becoming certified, the two had enjoyed numerous dives in the Savannah River, the Charleston Harbor, the Atlantic Ocean off Edisto Island, the Florida Keys, and even the Caribbean.

At each lesson, the instructor had stressed to his students that conditions differed in every body of water, but Aurora had not been prepared for the hazards awaiting divers in Smith Mountain Lake. Before this lake began to fill, construction crews cleared numerous hillsides, but trees in some low-lying areas were left standing. Those too tall to be covered by water were simply topped instead of removed. Dilapidated farmhouses, abandoned automobiles, barbed wire fences, and even a bridge slowly disappeared from view as the water level in the lake gradually rose. Now these unseen secrets of days gone by waited on the lake bottom as silent sentinels, providing safe havens to fish and other aquatic creatures.

But these same sentinels could kill a diver.

Once, in her eagerness to explore Spawning Run, Aurora failed to adhere to strict diver's rules. And it nearly killed her. *Never dive alone. Always carry a cutting tool.* Even as she entered the water, those words rang in her head. But she dismissed them. After all, she rationalized to herself, this was her cove; she'd swum in it for years, knew nearly every inch of shoreline. The instructor's words of warning screamed out to her again, but by then she had become hopelessly entangled in fishing line caught in a tree on the bottom of the lake. Even if she'd had an underwater light, she couldn't have seen more than eighteen inches in front of her. At first she struggled. Then she willed herself to calm down to prolong her air supply and to think through her predicament. Her air nearly exhausted, Sam miraculously found her. He'd seen Aurora enter the water and had hurried after her. With his cutting tool, he'd freed her from the fishing line. With the search line he'd attached to the boat's anchor, he'd guided them both safely back to the surface.

Aurora had never dived again.

Jerked back to the activity on the lake, she watched the boat's diver pull on diving gloves and a mask. He grabbed a light and stepped off the gunwale, the flash of a large knife in his hand briefly visible as he disappeared into the lake.

As soon as Clyde descended into the murky depths, Jimmy Ray pulled out his cell phone. He placed a bet with his bookie and hung up. He surely did like cell phones; that was a big perk in this job. Why, he could call chicks any time he wanted, could make obscene phone calls while being paid to work. No, he never again would be without a cell phone. He glanced at his watch, then dialed again. He would call that sweet young thing he'd been harassing for a couple of weeks. The fear in her voice always excited him. And he liked the change he'd noticed in her when she darted outside her trailer home to check the mail, the way she shot frightened glances up and down the street before hurrying to the presumed safety of her home. Little did she know he could get her any time he chose. She hadn't the foggiest idea her caller lived right across the street. He finished dialing, then got a better idea. He hung up and grinned, and dialed a new victim. The chance that Clyde's wife would recognize his voice or that Clyde would catch him talking to her only excited him more.

*

Intent on recording the man in the boat, Aurora almost didn't hear the incessant ringing of her own phone inside the house. She considered letting it ring, then thought it could be Sam. She left the camera running and stepped into the house.

"No, I'm not interested in changing long distance telephone providers," she said. "Why? Because my husband is a vice president of your biggest competitor." When the caller stammered her apologies and hung up, Aurora smiled. Yes, she had lied, but this particular lie was the only one she ever told, and she told it almost every time she received a telemarketing call. It just felt so good, so right.

Before she could return to the deck, the phone rang again. Still smiling, she expected the same telemarketer.

But she was wrong.

"Lady, a man just paid me $100.00 to read this message to you. Please don't interrupt me. Here goes.

Bring the diamond and ruby necklace, pictures, negatives, and any undeveloped film your father took before he drowned—and you know the ones I mean—to Cabin 171E in Smith Mountain Lake State Park. Enter the cabin, place the items inside the white Styrofoam cooler to the left of the entrance door, and leave. Do not look back. Do not bring anyone with you or tell anyone. Then drive to Hales Restaurant, take a seat by a window, and await further instructions. Do this by 4:00 p.m. today. If you fail to deliver as instructed, your husband will die the same way your father did. This is not a joke.

"This *is* a joke, right, lady?" the caller asked.

But Aurora had dropped the phone.

CHAPTER TWENTY-EIGHT

The descent wasn't nearly as treacherous as the actual underwater search would be. The only diving Clyde had done in the last four years was right here at the lake, but his diving experience that began three decades ago down in the Florida Keys kicked in now. Hand over hand, he followed the anchor rope to the lake bottom. From there he began searching for the body of J. Melton Lampwerth IV, confident that if he remained focused, he would find Lampwerth. But it wouldn't be easy. Try as he might, he couldn't shake the sense of foreboding, the feeling that Jimmy Ray had just about reached his breaking point. It wouldn't take much to set him off.

Every night for three months Clyde had dreamed the same nightmare. In the dream, he, Snake and Jimmy Ray would drown the old man, ignoring his desperate pleas. "Why don't you just shoot me? I don't want to drown! Please, don't do this!" the old man begged. Clyde would wake up in a sweat remembering that foggy morning in January when Snake wrapped the anchor rope around the old man's leg. He couldn't forget when he, Snake and Jimmy Ray hoisted the old man and the anchor over the boat's gunwale into the cold water, then capsized the man's red rowboat to make it look like an accident. Damn, he despised himself. How could he have done such a thing? The old man's words "You won't get away with this!" rang inside Clyde's head.

Clyde wondered how his peaceful life had changed so drastically. Growing up in rural Georgia, he'd gone to church every Sunday, even sang in the choir. He played second base on the church softball team, was a lineman on the high school football team, ranked number two in the state in high school wrestling in his weight division. Sure, he'd only had a high school education, but he'd been ambitious, a hard worker, a moral person. He had moved to the Florida Keys, taken diving lessons, and soon was earning big bucks working on an underwater salvage team.

Sheila, that's what happened. He'd fallen hard the first time he saw her, dressed in white shorts and sky-blue halter, drinking a gin and tonic on the sailboat's deck. In those days, Clyde had been tan, tall, muscular, not like now, and Sheila had succumbed to his charms—and his hard-earned money. She was so sexy, so sweet, so adoring. They were positive fate had created a special place just for them. Even now, after all these years and everything that had happened in their lives, he quivered with desire when he thought of his Sheila.

Six months after the quickie wedding, she had a baby. A preemie, they told family and friends, but everyone knew babies three months early never weighed eight and a half pounds. But who cared? After all, Sheila and Clyde loved each other, and both were devoted parents. And from the day she was born, Red, nicknamed after her mass of flaming red hair, never lacked for material things. Big mistake.

Then came the boozing and partying, which took their toll on both Clyde and Sheila. Clyde lost his high-paying job managing the salvage company. For a year they lived off the profits from the sale of their house while renting a tiny apartment. Then, nearly destitute, the family moved from Florida to Virginia where Clyde went to work for Sheila's brother at Smith Mountain Lake. Another mistake. Sheila's wealthy, can-do-no-wrong brother introduced her to drugs, and Clyde found himself plunged into a life of crime to pay for Sheila's habit. If not for Sheila, Clyde could be working somewhere else doing honest labor, but he couldn't abandon her. And so he stayed. Then Red, more interested in having a good time with the fraternity boys than studying, flunked out of Florida State and moved in with her parents.

Clyde snapped back to the job at hand, attached one end of the search line to the anchor rope, and held the free end in his hand. From this point on he began the tedious search pattern of fanning out in one direction, returning to the anchor, then out again, thus making the anchor the hub in an imaginary wheel. Groping his way with gloved hands, he knew that eventually he'd discover the body. He was positive it was here. After all, he and Jimmy Ray had tied Lampwerth to a couple of cinder blocks and dumped him in this spot only a little over a week ago. Time after time Clyde's hands touched tree limbs, fence posts, and even a deflated inner tube. Never the corpse. Even with his underwater light flipped on, visibility was so bad he could see only inches in front of him.

On the water's surface, Jimmy Ray's phone call to Sheila reached her answering machine. Knowing Clyde could surface any minute only enhanced Jimmy Ray's excitement. He grinned in anticipation, whispered a couple of perverted thoughts into the phone, and hung up. Leaving messages was good, but occasionally he'd need to hear the fear in her voice. He'd call again later.

When air bubbles signaled Clyde's ascent, Jimmy Ray put aside all thoughts of Sheila. *Later, baby.*

"Got it, Jimmy Ray. Pass me the line," Clyde said as he surfaced beside the boat and whipped off his mouthpiece and goggles. He tied the line to one end of the freshly sliced rope still attached to Lampwerth. He'd had no trouble cutting the cinder blocks loose. "Help me get him in the boat."

"Hell no, I ain't gonna help you drag that squishy body in this here boat. He looks worse than crap. Don't smell none too good, neither. Let's tow him behind the boat; it sure won't hurt his looks none." Jimmy Ray laughed.

Clyde, not eager to touch the dead man any more than necessary, agreed.

"Wait up a sec, Clyde. Gotta git his diamond ring. Don't know how I missed it before. The chicks go for flashy rings, you know. And this is a big 'un." Clyde gagged and looked away as Jimmy Ray pulled out his knife, leaned over the side of the boat and chopped off Lampwerth's swollen finger. He tugged at the two-carat diamond ring, but it wouldn't budge. Jimmy Ray swished the finger around in the water, then grinning, dropped the finger with ring intact in his pants pocket.

Clyde hauled himself into the boat, pulled up the anchor, turned the ignition, pushed the throttle forward, and began motoring slowly out of the cove.

"Uh oh," Jimmy Ray said, "look over there. We got company." He pointed to a pontoon boat loaded with sightseers about a hundred yards away.

"Let's hope they stay in the main channel," Clyde said. He throttled back to an idle and waited for the other boat to pass by. He and Jimmy Ray both relaxed an instant too soon. A passenger on the other boat pointed to the cove, hollered, and the pontoon boat suddenly changed course and headed straight for them.

"What'll we do, Clyde? If they git too close they'll see our dead dude."

"Ahoy there," shouted the pontoon captain. "Do you have a phone we can use?"

"Sorry, no," Clyde yelled back.

"I've got a pregnant woman here. She's just gone into labor, needs a doctor. How 'bout your marine radio?" The pontoon boat inched closer to the idling cruiser.

"It's broke. Been meaning to get it fixed."

"I could pick him off easy," Jimmy Ray said under his breath as he bent over and fingered his rifle resting on the boat's floor.

"Listen carefully, Jimmy Ray. Put the gun down. Move slowly to the stern and cut Lampwerth loose. Maybe they won't see him floating, then we can come back later and pick 'im up. We can't take a chance on them identifying us."

For once Jimmy Ray did as he was told without arguing. Clyde shoved the throttle forward full speed and the boat bounded out of the cove. Seconds later screams of horror from the sightseers echoed across the water.

They'd discovered J. Melton Lampwerth IV.

CHAPTER TWENTY-NINE

Field investigator Lieutenant Ian Conner slammed down the phone, twirled around in his desk chair, clapped his hands together, and said, "Got 'im!"

Sergeant Johnson pushed the filing cabinet drawer shut, turned and faced Conner. "Got who?"

"Reeves, Robert Reeves, that's who. At least I'm pretty sure we got 'im."

"What happened?"

"That call I just received? Seems a tour boat captain, a Bud Karnes, found a floater about two hours ago in Spawning Run. That's Reeves' cove. Captain said his marine radio was busted, had a pregnant woman on board go into hard labor, and he needed to get her to shore fast, so he didn't haul the body back with him. Didn't call us when he docked because he wasn't sure where he saw the body, couldn't remember the closest buoy marker number. After he dropped off his party, he went back to locate the body. This time he remembered to take his cell phone with him, and he used that to contact the game warden.

"Anyhow, it sounds like our missing Lampwerth has finally surfaced. This is our lucky day."

"Don't we need a positive I.D. before we jump the gun?"

"Yeah, but the coroner and the body are on the way in right now. And we already have a copy of Lampwerth's dental records, which will speed up the identification process. The boat captain will arrive here any minute to give us a statement.

"And get this. A confirmation fax came in earlier. The blood in Reeves' foyer and the blood on the baseball bat match Lampwerth's. And the bat belongs to Reeves."

Johnson said, "And the accountant at Lampwerth International says Reeves was embezzling money from the company. Lots of money. The way I figure it, when Lampwerth found out someone was dipping into the company cookie jar, Reeves lured him to the lake on some pretense or other, killed Lampwerth, disposed of the body, then took a quick trip to establish an alibi. Bet when we check, we'll find that he flew out of the lake airport. I think you're right, Ian. I think we've got our killer."

Conner slapped his hand on his knee and said, "We're gonna make an arrest today." Johnson just grinned.

"I'm going to Sheriff Rogers with this. Will let Judge Anderson know, too. Buzz me when Karnes gets here."

"Will do."

When Captain Karnes arrived a little later, Sergeant Johnson ushered him into the office and motioned for him to sit in one of the folding wooden chairs near the desk. Turning another chair around, its legs scraping on the worn hardwood floor, Johnson sat spread-eagled in his seat, one arm resting on the back of his chair. He leaned over and buzzed Lieutenant Conner.

"Mr. Karnes has arrived."

"I'll be right there."

"Mind if I smoke?" asked Karnes.

"Help yourself, Mr. Karnes. In fact, I think I'll join you." Sergeant Johnson opened the box on his desk, pulled out a cigar, lit it, and puffed until he was sure it would stay lit. It didn't, so he lit it again.

"So did the woman have the baby on your boat?"

"I was certain she would, but we made it back to the marina. Would you believe her luck? An obstetrician getting ready to go water skiing was just launching his ski boat when we docked. I was yelling at the top of my lungs for help, and he rushed over. Delivered twin boys right there on the dock."

"You're kidding."

"Nope, it's the truth. She's gonna name one after me, and the other after the doctor."

"Why was she in a boat in the first place if she was nine months pregnant?"

"Her husband said she was only eight months along, so they figured she'd be okay."

At that moment, Lieutenant Conner hurried into the room, introduced himself, and started questioning Karnes.

Aurora searched through the house again as she looked for any pictures that could pertain to the menacing message she had received thirty minutes ago. Stymied, she flopped down on the couch and sat staring into space.

Maybe there aren't any pictures. Maybe that call was just a silly, vicious prank. But he knew about the necklace. And where is Sam? He should have returned hours ago. I can't take the chance that he could be killed.

Fear for Sam gripped her, and Aurora stood up and walked the floor. In her mind she went over every place in the house where her parents had stored pictures in the past. No new ideas came to mind. *I've never given up on anything; I won't cave in now.*

She again thought about where she had already searched and what she could have missed. She jumped up and rushed to her dad's workshop in the basement. She wanted another look at the picture frame and the message she hadn't understood on the frame her dad made. Picking up the finished frame, she turned it over and read again "Ask Wyeth." Next she inspected the unfinished frame, realizing she'd not checked it earlier. There was a message all right, but also different from those on all the previous completed ones. The words "Phone lines cut" jumped out at her.

She leaned on the workbench and looked again at the two frames, reading "Phone lines cut," then "Ask Wyeth" aloud several times. She was sure the inscriptions were clues left by her dad.

Aurora laid the frames back on the workbench and raced upstairs with King right behind her. *Wyeth. Dad's collection of books illustrated by Wyeth!* Reaching the living room, she ran to the bookcase and pulled out Robert Louis Stevenson's *The Black Arrow.* She rifled through the pages, then looked for more books in the collection. "Where is *Treasure Island?* It should be right here with *Kidnapped* and *The Black Arrow.* And where are Dad's other books illustrated by Wyeth? Where are they?"

Thanks to the vandals, all the books were hodge-podged on the shelves. Aurora spent precious minutes finding and examining copies of the books she sought. When she finally finished checking each volume, she stood, puzzled, her hands on her hips. *I just knew the pictures were hidden in one of the books. I was sure of it. I was wrong.* "Ask Wyeth, ask Wyeth" kept running through her head.

And then she understood.

Dad's favorite painting. And the brown backing paper was slit. Aurora opened a drawer in the antique sideboard, removed a stack of place mats, and arranged them on the Hepplewhite dining room table for padding so she wouldn't scratch the finish. She took the beloved Wyeth from the wall and placed the painting upside down on the place mats. Excitement mounted. She picked up a pair of sharp scissors and carefully cut away the brown paper backing.

Five Polaroid photographs stared back at her.

The first photo she picked up showed a man hoisting a large black bag on what appeared to be a type of pulley. It was obvious to Aurora that the man was in her parents' boathouse; the *Maggie A,* their speedboat named for Aurora's mother, hung on the boatlift high above the water. She studied the man carefully, finally deciding she had never seen him before.

The second picture showed a man she had seen right here in Spawning Run; he was the one who had assisted the diver in *Bad Boat* just a short while ago. In the picture, he was modeling a hip-length fur coat, pointing to himself and grinning. Beside him a large, black bag dangled from a hook attached to the pulley.

Four men were in the third photograph. One she recognized as the same guy who was wearing the fur coat in the previous picture. Another, the man wearing the diving suit, she had seen in the same diving gear a short time ago in her cove. The third man in this picture was the same person in the first picture she looked at, someone she didn't recognize. He held a painting and, again, an empty-looking black bag hung from a hook. The fourth man in the photograph had his back turned to the camera.

The *Maggie A* was visible in each of the three pictures.

In the fourth photo, a large fish lay on the dock, its empty belly split open down the center. The cavity held what appeared to be a plastic bag stuffed full of something. Aurora thought the fish was a striper that weighed maybe 35 pounds. But something about it looked strange, almost artificial.

She set that picture down with the other three and picked up photo number five. She stared at the same fish, but in this photo the plastic bag had been opened, its contents spread on a pale yellow towel beside the fish. Aurora sucked in her breath when she realized the bag had contained precious stones, necklaces, bracelets and rings. She guessed the contents were worth a small fortune. Aurora grabbed a magnifying glass to get a better look. *That's the necklace I took off the grebe!*

All strength drained from her legs, and Aurora sank into one of the eight dining room chairs, their padded seats needle-pointed by her mother a lifetime ago. Or so it seemed to Aurora. "Oh, Lord. Dad must have become suspicious of the activities in the boathouse, investigated, and took these pictures," she said aloud. King put a paw on her leg.

She looked helplessly around the room as tears rolled down her cheeks. The knowledge that her dad hadn't drowned accidentally hit her. The pictures proved it.

Her dad was murdered!

CHAPTER THIRTY

When he looked through the peephole and saw investigators Conner and Johnson standing on the porch, Robert Reeves hesitated a moment, then jerked open the door. The tremor in his hands was barely noticeable.

"Hello, gentlemen, what may I do for you?"

"Mr. Reeves," said Conner as he flashed his badge, "you're under arrest for the murder of J. Melton Lampwerth IV. You have the right to remain silent. If you give up the right to remain silent, anything you say can and will be used against you in a court of law. You have the right to speak with an attorney and to have the attorney present during questioning. If you so desire and cannot afford one, an attorney will be appointed for you without charge before the questioning begins."

"What?" said Robert. "You've got to be joking!"

"Do you understand your rights as I have read them to you?"

"I don't believe this."

"Do you waive and give up those rights?"

"No, damn it! I do not."

Robert knew he was a suspect, but never did he expect to be arrested. After all, Jill would call any minute to say she and Louis Beale had examined all of Lampwerth International's accounting records and that Robert had been cleared of any wrongdoing. But for now he'd call his lawyer; no way would he waive his rights.

"I understand my rights, and I want my attorney present," Reeves said.

"You can call your lawyer when you get to the police station."

"I need to call Jill Hathaway at Lampwerth International, too. I believe I'm entitled to do that, right?"

"You are. But like I said, you'll have to wait until you get to the station." Johnson frisked Reeves, Conner hand-cuffed him, and the two men led him to the police car.

"Jill, I've been arrested. They're accusing me of murder-ing Melton," Robert said when they finally let him use a phone.

"What did you say?"

"You heard me; I've been arrested for murder. I'm at police headquarters right now."

"Robert, how could that happen? You weren't even in the country when Lampwerth disappeared."

"His body floated up today. And his blood is on my Babe Ruth bat. The cops say I had motive—the embezzling thing, you know—and opportunity. They believe I arranged for Lampwerth to come to the lake, killed him, dumped his body right there in Spawning Run, hid his car, then flew out of the country to establish an alibi."

"Have you contacted your lawyer?"

"Yeah, he's flying down tomorrow."

"I'll come tomorrow, too."

"As much as I'd like to have you here, I believe you'd be more help continuing your search of the records. How are you coming with that?"

"It would be easier if you would allow me to confide in Louis Beale, tell him what really happened."

"No, I want Tinsley's widow protected. She doesn't need to know what her husband did. You're smart, Jill. You and Beale can come up with something."

Before Jill could answer, Detective Conner reached for the phone, said "Time's up," and hung up. Shaken, Jill hurried to Beale's office.

She and Louis had worked ever since she returned to Washington that day examining Robert's bank records. They planned to continue late into the night. Something screwy was evident, but neither knew what. They discovered large deposits to Reeves' checking account over the past year, then large withdrawals. Where was the money coming from, and where was it going?

"Louis, can you get me Mr. Tinsley's personal bank records?"

"Why?"

"Because Robert told me something in confidence, something he wants kept secret. But I don't see any way we can clear him unless I tell you everything." She looked him straight in the eye. "Now is there any way you can get hold of Mr. Tinsley's personal bank records? Believe me, it's important."

"Maybe, if there's a good enough reason. And I have to know the reason up front, right now. I'm not going to prison to save Robert Reeves or anyone else."

"I can trust you completely?"

His black eyebrows shot up. "I can't believe you even asked that question. Of course you can trust me."

Jill knew Robert wouldn't approve of her telling Beale the truth, but she was sure that unless Beale knew what to look for, Robert would go to prison. She paused a moment, then began.

"Here goes, then. Mr. Tinsley and Mr. Lampwerth go way back to almost the beginning of Lampwerth International thirty-five years ago. Lampwerth was a nobody with an idea. He started the company, hired Tinsley as bookkeeper three years later, and paid him a minimal salary with the promise of huge financial rewards down the road. Tinsley believed in Lampwerth and agreed. Tinsley's wife June took a job working long hours as a seamstress in a sweatshop to help support them. Anyhow, Lampwerth International slowly grew. After six years, Tinsley moved into the position of accountant. Then he worked his way up to Senior Accountant, the job you now hold. Anyhow, June

166

worked for five more years, then quit her job to raise a family."

"What does Mrs. Tinsley have to do with this?"

"The years of working in the sweatshop had taken their toll. June's health declined. Ten years ago she became gravely ill. 'Lymphoma,' the doctors said. 'Sorry, but there's nothing we can do for her. She has two years at the most to live.' Tinsley wouldn't accept that. He searched this country for alternative treatments. When nothing materialized, he expanded his search to Mexico and Europe, and eventually located a doctor in Lyon, France, who agreed to use June in an experimental study. But it would be expensive.

"Doctors in the U.S. warned him that this French doctor was a quack, that Tinsley would be throwing his money away, said he should keep his wife comfortable and let her die in peace. He didn't listen. He worshipped June and vowed to sink every cent he had into her treatment if necessary. He moved her to Lyon, rented a small apartment near the research center, and hired a housekeeping staff and round-the-clock nursing care for her both in the apartment and when she stayed in the hospital.

"Very slowly she improved. Very quickly Tinsley spent his money. You see, not only did he shell out money for his wife's treatment, but he also had the additional cost of hiring a nanny and a housekeeper for his house in Fairfax. By that time they had a fourteen-year old daughter and a twelve-year old son in a private school, which also added to his expenses. When the doctor in Lyon announced June cured, five years had passed, and Tinsley had mortgaged his house to the hilt. His daughter was in college. He was close to bankruptcy."

"Why didn't he just sell the house? I heard it's worth a small fortune."

"Well, June was plagued with feelings of guilt for having been away all that time, for causing her husband to worry so much. And even though the French doctors deemed her cured, the treatment had left her weak and frail. Tinsley vowed not to cause her any more worry, so he never told her their true financial situation. Strapped for funds, he discovered the occasional rewards from betting on the horses at the racetrack up in Baltimore. Occasionally he won, so he placed larger and larger bets. And he couldn't stop. The bookies loved him."

"What does this have to do with Robert Reeves?"

"When Tinsley couldn't pay the money back, and the bookies threatened him and his family, he started embezzling from Lampwerth International. Then, on top of everything else, a year ago he had the heart attack that killed him. But before he died, he told Robert what I just told you. Ashamed of himself and what he'd done, he didn't want June to learn the truth. That's when Robert devised a scheme to pay off the bookies and even put the embezzled money back into Lampwerth International. He's been using his own money; that's why you've seen so many large deposits and withdrawals. Robert's not taking money *out* of Lampwerth International; he's putting it back *in*."

Louis Beale's mouth dropped open and he stared at Jill. "That's impossible."

"No, it isn't. Now help me prove it, Louis. Okay?"

CHAPTER THIRTY-ONE

Aurora dialed Uncle Charlie's home phone and prayed his answering machine would pick up. She couldn't talk to him, not right now. He would insist she tell him everything, wouldn't leave her alone until she did. The caller had instructed her not to notify the police, or Sam would die. Yes, a message would work better.

"Judge Charles Anderson here. Leave a message and I'll get back to you as soon as I can."

She left a message. "Uncle Charlie, this is Aurora. I can't explain now, but if you don't hear from me by mid-day tomorrow, Sunday, please come to the house and turn on the computer. You know where Dad kept a house key hidden out in the barn in Frosty's old stall; the key is still there. My password is 'crossstitch,' and the file name is 'Wyeth' located on drive C."

Then she gathered up the pictures and stuck them in a large Manila envelope. She pulled the necklace out of the junk drawer in the kitchen, wrapped it in paper towels, and stuck it in a zip lock bag. She stiffened as she started to close the drawer. Her dad's old scout knife stuck out from under a piece of paper. The motto "Be Prepared" stared up at her. *You're telling me something, Dad. And I hear you.* She snatched up the knife and wedged it inside her sneaker. She grabbed her car keys, fed King, and put him in the dog pen. He whined and looked hopefully at her.

"Sorry King, you can't go." Aurora climbed in the car and drove off.

Normally, the drive along Route 626 relaxed her, but the rolling fields, gray-blue mountains, and green forests didn't affect her today. She swerved to avoid hitting a dead skunk on the road. *Funny how buzzards don't pick skunks clean the way they do other animals.* She wondered if it was sight or smell that attracted buzzards. Soon she reached the park entrance and stopped at the gate to pay the park ranger.

Senses alert, Aurora drove into Smith Mountain Lake State Park. She met a few cars near the entrance gate, and passed a couple of hikers just as she turned onto Interpretative Trail Road. Were the two hikers part of the scheme? She decelerated, studied them through the rear view mirror, and decided the elderly women were harmless. On most days, she would stop the car to gaze at a red tail hawk circling high in the sky searching for prey. But not today. She slowed when she reached Overnight Road and began looking for Cabin 171E. Aurora didn't notice the young fawn, dressed in nature's spotted camouflage, that watched her progress, ready to bolt at the slightest provocation.

When she located Cabin 171E, she saw that the cabin was accessible both by car and boat. Blue jays squawked and crows cawed, upset over this human intrusion, but Aurora never heard them. She parked the car, shut off the engine, and re-read the instructions. She couldn't afford to foul up; Sam's life was too precious. Picking up the necklace and the picture packet from the passenger seat, she walked to the cabin and, per instructions, looked neither to the right nor left. She felt the hairs standing up on the back of her neck. She knew she was being watched.

She opened the cabin door, placed the envelope in the white Styrofoam cooler to the left of the door, and backed out the door. Resisting the temptation to look back, Aurora turned and walked directly to her car, climbed in and drove out of the park.

The deed was done. Now she would drive to Hales Restaurant at the bridge to wait for further instructions and for the kidnappers to release Sam. She prayed they would keep their part of the bargain.

"Do you believe it? Like, did he really think I would, like, fall for that old excuse?" The young woman seated at a table near Aurora waved her arms as she poured out her woes to her girl friend. Aurora's ears perked up, then dismissed the conversation when she learned it concerned a two-timing fiancé.

More snatches of restaurant conversations registered in her head, but none seemed relevant to her situation. A group of ladies from the Red Hat Society talked and laughed at two tables across the room. A building contractor and his foreman, each on his third beer, laughed about the money they would pocket by using cheaper grades of lumber, concrete, and roofing materials than specified in the contract. At the table next to Aurora, a lone woman sat by herself, tapping her foot impatiently as she looked at her watch. *She's like me. Alone, waiting for someone. Wonder if her husband is a prisoner, too.*

A tall, well-dressed man entered the room, glanced in Aurora's direction, and headed toward her. *This is it. This is the contact I'm waiting for.*

Aurora half stood as the man advanced. When he held out his hands and tenderly grasped those of the woman seated at the table beside hers, Aurora blushed, glanced around the room to see if anyone noticed, and sat back down. She felt like a fool. She picked up her fork and pushed the slice of sweet pickle around on her plate, bit into her grilled cheese sandwich, now cold, and sipped her white wine, now warm.

She jumped when a feminine voice beside her said, "Aren't you the lady who designs cross-stitch kits?" Not waiting for a reply, the heavy-set, middle-aged woman wearing red and white checkered slacks, babbled, "I've been looking at you from across the room for almost an hour, trying to figure out where I've seen you. Then it dawned on me; you're the lady who designs cross-stitch kits for fanatics like me. Your picture's on the back of the packages. My husband, he's the man over there in the parasailing T-shirt, said I've lost my mind. But I haven't, have I? I just love your creations. I collect your kits whenever I see one. Are you here to produce another?"

"No, I'm here for my mother's funeral," answered Aurora. *Is this my contact?* She wondered. She would find out soon enough.

"Oh, I'm so sorry I bothered you. But you do design cross-stitch kits, do you not?"

"Yes, I do."

"I'll leave you alone, but first, would you please auto-graph my napkin?"

"I'll be happy to," said Aurora as she dug in her purse for a pen. "What's your name?"

"Nadine."

Aurora forced a smile, signed the napkin, then expecting written instructions for her to follow, she turned the napkin over. No message was there.

"I can't wait to tell my friends in our cross-stitch club that I met you and show them your autograph. They'll be so envious. Thank you so much."

"You're welcome," Aurora said as the woman scampered back to her table and waved the napkin triumphantly in her husband's face.

An hour and a half passed. Nothing unusual had happened. The waiter looked in her direction and started toward her. Aurora wished she were invisible. She groaned. All this time she'd ordered only one sandwich and one glass of wine. The waiter had asked several times if she wanted her check. Now he was probably going to tell her that people were waiting to be seated. She glanced around the room and saw no empty tables. But instead of asking her to leave, the waiter handed her a slip of paper and walked off.

At first Aurora thought it was just her check, but when she fingered it, she realized there was a yellow note stuck on the back. She read the note three times. Then she put a ten-dollar bill on the table, drained her wine glass, gathered up her jacket and purse, and left the noisy, crowded restaurant. An acquaintance sitting with friends at a table recognized her and called her name, but Aurora only waved and kept going. Once outside, she hurried toward the marina per the explicit instructions the waiter had handed her.

All types of boats—pontoon, fishing, houseboats, speed-boats and high-performance boats—floated in the calm water, bobbing gently when some passing boat's wake washed against them. Aurora passed the rental boats and moved on to the wooden piers that stretched out from the shore like orderly tree branches. Today not even the gleaming Chris-Craft, the antique wooden Owens cabin cruiser, or the sleek Fountain Powerboat interested her. Tied up in the last and largest slip floated the houseboat she sought. The man standing on the bow waved her aboard. She stepped onto the gangplank.

I know we're in grave danger. But there's no way in hell I'll abandon you, Sam. She swallowed the bile rising in her throat.

Together Sam and I will live—or die.

CHAPTER THIRTY-TWO

Aurora recognized the man on the bow. He was one of the men in the Polaroid pictures. She had seen him diving in Spawning Run earlier that day. He stood back for Aurora to pass and pointed to the open sliding glass door. "They're waiting for you inside."

She wanted to punch him in his flabby stomach, whack his red-veined, bulbous nose. *If I had the chance, I'd rip your eyes out!* But she couldn't, and escape was impossible. She straightened her shoulders and stepped inside the houseboat. The man motioned for her to keep walking.

She noticed the compact kitchen with a dinette table and benches that she suspected would fold down into a double bed, and the upholstered seats under the wrap-around windows. That room afforded an expansive view of the lake. The control center, with a key stuck in the ignition, was tucked in the right front corner of the bow. An aluminum spiral staircase led to the flat roof and deck above. If this houseboat were like some of the other luxurious ones she'd seen, up top would be another control center, hot tub, and a sliding board off the stern.

Aurora stumbled slightly as the man prodded her back. "Keep moving," he ordered.

"I'm going, dammit. Don't push me." She heard a familiar bark from the room at the end of the hall.

"Run, Aurora!" Sam yelled. But even if the man follow-ing close behind her had let her go, she would never desert her husband. Little Guy barked furiously. Then he yelped.

"You didn't have to kick him. He knows Aurora's com-ing," Sam said to someone in the room with him. The door opened, and another man, the one Aurora had seen wearing the fur coat in the picture, grabbed her arm and yanked her into the spacious stateroom.

"You should have run," Sam said, as she rushed to him. Little Guy, recovered from the kick, ran to Sam and Aurora.

Sam sat in a wooden chair, his hands tied behind the chair back. Aurora bent over and kissed him on his cheek.

"Are you badly injured?" She squatted down in front of him. Her eyes searched his battered face, and she gingerly touched his swollen eye.

"Not really. My arms and wrists are sore, my eye hurts like hell, my head aches, and I'm sure there're some ugly bruises, maybe some broken ribs to add to the already cracked ones, under these clothes. But no, I'm not badly injured. Nothing life threatening, anyway. And I did manage to get in a few good wallops myself." He attempted a smile.

"I'm sorry you came, Susie-Q. I don't want you hurt."

"How could I not come, Sam? I love you. We'll get out of this. And we'll do it together." Or not at all, she thought to herself.

"Who did this?" She recognized Jimmy Ray and Clyde as two of the men in the Polaroid snapshots. But who were they?

Jimmy Ray, his face marred with several fresh bruises and cuts, thanks to Sam, yanked Aurora to her feet. "Shut up!" he growled.

"I delivered the pictures like you told me to do, I waited in that restaurant per your instructions, and I will talk to my husband if I wish!"

"Damn uppity woman! Who do you think you are?" Jimmy Ray slapped her and Aurora fell to her knees. Dazed, she wondered for a moment if her jaw was broken. She touched her lip and saw blood on her finger. Sam strained at the ropes that bound him. Little Guy growled and attacked Jimmy Ray's leg.

"Call that mutt off or I'll shoot 'im!" he demanded, pulling a .38 from his jacket.

"Stop it!" yelled Clyde over the noise as Aurora grabbed a still-furious Little Guy and held him in her arms. "Shots will bring cops. Use your head, Jimmy Ray." Clyde was tired of this mess with Jimmy Ray, tired of nice people being murdered. But there wasn't a damn thing he could do about it.

Jimmy Ray swung his pistol toward Clyde. For a brief moment, Clyde thought Jimmy Ray had read his mind, that the end of his life had come. Then Jimmy Ray lowered the gun.

"She ain't gonna talk to me that way! And I damn sure ain't takin' any crap from a dog!"

"Look," Sam said, "be reasonable. Little Guy will be a problem to you as long as he's on board. And you don't want to attract attention by firing that gun. Let the dog go. No one can trace him to you. Besides, you have what you want."

"I could cut him up," leered Jimmy Ray as he pulled a long hunting knife from its sheath on his belt. "Feed 'im to the cat fish." Aurora shuddered.

"You could do that, sure," said Sam, "but what's your boss gonna say when he sees blood all over his big, fancy boat? Think he's gonna like that?"

Clyde whispered to Jimmy Ray in a corner of the cabin. Aurora raised an eyebrow and shot Sam a questioning look. "Cross your fingers," he mouthed as he winked at her. She didn't know what, but she knew Sam was planning something.

"Hold the dog still or I swear I'll stick 'im," Jimmy Ray said to Aurora. Aurora glared at him, but wrapped her arms around Little Guy. Clyde looped a piece of rope through Little Guy's collar and dragged the snarling dog from the cabin, through the galley, and across the gangplank. Pointing his knife at Sam, Jimmy Ray warned Aurora, "Don't you try

nothing smart or I'll sure as hell kill him when I get back."
He left the cabin and locked the door.

"How did they get you, Sam? And who's behind this?"

"I met Jimmy Ray and Clyde on my walk. They drove up
in a black pick-up truck. They said you'd been in an
accident, that you were hurt. They described your Jeep.
When they offered to take me to you, Little Guy and I got in
the truck. I don't know who the ringleader is, but," he added,
"my guess is we'll find out soon enough. Check out that
framed photograph over there. Look like anyone we know?"

"What photograph?"

"The one over there on the corner shelf above the bed.
Go look at it."

Aurora, a quizzical look on her face, walked across the
room, stared at the picture, and dropped down on the bed.

"Sam, tell me that isn't Carole in the picture. Tell me,"
pleaded Aurora.

"My darling Susie-Q, I can't tell you that. I, too, think
the picture looks exactly like Carole." Sam ached for his
wife.

Aurora couldn't believe it. Carole—her friend, her
bridesmaid, her confidant, a person she loved and trusted—
had betrayed her! Aurora sobbed softly into her hands. Was
there anyone left she could trust?

"Aurora," Sam said. "Aurora!"

Aurora raised her head and looked at her husband.
"What?"

"See if you can untie my hands while we're alone."

"I'll do better than that," she said as she stopped snif-
fling. Reaching in her shoe, Aurora pulled out the scout knife
she'd wedged there before leaving the house.

"You have a *knife?*"

"Yep. One thing my Daddy taught me was to be prepared. This is his knife. And I'm prepared."

She worked furiously for several minutes before one
tough strand of the three-strand Manila rope snapped.

Footsteps sounded in the galley and continued down the
hall. Aurora thrust the knife in her pocket and quickly moved

beside Sam. Clyde opened the door and peered inside the cabin. "Just checking on you. I'll be back in a few minutes. Don't do anything stupid." He closed the door.

"I checked 'em. No need for you to. I tied the dog to a tree," they heard Clyde say to Jimmy Ray in the hall.

"Nobody saw me. Boss is coming aboard. Time to shove off." Both men hurried to haul in the gangplank and start the engines before casting off.

"We're underway; one of them will be down here any minute," whispered Sam as he heard the engine start and felt the boat move. He didn't need to urge Aurora to hurry or tell her the consequences if she were caught attempting to free him. She sawed harder, and suddenly the second strand broke. Beads of sweat covered her brow and upper lip. She heard footsteps coming down the stairs from the overhead deck and, returning the knife to her shoe, she moved around to Sam's side.

Jimmy Ray poked his head into the room. "Thought I'd better check on you two. Kinda sorry you ain't misbehavin'. Was looking forward to teaching the little lady some new tricks." A sickening leer spread across his face. He took a step toward Aurora. Clyde hollered, "Jimmy Ray! Get back up top!

"Guess we'll hafta wait 'til later, sweetheart," said Jimmy Ray. "But not too much later." Aurora knocked his hand away as he reached over to stroke her hair.

"Leave her alone!" yelled Sam.

Jimmy Ray laughed and blew her a kiss. "Later, Baby."

As soon as he left, Aurora whipped out her knife.

CHAPTER THIRTY-THREE

Charlie stuck a key in his front door. The afternoon on the links at Boonsboro Country Club in Lynchburg had exhausted him, but he'd needed it. He hadn't realized how stressed he'd become, and the golf outing with his retired buddies had relieved much of the pressure he'd been feeling. How could he have let himself get so tense? Maybe it was time to retire, to leave his legacy of justice to someone younger. He wondered how he would cope with a lot of time on his hands. If Annie were still alive, they could travel, take some of the trips to Europe they had planned. Before cancer claimed her, they'd had forty-nine good years together, but now all he had left were memories. Lord, he missed her.

Playing the front nine, enjoying a chili dog slathered with mustard and coleslaw, and then attacking the back nine had recharged him When he left his friends in the club parking lot, he'd promised them he would consider retirement.

He pushed open the door and heard the answering machine's beep. Five messages appeared. He groaned. All he wanted was to settle down in his brown leather recliner with a martini, maybe two. Later he'd fix a grilled cheese sandwich and a bowl of the delicious healthy-but-ugly lentil and spinach soup his widow neighbor brought over yesterday. He pushed "Play." The voice of a sweet young thing stated that the maintenance warranty on his dishwasher would soon run out and now would be the perfect time to renew. He erased it and listened to someone, probably a telemarketer, hang up. The third and fourth messages were equally unimportant. Maybe he'd get to his martinis after all.

But then he heard message number five.

Aurora's no-nonsense voice wiped out all thoughts of a relaxing drink. He dialed her number. "Come on Aurora, answer the phone!" he said aloud. He slammed down the receiver when the answering machine picked up. Aurora's message to him had said to check her computer if he hadn't heard from her by noon tomorrow, but he wasn't a patient man. She was in trouble. He called the lake police, told them to meet him at 210 Spawning Run Road, and sped toward the lake.

The drive took him fifty-one minutes. Investigators Conner and Johnson were waiting on the front porch when he arrived.

"You two check out the house while I turn on the computer," he said as he unlocked the front door.

"What are we looking for?" Johnson asked.

"Anything unusual or suspicious. You're the cops; I'm just a judge. Use your instincts."

Aurora's computer was slow to boot up. Judge Anderson went to C-drive, then typed in "crosstitch." Across the screen flashed "You have used an invalid password." Exasperated, he retyped it. The identical message reappeared. Several more attempts produced the same results. Pushing himself back from the computer, the judge closed his eyes and pressed his fingertips against his temples.

Irritated at the interruption when the doorbell rang, he shouted, "Someone get the damn door!" Seconds later, Conner and Johnson ushered Luke Stancill into the room.

"Look who just happened to stop by," said Conner. "Says he was fishin' for stripers near Spawning Run. Looked like a storm was brewin', and he figured Aurora and Sam would shelter him for a while."

The judge confronted Luke. "Really? Can you prove it?"

"Of course not. What's going on? Where are Aurora and Sam?" asked Luke.

"Why don't you tell me?" countered the judge. "No, tell Conner. I'm busy."

Luke peered over Judge Anderson's shoulder as another "You have used an invalid password" flashed across the screen.

The judge growled.

Luke read the password the judge had scribbled on a piece of paper next to the computer. "Are you typing two s's or three?"

"Two."

"Why don't you try typing three? Make it 'crossstitch'."

The judge scowled at Luke, but followed his suggestion. Words from Aurora flashed on the screen.

Uncle Charlie, today (Saturday) I received a phone call ordering me to go to Cabin 171E in the State Park with certain pictures, negatives, and a necklace I found if I wanted to see Sam alive. The caller said not to call the police and to come alone. I'll explain later, but I located some Polaroid pictures Dad had hidden. I'm pretty sure the men in the pictures murdered Dad. I assume this house is being watched, so since I can't go have copies made, I have scanned the pictures into the computer. After I drop off the photos and necklace, I'm to go to Hales Restaurant and wait for further instructions. Before the phone call came, I videotaped two men in Spawning Run. I think they were in the boat that tried to ram Luke and me. That tape is in my cross-stitch bag in my bedroom. If I don't return, please take care of King. He's in the dog pen outside. The dog food's beside the laundry tub in the basement. I feed him twice a day. I love you, Aurora. P.S. King needs snuggle hugs every day.

Charlie's watch read 6:45 p.m.; Aurora had called at 3:00. "Conner and Johnson, let's go!" he bellowed. "We'll take both cars. King will ride with me."

"Won't the dog just be in the way?" asked Johnson.

The judge scowled at him. "On the contrary. King and Aurora have something special between them, something you and I don't understand. Believe me, King will help us find my niece." As he hurried outside to get King, he uttered a prayer for his niece's safety.

"What about him?" asked Sergeant Johnson, pointing to Luke.

"I'll come with you," offered Luke.

"No you won't," the judge hollered over his shoulder. "We'll catch up with you later. Don't leave the lake area." The three men left Luke standing on the porch.

Luke hurried down to the water and looked up at the sky. He knew a bad storm was imminent. He'd always had a sixth sense about weather, and he'd learned to listen to it. Should he look for Aurora and Sam? He looked up at the security of the big house on the hill. He could wait on the covered porch until the storm subsided. He shrugged, turned and boarded his small fishing boat. He hit the throttle and headed out into the lake.

"Stay, King." The judge turned off the car ignition. Conner and Johnson pulled up beside him, and they all advanced on Cabin 171E. The deputies drew their guns and pushed open the unlocked door.

Conner entered the cabin first. "Looks empty to me. We'll have a look-see, though."

The cabin was neat and free of dust. No shoe prints showed on the vinyl floor. The empty refrigerator shone, as did the oven. Neither the two bedrooms nor the bathroom yielded any clues. The place was immaculate.

"Call the station and get forensics in here," Conner ordered Johnson. "Find out if there's been a recent rental. If so, get a name, address and phone number."

Charlie returned to his Lincoln, snapped the leash onto King's collar and let him out. "Find Aurora, King." The dog whined, sniffed the ground, and dragged Charlie up to the cabin door, then turned and backtracked to where Aurora had parked her car hours earlier. Charlie saw tire prints in the dirt.

"She's been here," the judge said. "I won't take King inside; don't want to destroy any potential evidence. King and I will drive on over to Hales Restaurant and check it out. I'll call if I find anything." After putting King in the car, Judge Anderson drove away.

"Do you believe him? Looks to me like he thinks he's still a cop," said Johnson.

"Cut him some slack, man. His niece is in trouble."

CHAPTER THIRTY-FOUR

"Somebody's coming!" Sam whispered.

Aurora put the knife in her shoe and sat down beside Sam. She'd been so close to freeing him.

"Hello, Sam, Aurora. Surprised to see me?" Harold Johns sauntered into the room.

"That's an understatement! Yes, I'm surprised to see you. How'd you find us, Harold? Guess there's time for explanations later, though. We'd better go before they find you here."

Suddenly Aurora understood. "I don't think you and I will be leaving with Harold, Sam," she said in a quiet voice.

"Why not?"

"Your little lady here is astute. I bet she's guessed the truth."

Sam looked from Aurora to Harold. "Oh, no. Not you, Harold. Don't tell me you're responsible for robbery and kidnapping."

Harold smiled. "I like you Sam, always have. Admire you, too. But you're naïve. You accept people for what you see, what you want them to be. Miss Aurora here, though, is a better judge of character." He grinned at Aurora. "I don't believe you like me anymore, Aurora."

"I've never liked you. You're a creep, a jerk. Now I can add 'sick' to the adjectives describing you. Just wish I'd told Sam how I felt."

"Pity. I really admire you both. Was hoping you could get out of this alive. Even the pictures Aurora delivered to the cabin can't identify me. You see, Aurora, I really didn't want you dead, either." Aurora glared at him. "But I learned just thirty minutes ago that the cops searched the cabin in the park. Won't be much longer before they'll trace Sheila's involvement."

"Sheila?" Aurora wondered how Harold knew Sheila.

"Yeah. She helped clean your house. Sheila's my sister. It's only a matter of time before she squeals. She'll do anything to get her drugs. My guess is she's either finished her supply or is close to it. She's really not a bad person, just a typical addict—and she's under my control." Harold stroked his chin.

"Pity both of you have to die. What a waste."

"You have everything, Harold. Why'd you ever get in volved in crime?" asked Sam.

"For the money and the power, of course. And revenge. This lake cost me my inheritance. Haven't I told you about that sad period of my life? That's a story I'd like you to hear, but I'm afraid there's no time."

"Is Melinda involved, too?" Sam asked.

"That empty-headed, perfect little heiress wife of mine? Hell no, she's too busy with the spa I bought her in Paris. One of the best moves I ever made; keeps her out of my business. Occasionally she comes home for a week or two, maybe a month, but she always returns to her precious Paris. She flew back yesterday, got furious when she saw a certain photograph in my wallet. Stupid of me to forget I'd left it there.

"Do you want to see it?" he asked, and he pulled out the picture of a beautiful woman standing on the houseboat's upper deck.

"Not a smart thing to do, Harold, to let your wife see a picture of your girlfriend," Sam interrupted. He didn't know why, but he didn't want Harold to know they recognized Carole.

"Turn yourself in to the police. I'll testify on your behalf. So will Aurora." Aurora shot Sam a speak-for-yourself look.

"You'd never suggest that if you had any idea of the things I've done. Earlier you mentioned robbery and kidnapping. Add drugs and murder to that. Or maybe you didn't know about those?" Harold shrugged. "I'm not sorry for past transgressions, mind you, only sorry you two got in the way. But I do what has to be done to accomplish my goals.

"Look around you, notice the paintings, the art objects. They're priceless. I could sell every one of them in a heartbeat if I wanted to, but these particular ones are my favorites, my private collection, you might say." He hollered out the door. "Clyde, bring me the Perigal. I want them to admire my most recent acquisition before we kill them."

Aurora had an uncanny feeling that the painting they were about to see was the same one that had hung in Robert's house. She was right.

"Ah, Aurora, I see by your expression that you know the painting."

"Yes, I recognize it. The Scotsman A. Perigal painted it in 1865. You stole it out of Robert Reeves' house. Murdered Lampwerth, too, I bet."

"Actually, Lampwerth's murder is one of the few I didn't order. My men killed him when he surprised them at Reeves' house. Not too bright, those two."

"I used to think you were smart, Harold," Aurora said. "But you're not. These items you've stolen, killed for, don't make you important. And you know why? Because—and I'm so glad—you can't show them to anyone. You can only view them in your small confines with small people who bow and scrape when you say 'Jump.' These so-called priceless objects only serve to make you smaller, a peon. And even if you kill us, you'll still be a peon, a nobody. You're stupid, Harold. And you're small."

Harold raised his fist, but checked himself. "Killing you won't be so bad after all. Jimmy Ray's been begging to have some fun with Aurora first, though. Sam can watch. I'll enjoy your screams immensely." He smiled and left the room.

The second she heard the door lock, Aurora pulled the knife out of her shoe and began cutting on Sam's ropes. If she could free him they stood a slim chance of escaping. If not. . . .

"Hey, mister, you cain't bring a dog in here," said the restaurant hostess. "It's against the law."

"Lady, I *am* the law," Charlie said. He whipped out his identification. "I'm a judge, and I'm on police business. The dog stays."

"Sorry, sir. It's not that I have anything against dogs, you understand. Just tryin' to do my job."

"I understand." He pulled a photograph from his wallet. "Did this woman come in this afternoon? Her name is Aurora Harris. She's in great danger."

The hostess studied the picture he shoved in front of her. "I don't remember anyone who looks like her coming in today. But my shift didn't start until six this evening."

"Please send the wait staff to me right away. Maybe one of them remembers her," he said as he put his I.D. away.

"Yes, sir." The hostess hurried from the lobby.

One by one the waiters and waitresses tramped out to peer dutifully at the picture. They all shook their heads and returned to their customers.

When the hostess came back, Charlie asked, "Could I see a list with names and phone numbers of those who worked earlier today, say from three o'clock on?" His fingers drummed on the counter as he waited for her to look up the information he needed.

"Hey, Doreen, like, what's happenin', girl?" called a young blonde to the hostess as she entered the restaurant.

"Tami, you're the person this man needs to see. I was just fixin' to give him your name," answered Doreen, relieved to see her co-worker. "What are you doing back here?"

"Got lonesome and hungry, thought this place would be swinging, so here I am. Besides, I wanted to see the Mr. Muscle contest across the road later. Where the loser, like, French-kisses a carp? Wanna go?"

Yuck, thought Charlie.

"Oh yeah, I forgot about the contest. I have to work, though. Cain't go.

"This here's a judge; he wants to ask you some questions. Judge Anderson, this here's Tami Pittman. She hostessed the noon-to-six shift. Maybe she can help. Excuse me, I've gotta get back to work."

"Miss Pittman, you certainly walked through that door at the right time. I'm searching for a missing person, someone in a lot of danger. I understand she may have come to this restaurant today, sometime between three-thirty and six. Do you recognize this photograph?"

"Sure do. She, like, sat at a table in the next room. Asked for a seat over by the window there. Lady ate, like, only one grilled cheese sandwich and drank one glass of wine the whole time. She must have stayed close to two hours. Seemed, like, well, real fidgety, kept lookin' up every time someone came in the room. Finally jumped up and left when the waiter gave her the check."

"Did anyone meet her?"

"Cain't be sure, but I don't think so. You could, like, ask her waiter, though. He probably knows more about her than I do."

"What's his name?"

"Rick." Tami pointed to the list on the counter. "That's him. His phone number's there, too. Don't think you'll catch 'im tonight, though. He, like, bar hops nights, crashes mornings, and works here afternoons. But there's a chance he could, like, come for the contest. I'll have him call you if he shows up. I won't be going anywhere except across the road later on.

"Oh, I just thought of something. Hey, Doreen," she called when the hostess walked by, "Do you, like, still have Rick's cell phone number? The judge needs it."

"I think it's in my purse in the back room. I'll go check," said Doreen.

"That would be helpful." Charlie pulled out his wallet again, handed Tami one of his business cards, and put one on the counter to give Doreen when she returned.

"By the way, Tami, the carp you're talking about. That's a fish, right, the kind the kids throw popcorn to?"

"Yeah, like a really gross fish with big lips and all."

"Ugh," Charlie said. "And just what does the winner get out of this contest?"

"Who cares," Tami answered. "We all want to see the loser."

King whined and tugged on the leash.

"Wait, King, you can't go out yet," the judge said.

Ignoring Anderson, the big dog pulled harder and barked.

"He's upsetting the customers, Judge. Cain't you just take him outside and let the poor dog pee?" asked Doreen when she came back and handed him a piece of paper with Rick's cell phone number on it.

"Guess I could do that," he said. He pushed his business card over to her. "Be sure to call me if you think of anything." He stuck Rick's phone number in his shirt pocket and folded the paper Doreen gave him. "You don't need this back, do you?" he inquired over his shoulder as King pulled him out the door.

Once outside, King stood, nose twitching, as he analyzed the scents floating in the wind. A distant, high-pitched bark traveled through the night air and King bounded from the restaurant parking lot. The judge stumbled along behind as he fought to maintain his footing on the damp grass and still hold onto the leash. Man and dog crossed the wide expanse of grass, then veered toward the marina on the other side of the road. King ran to the finger of piers and turned right, casting, nose to the ground as he picked up a familiar smell along the bank.

A high crescendo of barks and yelps greeted them. Tied to a cedar tree near the shore, a Jack Russell terrier wiggled and jumped at the end of a short rope. A heavy-set woman in lime green and royal blue striped polyester slacks and matching jacket attempted to calm him. She looked up when King and Charlie rushed up.

"Mister, is this your dog? How dare you leave him tied to a tree! I should report you for cruelty to animals. You didn't even leave him food and water. I supplied that. What kind of low-life are you? I've half a mind not to let you have him back."

"Ma'am, he's not my dog." The judge frowned up at the sky when he felt a few drops of rain.

"Right," she answered sarcastically. "Do you expect me to believe that? I can see how glad he is to see you, although I don't for the life of me understand why."

"Ma'am, he's glad to see King here, not me. He's not my dog. He looks like one my niece recently adopted, though. She's in danger, and we're searching for her. I'm Judge Charlie Anderson. What can you tell me about this dog? If he's the dog I think he is, my niece Aurora's been calling him Little Guy. Do you know how he got here?" He knelt down to check the collar for identification.

"Whoa, what have we here?" he asked as he fingered the thick, studded collar. Looping the rope around Little Guy's neck so he wouldn't run off, he shoved the end of the rope toward the irate woman. "Hold this." Then he removed the dog's collar. On the inside was a thin zipper. "Interesting. It's like a man's money belt." He pulled the zipper and removed a piece of folded paper from the collar.

Taking a small flashlight from his pocket, he aimed the beam at the note. The words that leapt out in the dim light read: *Help! Held prisoner on big houseboat at Hale's Ford Bridge. Call police! Sam Harris.* The judge whipped out his cell phone and punched in a number.

Within fifteen minutes, police, including Conner and Johnson, swarmed the marina, but found no boat matching Sam's description. The judge put Little Guy's collar back on, removed the rope from around his neck, and followed as the terrier dashed toward the boardwalk leading to the end of the piers. He skidded to a stop at the last berth. It was empty.

"What's all this here ruckus 'bout?" asked a man lounging on the deck of a small cabin cruiser. "You're disturbin' the peace," he slurred. He drained a beer, then pitched the can into a five-gallon bucket. Anderson noticed the stash of empty beer cans in the bucket, and a woman, two sheets to the wind, stretched out on a chaise.

"How long have you been tied up here?" asked Charlie.

"Don't see as how that's any of your damn business."

Anderson sighed and pulled out his I.D. for what seemed like the umpteenth time that day. He remembered the thrill this simple act gave him in the past. Now it seemed a chore. Maybe his golf buddies were right; maybe he should retire. He shook his head and focused on the obviously inebriated couple on the boat.

"We're the police. Once again, how long have you been docked here?" asked Lieutenant Conner.

"Since noon, I reckon." The man leaned over and shook the woman. "Paige, how long we been here, darlin'? Paige?" He glanced at Anderson, then whispered in his companion's ear. "Paige, baby, it's the cops. Please, baby, wake up."

"She's asleep. But I'm sure we docked 'round about noontime today." He burped loudly.

"More like passed out," Anderson mumbled to Conner. Then he asked the man, "Was a large boat berthed over there earlier today?"

"Sure was. A houseboat, a real honey. Bet it was fifty feet long, maybe more. Anyhow, it was long. Left 'round six o'clock. I remember 'cause Paige and me'd just started on another case of beer."

"How many were on board her?"

"Saw two, naw, reckon three guys. Then a woman joined 'em, a real knock-out. Little old for my taste—I like 'em real young like Paige here—but hell, to each his own, right? Figure they called her. Know what I mean? A call girl? Get it?" He laughed, and grabbed the railing to steady himself.

By now the rain beat so hard on the tin roof that Judge Anderson could barely hear the intoxicated man. He turned to leave, then stopped and pointed to Little Guy. "Did you see this dog on the houseboat?"

"Naw, didn't see no dog. But I heard one. A real yapper. 'Bout drove me crazy. Paige and I were down in the cuddy cabin tryin' to get a little, uh, rest, see. Started to go complain, but Paige wouldn't let me, said I could go later, when we finished restin' an' all. Then the barking stopped." He put his hand over his mouth. "Hey, can I go now? Gotta barf."

The man and his companion disgusted Charlie, but he'd learned a lot. He smiled, then walked away with King and the deputies, dreading the soaking they'd get as soon as they left the protection of the covered boat slips.

CHAPTER THIRTY-FIVE

The air felt damp and cold. Luke pulled his foul-weather jacket tight around him. He scanned the sky, hoping for stars. The darkness didn't bother him, but he didn't like thunderstorms, especially at night in a boat on a lake. He'd meant to fix his marine radio, but a fishing buddy had hollered over to him on the dock—told him the stripers were biting—and Luke had forgotten all about the radio repair. When the fishing was good, Luke had to go. His marine radio was important, but so was the chance of landing a citation striper.

Now, however, his thoughts centered on Aurora and Sam. Where could they be? Lightning sliced through the sky and thunder roared. That was close. Luke knew the lake could quickly change from a smooth, slick surface to angry waves with whitecaps. Time to vamoose. The State Park wasn't far; maybe he could make land before the downpour began, find shelter in one of the buildings there, possibly check out Cabin 171E at the same time.

He motored slowly, searching the water as best he could for obstacles as he crossed the main channel and guided the boat toward the park.

Too soon, huge drops of rain pelted him. The lake turned rough and choppy. He hugged the shoreline as closely as the buoy markers allowed, attempting to maximize any shelter from the wind and pounding rain. Good thing he knew the lake so well. Landlubbers didn't realize it, but you could get disoriented, even lost, on this lake at night.

The boat dropped hard into a trough of water, then rode the swell back to the top. Lightning flashed. Luke got a split-second glimpse of a large houseboat bouncing and straining at anchor ten yards ahead, running lights off. Any good boater knew that watercraft not docked should have running lights on after sunset, even if just anchored out in the lake, but some boaters ignored this. He yanked back on the throttle and carefully navigated around the houseboat.

"Whaddaya know. That's the boat that attacked Aurora and me." Tied parallel to the starboard side of the houseboat, protective fenders between the two craft, the hated speedboat sat in the water. A short rope ladder dangled from the deck of the houseboat. Luke attached a line from his boat to the stern of the speedboat. He waited for a large wave to pass, then struggled quickly into the speedboat. He checked to see if the keys were in the ignition. He couldn't find any. Grabbing the rope ladder, Luke hauled himself up on the houseboat. The wind tore at his footing.

On board, he crouched low and listened for any sounds. When the sliding glass door on the bow opened, he pressed his body against the side of the boat. He saw, silhouetted in the doorway, the two men who had tried to capsize him. Between claps of thunder, Luke heard enough to tell him that Aurora and Sam were captives on the boat.

"Think the boss is gonna kill 'em?" asked Clyde.

"You can bet on it." Jimmy Ray laughed. "But first we'll have some fun with the woman."

Damn, Luke thought, Aurora's gotten herself in a real jam this time. Sam, too. Where are the cops and her Uncle Charlie? If I go for help, the houseboat might pull anchor and leave before I can get back. Damn! Why didn't I fix the marine radio? And put new batteries in the cell phone. He scratched his rain-drenched head. I'll stay. Somehow I'll find a way to help Aurora and Sam escape.

"Yes!" The last strand of rope snapped.

"Good job, Aurora!" Sam said.

"Oh, Sam, your wrists are rubbed raw."

"We'll worry about that later. Someone's coming. I hear footsteps."

Sam grabbed the chair and hoisted it high in the air, ready to crash it over any head that came through the door. Determined not to be left out, Aurora crouched beside the closed door.

"Time to git ready for Jimmy Ray, sugar pie. I'm shore nuff ready for you!" Grinning, Jimmy Ray pushed open the door, only to be hit hard as Aurora slammed the door back into him. Jimmy Ray dropped to his knees. "Wanna play rough, huh?" he said as he stood up and pushed the door back open. Sam smashed the chair across Jimmy Ray's back, knocking him flat on the floor.

"Now's our chance!" Aurora called to Sam. "Let's go."

"Right behind you, Susie-Q."

Aurora dashed through the doorway and ran smack into Clyde. He grabbed her, but Aurora kneed him in his groin. Clyde yelled and doubled over in pain. Sam, still in pain himself, delivered a heavy uppercut to Clyde's jaw with his right, then a belly-wrenching punch with his left before following Aurora to freedom.

Once on the deck, Aurora hesitated. *Which way to go? And where to go? We're trapped somewhere on a forty-mile long lake.* She screamed when a flash of lightning revealed a man coming toward her.

"This way!" shouted Luke. "I've got a boat!"

Aurora and Sam darted toward Luke's voice. Another flash of lightning showed the rope ladder flapping off the side, but before they could scurry down, a hard, familiar voice stopped them.

Harold Johns held a flashlight in his left hand. "Where in hell do you think you're going?" In his right hand was a .38. He pointed it at Sam and Aurora.

"Jump!" yelled Luke. He threw his weight against Harold. Harold dropped the gun and fell to the deck. Luke plunged over the side of the boat and into the water.

"It's our only chance!" Sam yelled as he shoved Aurora overboard.

Harold snatched up the gun and struggled to his feet. He pointed the gun at Sam.

"I should have killed you a long time ago, Mr. Perfect."

Before Harold could pull the trigger, Clyde rammed into Harold and knocked him off balance. Clyde grabbed three orange life jackets and flung them over the side.

Sam hurried to the side of the boat and pulled himself over the railing. He dropped into the angry water.

"Grab the jackets!" Clyde yelled. He glanced around for the life ring to toss to the struggling swimmers, and froze. Jimmy Ray, his face bloody, stood in the doorway. A large knife was in his right hand. He glared at Clyde.

Clyde knew he stood face to face with a devil. Jimmy Ray had cracked.

"You shouldn't have done that, Clyde." Jimmy Ray advanced. "I'm gonna really enjoy this."

Clyde backed up slowly, stumbled over the life ring, and fell to the deck. He looked up into the hate-filled, maniacal faces of Harold and Jimmy Ray.

Harold beamed his light at Clyde's eyes. "Can't tolerate a traitor. He's all yours, Jimmy Ray," Harold said as he kicked Clyde's ribcage. Treading water, Aurora, Sam and Luke heard Clyde's scream.

Harold picked up the dropped pistol and fired randomly into the storm-tossed lake until the chamber clicked empty. Then he turned and entered the galley.

"Finish up, Jimmy Ray, and let's get the hell out of here," he called from inside the houseboat.

CHAPTER THIRTY-SIX

"I respect your position, I really do. I know you're worried sick about your niece, but you can't ride with us. You may be a judge, but you're still a civilian, and our policy is no civilians on board during a criminal investigation." Then Captain Vincent, game warden, waved curtly at the judge and maneuvered the Virginia Game and Inland Fisheries boat slowly out of the harbor and into angry water.

Helpless, Charlie Anderson—judge, former cop, former district attorney, and now worried uncle—stood in the rain and watched the boat's bright search lights barely pinprick into the night. Spears of lightning punched the turbulent water. "They won't let us go, fellows," he said to the wet dogs whining beside him."

Sergeant Johnson tapped Charlie on his shoulder. "We can wait in that building over there, judge!" he hollered over the wind. "There's a phone inside. Lieutenant Conner will call if they find anything. No point in makin' yourself sick."

The game warden's boat was no longer visible. Charlie knew a search during such weather was near futile, but he said nothing. He wanted to be on that boat. He felt useless, like he was deserting his niece, letting his brother's killer escape. He took one last look at the lake, then he, Little Guy and King followed Johnson inside the building.

*

"We've gotta turn back!" yelled Captain Vincent. "Visibility is near zero. And it's too rough."

"Judge Anderson will throw a fit!" shouted Lieutenant Conner. "We can't give up now!"

"It won't do his niece or us any good if we sink. Use your head, man." Vincent pulled his rain hat firmly over his head and his slicker tighter around his neck, but rivulets of water still trickled inside his gear. The captain then barked to his crew, "Head to port. Pronto." He patted Conner on the back. "We'll start again at first light tomorrow. We'll find her."

Aurora treaded water and tried not to swallow. Where was Sam? She saw him jump off the boat. Something bobbed up and down nearby. Was it Sam? A flash of lightning showed her a life jacket. She swam to the vest and fought against the rough water as she buckled it on.

"Sam, where are you?" she shouted into the blackness.

"Aurora, help me!" yelled Luke. "Sam's hurt!"

That was Luke, and he's close. But what did he say? Did he say something about Sam? She dog-paddled toward Luke's voice.

"Say something so I can find you!" she shrieked.

"Over here."

Lightning flashed, and Aurora spotted Luke fighting to stay afloat a few yards away. He wasn't alone; Sam was with him. But Sam wasn't moving.

"Sam!" she screamed.

"I think he took a bullet after he jumped off the boat. Can't tell how badly he's hurt, but he's alive." Luke coughed as a swell of water slapped him in the face.

Yanking off her life jacket, Aurora and Luke strapped Sam into it. She knew Luke must be exhausted, even more than she. After all, he'd been fighting to keep both Sam and himself afloat.

"Grab hold of the vest, Luke. Maybe it'll keep you both up."

She thanked her good fortune when the next lightning bolt showed her two more life jackets bouncing around in the rough water. *"Don't know how they got here, but thank you, Lord."* Tiring rapidly, she struggled toward them.

Aurora put on one of the jackets, then fought her way back to Luke and handed him the other jacket. The three of them bobbed in the raging water for a few minutes. Then Luke tapped her shoulder.

"I'll swim for shore and bring help!" he hollered.

"We should stay together, help each other."

"We could all drown if we stay here," he answered. "Or freeze to death."

While not freezing, the April water at around 50° could still kill. The cold rain didn't help. Hypothermia could set in. Aurora worried about Sam. He couldn't swim or tread water, so his body generated very little heat. "You're right," she said. Luke swam away. Hoping to keep Sam's circulation going, she massaged his arms and legs.

"My poor, darling Sam. You're hurt again. And all because you drove up from Augusta to surprise me. Some surprise." In the darkness, she hadn't located his gunshot wound. She hoped the frigid water would slow any bleeding.

Uncle Charlie would start searching for her at noon tomorrow—if he got her message on the answering machine, that is. Aurora regretted telling him to wait; she and Sam could be dead by then.

"Luke's right. There's nothing to gain by just bobbing around in the lake. Besides, I'd like to put more distance between us and Harold Johns." Aurora hooked one arm through Sam's life vest and side-stroked after Luke.

Aurora had just about reached her limit of endurance when her outstretched hand struck something hard. *Have I finally reached land?* Dog-tired, she lowered her legs and scraped against a rocky bottom.

When she found a bank level enough to navigate, Aurora half-lifted, half-dragged Sam onto shore.

Aurora wept. She was too tired to move. *Stop it, Aurora. Crying won't help Sam.* She hugged him close and felt his breath on her cheek. In the darkness, she couldn't see Sam's wounds, but she could use her hands to feel all over his body for injuries. She stroked his head. Above his right temple, she felt something sticky. Was it blood? She couldn't feel a wound big enough to account for his present condition. *There must be something else.* She felt for other wounds.

Aurora unfastened the jacket and felt Sam's chest and abdomen. Nothing. Carefully rolling him onto his right side, she inched her hands under the jacket and along Sam's left side. Bingo! At his waistline she felt something warm and sticky. Aurora knew it was blood. *How much blood has he lost? What can I do? Well, I'll just have to do the best I can.* Taking off her windbreaker, she rolled it up and put it against the wound. Then she pulled the life jacket as tight as she could get it. She hoped this would staunch the bleeding.

She stood and yelled, "Luke!" No answer. "Anybody! Hello?" Aurora looked up toward the sky and realized the storm was over. She wondered when the pounding rain had ceased. *I don't know and I don't care. Only Sam matters.* Hoping to see house lights, Aurora stared into the darkness. She saw nothing. *Where are we?*

Aurora felt around for rocks and other debris near Sam. When satisfied she had removed the larger obstacles, she dragged him to the cleaned area. She considered making a bed of pine boughs for him, but decided that would be almost impossible in the dark. She removed her life jacket, slipped it under Sam's head, then stretched out on the cold, wet ground and snuggled up to her husband to warm his body.

When daylight came, she would know better how badly he was hurt. Tears welled in her eyes when she heard him utter a barely audible "I love you, Susie-Q."

"I love you too, darling. Rest now."

CHAPTER THIRTY-SEVEN

A Carolina wren chirped trip-trip-trip in the pre-dawn hour, a mourning dove sang, and an orange-breasted robin whistled a come-hither tune to his mate. Aurora, waking from a fitful sleep, stretched out her arms, not yet cognizant of the events of the preceding day. A raucous crow, perched in the tree above her, cawed his disapproval at her presence.

Aurora struggled to a sitting position and groaned. Every bone, muscle and joint in her body ached, and she shivered from the cold air that dripped with a heavy blanket of fog. For a brief second she wondered why, then remembered the harrowing events of the previous day and night. *Sam, I must check Sam!*

She leaned over her husband and touched his face with her cheek. *He's not breathing!* Quickly she unfastened the life jacket she'd used to help stop the bleeding and prepared to start CPR. Again she put her face close to his. This time a whisper of warm breath caressed her cheek. *He's alive! Thank you, God.*

Aurora looked up at the sky. Soon she'd be able to see Sam's injuries. Once the sun came up and the fog lifted, she would try to figure out where they were and how to get them out of this mess—and get medical attention for Sam.

"Susie-Q." Sam's eyes fluttered, then opened. "What happened?"

"Shh. Don't try to talk, Sam." She kissed his forehead. "Everything will work out. You'll see." Tears ran down her cheeks.

"Did ten mules kick me? I feel like they did."

"I know, darling. Hush now. You need to save your strength."

Sam closed his eyes. Aurora breathed a sigh of relief when she noticed the faint, but rhythmic rise and fall of his chest.

"We'll beat this, Sam. You'll see."

Aurora waited for the sun to burn off the fog and thought about something her mother said to her years ago: "It's not what happens to you in life that matters, Aurora. The important thing is how you react. You can sit around and feel sorry for yourself or you can do something about your problem." Aurora smiled at the memory.

A few minutes later the fog lifted. Smith Mountain loomed straight ahead. Aurora pushed her way through the trees. In front of her towered the 230-foot tall hydroelectric dam.

We're on Dam Island, the closest island to the dam. And the closest to the huge penstocks—or tubes—that carry water from the lake to the turbines. She gasped when she realized how close they'd come to being sucked into the turbines. *Surely the intake screens, designed to keep debris out of the penstocks, would have stopped us. Or would they? Luke! Had he escaped the dam, too?*

Aurora sat on a pine log and watched the water that surrounded their little island. *Actually, this isn't a bad spot to be. Fishermen pass this island daily, especially this time of year.* Images of King flashed in her mind. She knew he missed her as much as she missed him, knew he would be searching the house and yard for her when Uncle Charlie opened the gate to the dog pen sometime after noon. Noon seemed like a lifetime away.

Hope soared when she spotted a boat zipping over the water. "Help! Help!" She waved her arms to attract attention, but the boat continued on its course. Minutes later she spotted another boat, but no one on that boat saw her, either. Several more boats passed in the distance. Her spirits plummeted.

They can't hear me; their engines drown my voice. And they can't see me because I blend with the trees. I need something to attract their attention. The life jackets! Surely someone would notice their orange color.

Crossing back over the island, she checked Sam again, then eased the life jacket out from under his head. She faced the main channel, ready to wave the jacket when another boat appeared. Soon two boats were visible, and she jumped up and down, wildly swinging the orange jacket from side to side. *Hooray! It worked!* The closer boat changed course and headed straight toward Dam Island.

They were saved.

"Hooray! Now you can get medical care, Sam!" Then she froze.

The oncoming boat looked like the speedboat that had tried to capsize her, the boat she'd seen in her cove, the boat in one of the pictures hidden in the Wyeth painting, *Bad Boat*. What could she do? "King, where are you?" she screamed into the wind.

Aboard the cruiser, Lieutenant Conner, Captain Vincent and the crew searched the water and shore through binoculars for any sign of Aurora and Sam. Conner hoped they were safe, but he was worried. He put down the binoculars and poured a cup of steaming coffee from a thermos. If he were this tired, this cold, he figured Sam and Aurora would be near freezing. If they were still alive, that is. Or they could be prisoners, maybe even dead, on a fifty-foot houseboat somewhere on Smith Mountain Lake.

Boats other than Conner's were looking for the missing couple. Some concentrated on stopping and boarding boats resembling the descriptions of the speedboat in the picture, and of the houseboat the drunk in the small cabin cruiser had described. But Conner knew Aurora and Sam could be anywhere.

For a while early this morning, Lieutenant Conner thought they would have to handcuff Judge Anderson to keep him off their boat. Conner understood the judge's desperate need to help search for Aurora and Sam. The judge finally relented after convincing Conner and Vincent to take King with them.

"That dog has senses we humans can't conceive of. And he loves Aurora with his whole heart and soul. I know it sounds strange, but the two of them seem to communicate with each other. Pay attention to King, and he'll take you to Aurora," the judge said. Little Guy whined.

The crew scanned the water and the shoreline with their binoculars. Twice they stopped boats fitting the description of the speedboat they sought. Both vessels, however, belonged to anglers fishing for stripers.

King stood, put his front feet on the gunwale, sniffed the air, and cocked his head. Then, with a high-pitched whine and eager bark, he leaped into the water. Using his tail as a rudder, the dog paddled straight toward Dam Island.

"Slow down!" yelled Conner to Vincent. "King's overboard!" When the boat stopped, Conner hollered, "King, come!" But the dog ignored the command and increased the distance between them.

"Follow him! Maybe he's scented Aurora!"

The police cruiser turned and followed the Lab. With their binoculars, the crew searched the water and land ahead of King. Conner spotted a fast-moving boat to his left. He recognized it as the boat in one of the pictures hidden inside the painting.

"Look over there!" yelled a crewman. Everyone stared in the direction the other boat was heading: Dam Island. A flash of orange disappeared in the woods. *Could it be Aurora?* Vincent changed course, steered the boat around the swimming dog, and headed after the speeding craft.

"Shouldn't we pick up King?" shouted one of the men.

"No time. We've gotta reach Aurora before that other boat does." Conner, an avid duck hunter and owner of two

Labs himself, knew King's ancestors were bred for just such swims.

The blood from generations of champion Labrador retrievers coursed through the big dog. Undaunted, King swam strong, his webbed paws propelling him through the water.

The instant she recognized *Bad Boat*, Aurora left Sam's side and ducked into the woods. Determined to protect Sam no matter what, she broke off a stout hickory stick, sat down, jerked the shoelaces from her wet sneakers, and knotted the laces together. Next, she reached in the side of her left shoe for the pocketknife. She hoped it hadn't slipped out into the water during her swim. *Hallelujah!* Her fingers found the knife. She opened the three blades and lashed the knife to the stick, crisscrossing the laces over the knife body and the stick until she was confident the knife wouldn't fall off. *Voila!* She had a weapon. *Not pretty, but then I'm not entering it in a weapons beauty pageant, either.*

At the far end of the island, Aurora stepped out into the open. She intended to draw attention away from Sam. Maybe the kidnappers would think he'd drowned. She watched as *Bad Boat* changed course and headed toward her. She ducked back into the woods. Jimmy Ray raised his rifle and fired. Aurora heard the bullet splinter into a nearby tree. She knew her only chance was to lure them onto the island, somehow get behind them, then attack. "Lord help me," she whispered.

Harold navigated his boat as close to shore as he dared. Jimmy Ray jumped out into the knee-deep water. He swore as water ran over the top of his snake skin cowboy boots.

"Get her, Jimmy Ray!" hollered Harold.

Aurora crouched in a thicket of mountain laurel. She heard Jimmy Ray running through the underbrush, then silence. She strained to hear any sound. *Where is he?* A twig snapped nearby. Jimmy Ray was close. *Come on, come on! Don't stop now!* For her plan to work, she'd need to attack before he could get off a shot. Another twig snapped and Jimmy Ray stopped four feet away from her. *Now's my chance!* She readied her weapon and started to rise.

From the speedboat, Harold saw the police cruiser bearing down on them. "Get back here, Jimmy Ray! Now! The cops are coming! Hurry!" he screamed. Aurora eased back down in her hiding place. Jimmy Ray turned and ran toward the water. He tumbled back into the boat and Harold gunned the engine.

Aurora ran out of the trees and onto the shore. Waving wildly to the police, she signaled them to come ashore.

"Aurora looks like she could use some help! Let's go!" shouted Captain Vincent.

"But the speedboat's getting away!" yelled a crewman.

"We'll radio another cruiser to pick them up. They won't get far," Vincent answered.

"No cavalry, no army artillery, no green berets could look as good to me as you guys do this minute!" cried Aurora before Vincent even beached his boat. "I've never been so glad to see anyone in my life!"

"Me too, Aurora," replied Conner. "Me too."

"Hey, there, I'm your friendly neighborhood game warden. Vincent's my name." He extended his hand.

"It's really, really nice to meet you," Aurora said as she shook his hand. "I'm Aurora Harris. My husband is hurt. Please follow me. Hurry!"

"You go, Conner," said Vincent. "I'll radio the other boats and headquarters. Also need to let the judge know Aurora's safe. Join y'all in just a minute."

Aurora led Lieutenant Conner and a crewman through the woods. Reaching Sam, she leaned over him and said, "Darling, help is here. Won't be long before you'll be safe in the hospital."

"Yeah, we'll get you to a doctor right away, Sam. You'll be good as new." But Conner wasn't so sure. Sam didn't look so good.

"I've radioed for help. Won't take 'em long to arrive," said Vincent as he joined them. "Also sent a description and the registration number of that other boat to all the cruisers on the lake. They won't get far."

Aurora helped the men spread blankets from the game warden's boat over Sam's shaking body. Suddenly she was bowled over by a dripping, whining King. He stood over her and licked her face. "King, old boy, I was afraid I'd never see you again." She wrapped her arms around him and buried her head in his wet neck.

"He led us to you; he's a true hero," said Conner. "If not for King. . . ."

"If not for King, Sam and I would probably be dead by now," interrupted Aurora. "But I guarantee they would've been sorry they'd ever tangled with me. I would not have gone down easily, I can assure you." She pointed to her jack-legged stick with the knife still attached.

Conner and Vincent both laughed. "I do believe you're right. They're damn lucky you didn't get to them before we did," Vincent said as he examined her weapon.

CHAPTER THIRTY-EIGHT

Jill Hathaway, wearing a battle-black knit suit and a rage-red silk blouse, stormed into the police station, marched up to the desk, and demanded to see the officer in charge of the Reeves case. Louis Beale followed at a distance.

"Sorry, ma'am, he's out."

"Then I want to see Robert Reeves. Now. His lawyer will arrive later today, but I must see Mr. Reeves right this minute. I have information that will prove him innocent."

"Wait here," said the desk sergeant as he pushed his brawny frame up from the chair. "I'll see what I can do."

Louis Beale sat down on a long, high-backed bench. As best he could, he balanced his briefcase and the two boxes of official papers on his lap.

Beside him, Jill glared at the No Smoking sign on the wall, lit up, and inhaled deeply. She and Louis had left D.C. at 9:00 p.m. yesterday in the midst of a dreadful thunderstorm, and didn't arrive at Robert's house until 3:00 a.m. Jill had tumbled into bed just before four, but couldn't fall asleep. Now she was exhausted, irritable. And, she admitted to herself, worried sick.

"Mr. Reeves is in the conference room. I need to check your briefcase and those boxes before you can join him, then a deputy will escort you," said the sergeant when he returned to the room. He thoroughly searched the boxes and rifled through the black leather briefcase. Frowning, he looked at Jill, and said, "You can see Mr. Reeves, but not until you put out that cigarette." Jill almost told him to go to hell, but instead she crushed the cigarette in the stained metal ashtray the sergeant pulled from a desk drawer. She and Louis followed the deputy out of the room.

"Jill, I can't believe you're here. So relieved to see you," said Robert as he wrapped her in his arms. Spending a night in a cell had given him time to think. He wanted to spend the rest of his life with this woman, and the only way he could do that was to forget his pride and tell her how much he still loved her. He hoped she still loved him, too, that she would agree to be his wife. He wanted to kiss her passionately, to tell her he couldn't live without her, that he couldn't continue pretending they meant nothing to each other. But the deputy cleared his throat, and Robert was jerked back to the present. He gently pushed Jill away and reached over to shake Louis Beale's hand.

When Jill got a good look at Robert, she fought to hold back her tears. He looked tired, pale, even defeated. He'd been in jail only one day and night. How would he fare if he had to spend weeks, months, or, heaven forbid, years locked up? She shuffled the papers Louis handed her until she gained control of herself. Then she said, "Louis, please explain to Robert what we've found and what explanations we need from him."

"Okay," said Beale. "To begin, Mr. Reeves, I believe that what you told Miss Hathaway is the truth. Can't honestly understand why you did it. You've risked losing all your savings, investments, reputation and your freedom just to keep a widow from learning what a jerk her husband was and to keep her out of the poor house. Didn't know there were people like you."

"There aren't many," said Jill. "He's an exceptional man in many ways." Then she added, "Your lawyer will be here later, Robert. When we're through with this legal battle, people all over the country will be astonished at what you've done. You'll see."

"I want this kept as quiet as possible, Jill. Don't want to expose all of Tinsley's dirty secrets to the world. In fact, I didn't want you to tell Beale here. You know that."

"But you could go to prison if Louis isn't allowed to use all the information he's obtained." She looked at Beale. "Isn't that right, Louis?"

"Well. . . ."

"Tell you what," said Robert, "Let's release only a little information at a time, just enough to keep me from being locked up. We can see how that goes. If you have to—if everything else fails—then I'll agree to let you use what you've put together. I don't want to spend the rest of my life in prison." He looked into Jill's eyes. "I've got too much to live for."

Harold Johns pulled a remote control from the boat's cockpit and punched in a code as he pulled back on the throttle. A smile spread across his face as one of the two wide doors to a boathouse rolled up. He steered the speedboat inside, pushed the remote, and watched the door roll down. The only sign that they'd even entered the boathouse was the boat's slight wake. Even that would vanish soon. The cops would never catch him now. He was safe.

"No one will outsmart Harold Frederick Johns," Harold declared to Jimmy Ray. "No one. I spent months planning before moving my operation here. Took every precaution. Cruised the entire five hundred miles of shoreline for days before I settled on this spot. The owner didn't want to sell, but he changed his tune fast when I shoved stacks of hundred dollar bills in his face. Money, Jimmy Ray. Money gets you power, everything you want. Remember that."

To Harold, this location on the lake that best suited his needs was especially sweet. This plot of land was the only property left from his family's holdings not covered by water. Only Sheila had any idea what this land meant to Harold. He couldn't understand why she didn't feel the same about it. They'd both grown up here in an old log cabin built over 150 years ago. His great-great-grandfather had felled the mighty chestnut trees himself, cut, trimmed, built his two-room cabin, then chinked the logs. Later generations added electricity, indoor plumbing, a small bathroom, a kitchen, and three more bedrooms.

The land, all one thousand acres of it, passed down through the male heirs. Over the years, 500 acres were sold off. Eventually, only two 250-acre parcels were left, one owned by Harold's dad Chester. His dad's brother Garvey, Harold's uncle, owned the other parcel, but sold off acreage when he needed cash. Harold's Aunt Lilly despised living in what she called "the boonies with all those gun-toting, tobacco-chewing hillbillies." Aunt Lilly insisted she needed a fine, two-story brick house with a swimming pool, expensive furniture, nice cars, a maid. "Told Garvey more than once he should never have brought such a high-fallutin' big city woman to the country," Chester had said. "But would he listen to me? Naw, and that's why he's selling off prime farmland bit by bit to hobby farmers and cattle breeders. Mark my words, he'll rue the day Lilly came into his life."

Harold grew up knowing his dad's 250 acres would one day belong to him. Chester had told him almost from birth, had said, "There weren't no way in hell Sheila would inherit any of it. After all, she was only a girl, and all girls was good for was to cook, make babies, and kowtow to their men folk." From the time he could walk, Harold explored the property's caves, hollows, streams and rocks, and dreamed of what he would do with each acre, even planned to go to VPI and get a degree in agricultural engineering. On the bottomland near the Roanoke River, he would raise tobacco and corn. His beef cattle would be top of the line, his bulls known all over the country for their get, the envy of all cattlemen in the state, the South, the nation. He dreamed splendid ideas for the old place.

Then the Army Corps of Engineers and Appalachian Power Company stepped in, built a dam at the base of Smith Mountain in Pittsylvania County to catch the flow of water from the Roanoke and Blackwater rivers, and created Smith

Mountain Lake and the smaller Leesville Lake. Property owners, whose land was covered by the rising water, were paid a pittance of what their land was worth. At least Harold thought so. He saw his future inheritance, except for fifty acres, slowly gobbled up by water. The farmland, log cabin, wild game, and pastures, were wiped out, all gone forever. The only thing Harold got was angry. He vowed to get even. Years later when the new breed of people—transplants and big city folks like his Aunt Lilly—flocked to Smith Mountain Lake, he schemed to take away the valuable possessions they had acquired.

Then, in spite of Harold's pleading, Chester Johns sold the remaining fifty acres—the last of Harold's due—and moved to West Virginia with his wife, Harold and Sheila. Sheila left home and moved to the Florida Keys when she was eighteen. Harold entered the University of West Virginia and in five years graduated with a Master's degree in electrical engineering. He went to work for an engineering design firm in Columbia, South Carolina, where he met and married Melinda, a voluptuous heiress from Aiken, and made a big name for himself in the engineering world. But Harold wasn't happy. His insatiable desire for vengeance drove him back to Virginia, and seven years ago he started his own electrical engineering firm in Lynchburg.

Even with all his success, Harold never stopped plotting his revenge. Five years ago he discovered this weekend cabin built in the mid-1970s. The cabin, he realized when inspecting the property, stood on three acres originally owned by his family—land he believed was rightfully his.

When Harold first saw the cabin at the lake's edge, it consisted of a two-bay boathouse built out into the water with a small apartment and a deck on top. Unlike most boathouses on the lake, this one had solid sides and two extra-wide garage-type doors that opened to the water.

Melinda hadn't approved of the small, old cabin. "If you expect me to live on this stupid lake with you, then you'd damn well better buy me a nice house. And I mean a really nice, big, elegant, expensive house, suitable for entertaining my high society friends." She stood with her hands on her hips in the middle of the cabin's tiny kitchen and looked around. "I will not live in this dump!"

Because he needed Melinda and her rich and influential contacts, he acquiesced and purchased an ostentatious mansion across the lake in Franklin County. He told her he'd sold the cabin, but that was a lie. He knew she'd never discover the truth; she was too busy traveling, socializing, having facelifts and tummy tucks, buying more and more cosmetics, working for charitable causes. When she begged for an apartment in Paris, he gave her what she wanted. Harold couldn't care less about what she did.

He hired a contractor to dismantle the cabin's deck and build in its place what looked like additional living space over the boathouse. He hung curtains in all the small windows and installed window boxes on the side facing the water. During the spring and summer months, the window boxes blossomed with marigolds and petunias. To anyone cruising by in a boat, it looked exactly like a cozy little cottage. But the addition wasn't living space. The new area had no floor; it was extra headroom with two heavy-duty boatlifts. Harold's ingenious design made it possible to hoist two thirty-foot long boats, one over the other, so anyone looking at the space between the water and sides of the building would think the boathouse empty.

The second bay concealed his fifty-foot houseboat. That monumental task had cost him a bundle of money. The original boathouse measured only thirty-five feet deep, not large enough for a fifty-foot boat. Per Harold's order, the contractor excavated twenty feet into the hillside and reinforced the dirt walls, thereby making the bay large enough.

Harold punched another button and the speedboat lifted out of the water. No one could see it from outside. He and Jimmy Ray stepped onto the wooden gangplank. They climbed fifteen steps and entered the small apartment.

Jimmy Ray sank into a brown leather swivel rocker, plopped his feet on the inlaid mahogany coffee table, and flicked a chunk of dried mud off his snakeskin boots onto the antique Persian carpet. A hard fist caught him under his chin, lifted him out of the chair, and sent him crashing to the floor.

"If you ever put your boots on a piece of my furniture again, I'll slam you through the wall!" Harold said.

Jimmy Ray slowly pushed himself into a sitting position and rubbed his throbbing jaw. He knew there would be a big, ugly bruise amidst the swelling. He wondered briefly if that would appeal to the chicks.

"Do you understand me, Jimmy Ray?" Harold tossed him a rag.

"Yeah, I understand. It won't happen again." Inside, the rage boiled as he cleaned up the mud. Jimmy Ray fought to stay in control. Now was not the time to get even. Not yet.

Harold mixed himself a gin and tonic and passed a cold beer to Jimmy Ray. "Just don't set it down on the coffee table without a coaster under it." He sipped his drink. "Clyde was second in command here, but he's gone. You want his job?"

"Was wonderin' when you was gonna ask me. I'm smarter than Clyde." Jimmy Ray grinned slightly, wincing at the pain in his jaw.

"Speaking of Clyde, you finished him off like I ordered?"

"Yeah. Dumped his body in that fishin' boat and set it loose."

"Good thinking. If the boat didn't sink in the storm, then the cops will blame Luke Stancill for Clyde's death and arrest him. If Stancill's still alive, that is. Now let's get busy. We've serious work to do."

Harold removed a huge picture from the rear wall, exposing a large rectangular cork bulletin board. Outlined on the board was a big, detailed map of Smith Mountain Lake marked with locations of some houses, docks and businesses. Green, red, orange, white, yellow, and silver thumbtacks dotted the map and corresponded with the colored bar graph at the bottom of the board.

"What's this blue one? It's bigger than the others." Jimmy Ray rubbed the blue tack with his trigger finger.

"That marks our headquarters—the nerve center, so to speak. You're standing in it." He watched as bewilderment spread across Jimmy Ray's face. "You thought this was just a cabin, didn't you? I could see it in your face. Like all the others who work for me, you believed I was a little dim-witted, didn't you? Here I have all this money, expensive boats, a big house on the lake, a classy ding-a-ling of a wife, but this little boathouse cabin is the place I prefer. Clyde knew the truth behind this place. He, Sheila, and my niece Red are the only ones who know. Well, not Clyde anymore. Soon you'll learn the secrets of the boathouse cabin, too."

Remembering Sheila, Harold frowned. *She must die. Pity. I hate to kill my own sister, I'm actually fond of her, but I know she'll sing her head off if the cops get to her before I do. No need to worry about Red. My niece's nerves are like mine—all steel. She's cold, calculating, power and money hungry. And smart.*

Jimmy Ray studied the map. Thumbtacks, thick in some areas, were placed on houses and boathouses around most of the shoreline. He read the graph at the bottom. Beside each color was one word: red for "Stop," green for "Go," orange for "Caution," white for "Done," blue for "Operations." Yellow meant "Valuables," and silver meant "Money." Even though he didn't understand the codes, he was impressed.

"This is some sweet setup," said Jimmy Ray. He opened his pack of Red Man.

"None of that chewing tobacco stuff in here. Put it back in your pocket," Harold said as he hung up the telephone.

"Sorry."

"You said this was a sweet setup? You've no idea." Harold picked up a remote control and pressed it. Slowly, the rear wall of the apartment opened to reveal electronic tracking equipment and a detailed computer system. He motioned for Jimmy Ray to follow and walked into the secret room. He pressed a button. Another movable wall opened. Boxes, wooden crates, and packing materials took

215

up a large portion of the room. Scattered around were small antique tables and chairs, oriental rugs, and valuable paintings. Jimmy Ray stared at wall shelves loaded with gleaming silver services, large footed tea pots, trays, sugars and creamers, candle sticks, coffee urns. Jewelry, sorted by value, filled several small see-through bins. Numerous patterns of sterling flatware rested in stacked divider trays.

"How much is all this stuff worth, Boss?"

"A fortune." Harold removed the diamond and ruby necklace from his pocket and put it on a shelf. "For instance, this'll fetch a big wad, upwards of a hundred thou."

"Whatcha gonna do with all this stuff?" Jimmy Ray asked.

"Sell it, Jimmy Ray. And get filthy rich."

CHAPTER THIRTY-NINE

The strong antiseptic hospital smell irritated her nostrils. From the nurse's station an urgent "Code Blue!" blared through the halls. A gurney returning from the recovery room rumbled down the corridor. Aurora groaned and tried to ignore all her aching bones and muscles. When she heard a knock at the door, she pushed herself into a sitting position. A pleasant looking, middle-aged nurse pushed open the door and smiled at Aurora.

"You're awake. How are you feeling, Mrs. Harris?"

"Awful."

"That's understandable. You've been through a lot."

"How's my husband? And is he still in Intensive Care?"

"I heard he's doing better. I think they'll move him out of ICU some time today." The nurse smiled. "I understand you created quite a scene here earlier."

"Yeah, I guess I did. I can understand the need for Sam to be in Intensive Care. That's where he needed to be. But I wanted to be with him, or at least be where I could see him. I couldn't understand why I wasn't allowed to be on a gurney in the hall where I could watch my husband through the glass." Aurora grinned. "Think I acted a little irrationally?"

The nurse smiled, patted Aurora on the hand, and said, "Perhaps just a tad. I'm Estelle. Let me know if you need anything. And by the way, a guard is stationed outside this door. Seems the police are concerned your attackers will try again."

"Is someone guarding my husband, too?"

"That's my understanding. Don't worry, Mr. Harris is in good hands."

"Nurse, uh, Estelle, will my husband and I be allowed to share a semi-private room once he's moved out of Intensive Care?"

"I don't know, but I'll be happy to check on that for you." She patted Aurora's hand again, turned, and left the room smiling.

Aurora swung her legs off the bed and onto the floor. She clutched the open back of her dull-green designer hospital gown with one hand as she padded across the room in her bare feet, quietly opened the door, and peeped out at the uniformed guard seated, legs crossed, in a metal folding chair. He was a large, black man with curly black hair and a neat mustache. A pistol rested snugly in the holster at his side. He looked up from his NASCAR magazine and smiled at her.

"Just checking," she said as she shut the door. For the first time in days, she didn't feel anxious or afraid. She climbed back in the hospital bed, pulled up the covers, and slept.

Hours later, Judge Anderson flashed his I.D. at the cop guarding Aurora's door. Yep, time to get out of this business, he thought. Dick knew him, had appeared as a witness in his court a few times, but still insisted on seeing the judge's ID. Anderson knew this was standard operating procedure, but the act still irritated him. He knocked lightly on the door and slipped into the room.

Aurora opened her eyes and recognized Uncle Charlie sitting in the chair beside her bed.

"Aurora, dear," he said, "how are you feeling?" He bent over, kissed her gently on her cheek, held her hand.

"Better, thank you. Much better. Guess I must've needed that sleep." The relief on her uncle's face caused her to smile. "Thank you for all you did. And I'm glad you didn't follow my instructions, or Sam and I would probably be dead. Is King okay? And Little Guy?"

"Both dogs are great. I think they rather like the rewards that come with hero status." The judge laughed. "Lieutenant Conner, Sergeant Johnson, and Captain Vincent have bought each of them all-beef hamburgers, not those already-cooked burgers at the fast food places. I'm talking going to the grocery store, buying high-quality, lean ground beef, then cooking the burgers medium-rare on the George Foreman Mean Lean Grilling Machine that Conner brought to the police station."

She laughed. "I can hardly wait to see them. They both played a part in rescuing Sam and me. King saved my life, you know."

"I know."

"How did he happen to be on the coast guard boat?"

"I insisted. They wouldn't allow me or Little Guy on board, but when I told them about the uncanny bond you and King have, the way you seem to communicate with each other, they agreed to take him."

"Uncle Charlie, the nurse said Sam is doing better, but I really need to see for myself. Would you get a wheelchair from the nurses' station and push me to ICU? I don't think they'll let me go under my own power yet."

He planted another kiss on her cheek and left the room. He returned several minutes later with the wheelchair.

"I'll be back soon," she said to the guard as the judge wheeled her from the room.

As she and Charlie entered ICU, she saw her husband lying in bed, a puzzled expression on his face as he softly hummed "Blue Suede Shoes."

"Sam?" She touched his arm.

"Susie-Q. Are you okay?" he asked.

"I'm fine. How are you?" She pulled his blanket up over his legs.

"All things considered, I'm not feeling too bad. The nurse told me I was lucky; the word I would use is blessed. The gunshot wound in my forehead is more of a deep graze than what I would call an honest-to-goodness gunshot wound. The one in my side is deeper, but no vital organs, arteries or veins were hit. And they removed the bullet easily, I understand. I wouldn't want to run a marathon any time soon, though. Or even walk down the hall. Bet my headache would improve if 'Blue Suede Shoes' would stop stomping around in my brain.

"You look well, Susie-Q." He smiled and shook hands with Charlie, then turned his attention back to Aurora.

"I am, but tell me about 'Blue Suede Shoes.'"

"I can't get that song off my mind."

"You were singing it several days ago," Aurora said.

"I know. There's something about it that's nagging me, ready to surface any minute. It'll come, just hope it's soon. Do blue shoes, or suede shoes, or blue suede mean anything to you?"

"When I was in high school," Aurora said to Sam and Uncle Charlie, "I owned a pair of royal blue shoes. They were my favorites. The heels were three inches tall with pointy toes, my first pair of spikes, a perfect match for my royal blue Easter suit. I wore it with a white silk, jewel-neck blouse. And there was this little matching purse. . . . But I digress. I don't think my old shoes are the ones you're singing about. Other than those, blue shoes mean nothing to me. But I'll think about it."

"So you say you're doing okay, Sam?" asked Charlie.

"I am. Dr. Cameron came by a little while ago, said I'm mending. Plans to release me in a couple of days if nothing unforeseen develops. Will probably move me from ICU to a private room later in the day."

"If I'm still here, would you be willing to make it a semi-private room so we can be roomies, Sam?" asked Aurora.

"You betcha, sounds good to me."

Sam paused, then drawled, "So have the good guys corralled the bad guys yet?" He started humming "My Baby Loves A Western Movie." Aurora stifled a giggle.

"Afraid not," answered the judge. "They've vanished. Even their houseboat's disappeared. How do you conceal a fifty-foot boat on a body of water this size? I'd understand the problem if we were looking on the ocean, but not on

Smith Mountain Lake. Helicopters continue searching the lake, police are checking all marinas, but no luck yet.

"We've located Luke Stancill, though."

"How is he?" Aurora asked.

"Okay. He made it to shore during the storm, took shelter in a boathouse until dawn, then found a kind woman who invited him into her house and called 911. When the cops arrived, Luke was feasting on a Texas-size breakfast the woman cooked for him. Doesn't seem to have any injuries other than bruises. He's already left the hospital."

The three discussed Luke's heroic actions of the night before. "Guess I've misjudged him," offered Charlie. "If he had something to hide, it's unlikely he would have risked his life for yours."

Sam asked the question he knew was troubling Aurora. "What about Carole? Do you know the part she played in this?"

"I was just about to get to her. Appears she was engaged to Harold Johns, but broke up with him several months ago when she discovered he was married."

"But she was engaged to a Fred, she told me so," Aurora said.

"Harold Johns' middle name is Frederick; Carole knew him as Fred, not Harold."

"But the pictures of her, the one on his boat, the other one in his wallet? And how do you know all this, Uncle Charlie?"

"Lieutenant Conner called me about an hour ago. He and Johnson checked out your friend's story, everything she told them can be proven. And a mutual friend of Harold and Carole said that Johns kept pictures of his conquests, has an album somewhere in the houseboat full of photos of unsuspecting women. Even has the dates when each affair began and ended. The friend hadn't told Carole because of that good-old-boy mentality that never rats on a cheating buddy. It's a guy thing."

"Are you sure of this? Have you talked with Carole yet?" Aurora felt relief. Her friend had not betrayed her after all.

"I believe Lieutenant Conner has interrogated her. I know she's very concerned about both you and Sam. She wants to talk to you as soon as you're up to it."

"You will have to leave now," the nurse said to Aurora and Anderson. "We don't want to tire our patient, now do we?"

Aurora stood up and gave Sam a quick kiss on his lips. "See you soon, darling. Get some sleep, now."

As her uncle pushed the wheelchair into Aurora's room, his cell phone rang. "Excuse me," he said, and reached in his coat pocket. Several minutes later he hung up and said, "Well, well, well. We've had some interesting new developments." He smiled and withdrew a small pad from his breast pocket, fumbled in his coat pocket for a pencil, and jotted down some notes. After returning the pad and pencil to their proper places, he strolled over to the window. "Not a bad view," he said. "Nice little flower garden out there. Have you seen it?"

"For heavens sake, Uncle Charlie, what's happened?"

"Seems Mr. Stancill's fishing boat washed up on shore."

"And?"

"There was a body in it, a man. He'd been stabbed several times. Fortunately, he's still alive. The boys are running a check on him right now."

"Is he here in the hospital?"

"Yep."

"What room?" Aurora pushed the wheelchair's footrests back, stood up and, remembering to hold the gown shut in the back, hurried to the room's one tiny closet. From the paper bag, she removed the fresh clothes Uncle Charlie had brought her, disappeared in the bathroom, and called out through the closed door, "What room did you say?"

"I didn't."

"You might as well tell me, Uncle Charlie. Maybe I can identify him, save us all some valuable time." Dressed, she emerged from the bathroom and smiled sweetly at her uncle. "You know I can find out for myself. You might as well tell me."

"Your physician hasn't dismissed you yet."

"I'm still in the hospital, aren't I? Just clothed instead of baring my *derriere* to the entire world."

"Okay, he's in Intensive Care, too. I'm going there now. You may as well accompany me."

Aurora and Charlie had just passed the nurses' station when one of the nurses called them over to the desk. "Mrs. Harris, your husband just buzzed, asked us to call your room, tell you to go to ICU fast. Something about 'Blue Suede Shoes'?"

Aurora didn't wait for the judge; she stepped out of the wheelchair and ran ahead of him down the corridor to ICU.

"Stop, ma'am. No visitors allowed," said the guard stationed outside the Intensive Care unit.

"It's me, the lady in the green hospital gown you saw earlier, just clothed this time. I was in the wheelchair . . ."

He looked her over carefully and smiled. "Oh yeah, I recognize you now." He stepped back for her to enter.

Sam sat up as best he could in the bed, his face twisted with pain. "The shoes, Aurora. They were blue leather sandals. And they were standing beside my head at the lake house, the last thing I remember seeing before passing out."

Aurora stared at him. "I've seen them, too. And I know who was wearing them."

CHAPTER FORTY

Sheila stared at the bleached-blonde hairs clinging to her brush. She tried to tell herself the hair loss was normal, nothing to worry about. *Who am I kidding?* She flung the brush down on the dressing table and picked up the magnifying mirror. *Is that a new wrinkle around my mouth?* She stroked it and gazed at her reflection in the oval mirror. Red glazed eyes stared back at her.

How had she come to this? Why, she'd always been the best looking, sexiest girl wherever she went. Everyone said so. All heads turned when she swept into a room. The guys' eyes radiated appreciation, lust; the gals' stares shot daggers of pure jealousy. And Sheila thrived on her looks. Never did she lack for boyfriends, but when their compliments came less often, when she thought they were taking her for granted, she moved on to someone new, someone who would be impressed with her beauty, her sexuality, and her ability to use both. Until she met Clyde, that is.

He was such a hunk, like a suntanned Greek god, his light brown hair clipped crew-cut style to suit his diver's occupation. The instant she saw him, she wanted him. Somehow this man was different. For the first time in her promiscuous life, she played hard to get—and it worked. Since that day, she'd never had another man, never needed one. And Clyde—dear, sweet Clyde—after all these years of marriage, he still adored her and sacrificed everything for her. They were in all this trouble because of her, and she hated herself for that and for what she'd become.

She glanced at the gold-framed picture on the vanity, the one of their daughter Red standing beside Clyde on the family's 60-foot yacht only days before the mortgage company repossessed it. Sheila had to admit that her daughter was gorgeous, looked a lot like she had years ago, except for the flaming red hair. Sheila's hair had been blonde through third grade, then it turned a dull brown. Her loving mother had started then to bleach it. "No mousy-colored head of hair for a daughter of mine," she'd said.

Sheila remembered how thrilled, how proud she was when she brought her perfect newborn daughter home from the hospital six months after she and Clyde married. Red always looked so pretty, so sweet. Sheila loved to dress Red in dainty outfits, put matching bows in her bright-red hair. Sheila would smile demurely and say "Thank you" as strangers stopped her on the street, looked in the baby carriage, and said, "Honey, I declare, you just don't look old enough to have a baby." And she heard these magical words for years, changed periodically to say, "You don't look old enough to have a child five (or ten or twelve) years old."

But Sheila's world fell apart when her daughter turned 16. On a family vacation to Aruba to celebrate Red's birthday, Sheila and Red returned to their hotel after a day of shopping, and discovered the lobby full of men attending a plumbers' convention. Sheila watched as her daughter—poised, beautiful, and sexy—sashayed across the lobby. Conversation ceased as every man turned to stare. When Sheila crossed the room, no one even glanced her way. From that day on, Sheila never took Red with her in public, ceased being a loving mother. Red rebelled at Sheila's sudden coldness and vowed to get even with her mother. At the same time, Sheila began to drink heavily.

Sheila grabbed the tweezers to pluck her eyebrows, but her hand shook too much. *Damn, I need a fix bad. Where the hell is Clyde?*

Sheila jumped when the doorbell rang. She wiped a tear from her cheek, checked her appearance in front of the full-length gilt-framed hall mirror, sucked in her stomach, and answered the door.

"Good morning, ma'am. I'm Field Lieutenant Conner, and this is Sergeant Johnson." Johnson nodded a greeting. "Could we talk with you for a minute?" asked Conner.

"What's this about?" asked Sheila.

"Ma'am, if we could come inside, I'll explain."

"I do not let strange men in my home. I don't see a badge. How do I know you're really cops?"

Both men flipped out their badges.

"A woman can't be too careful these days. I want to see your driver's licenses, too." They groaned, but complied.

"This is about Clyde, isn't it? Is he okay?"

Conner and Johnson exchanged glances. "We don't know anybody named Clyde. This is about something else," said Conner.

"Did Harold send you?"

"No, ma'am. Can't we come in?"

"I guess so."

Sheila walked to the coffee table, pulled a cigarette from the half-empty pack, and stuck it in her mouth. She tried to light it with the gold lighter beside the ashtray, but her hands trembled too much. Johnson walked over to Sheila and cupped his hand over hers, steadying the lighter.

After two deep drags, Sheila motioned to the sofa covered in pink chenille. "Please sit down." She remained standing for a moment, then sat across from the deputies in one of the two matching chairs. She straightened the straps of her halter top and fluffed her hair. "Would you like a vodka and tonic?"

"No, thanks."

"You don't mind if I have one?" She was already out of the chair and at the bar. The Waterford crystal decanters on the sterling silver tray glittered in the sunlight.

"Ma'am, we need to ask you some questions," Conner said softly. "Can't the drink wait?"

"No, it can't wait!" Sheila snapped. "I'm sorry, of course it can." She set the half-raised decanter down and walked back over to the chair. "I'm on edge. My husband didn't come home last night, and I'm worried about him, that's all."

"We're checking out everyone who is known to have a key to the cabins at the State Park, specifically Cabin 171E. You clean there on a regular basis, don't you?"

Sheila chewed on her bottom lip and looked down at the floor. "I manage the cleaning company that sometimes services the cabins. I don't clean very often myself, only when one of the girls is sick or something. Usually I assign one of the others to do the cleaning. Don't think I've cleaned there in over a month."

"Did you visit Cabin 171E yesterday?"

"No."

"A park employee cutting the grass says he saw you drive up to the cabin early yesterday afternoon."

"I told you I wasn't there."

Johnson flipped back a page of his small notepad. "You drive a white convertible, don't you?" He pointed out the window at the white convertible parked outside.

"Lots of people around the lake drive white convertibles."

"But few ladies who drive white convertibles are as attractive as you, ma'am," Conner said in a soft voice. "The employee described you perfectly." He watched as Sheila crossed her legs seductively and casually flipped one of her halter straps lower on her shoulder. Ten years ago she probably was a real looker, he thought. Still was, only now she had that faded-flower look.

"You think I'm attractive?" She glanced his way and batted her eyes.

"A woman with your looks is always noticed, not one a man would soon forget. And the grass cutter watched you drive up to Cabin 171E. He said you carried a white cooler inside. Only stayed a couple of minutes, according to him."

"Maybe I was there yesterday. I vaguely remember going to the park. It's just that I've had so much on my mind lately." She put a hand to her temple, thought a minute, then said, "I remember now. Yes, I was there. I returned a cooler that I took home the last time I cleaned the cabin. Yes, that's it. The renters had left a dead fish in it, and the cooler reeked to high heaven. Didn't get around to returning it until yesterday."

"We'd like for you to come down to headquarters with us for questioning."

"Am I under arrest?"

"No, we just need to ask you some questions."

As they walked to the police car, Sheila put an exaggerated wiggle in her walk and asked in a throaty voice, "So do you really think I'm attractive?"

Hero. That's what the nurses had called him. Exhausted is how Luke Stancill felt, not like a hero. All he wanted was to go home, take a long shower, and go to bed. A little comfort from Vanessa would be nice, too. He looked at the clock on the taxi's dashboard. If the cab driver hurried, Luke could get there before Vanessa left work for the day. Maybe she'd stay with him, not spend the rest of the day at her second job. He leaned over the seat and urged the driver to go faster. Engrossed in warm thoughts of his part-time secretary, he didn't see how close the taxi came to hitting the doe and fawn that bounded across the road directly in front of them.

The driver slammed on his brakes and jolted Luke back to reality. "Close call," the driver said.

"Yeah. I've had a lot of those recently." The two men watched the deer disappear into a dense pocket of tall pines.

Vanessa's red Camaro occupied its customary spot in the gravel parking lot beside the two-story building. Luke thought briefly of going upstairs to his apartment first to take a shower, but decided against it. He needed to see Vanessa, feel her arms around him, listen to her sexy voice praise his actions, boost his now-inflated ego. He paid the driver and went inside. The tweed carpet in the downstairs office cushioned his footsteps, so Vanessa didn't hear Luke come in. He hid behind the door to surprise her when she came out of the supply room.

Vanessa, her back to the door, spoke into her cell phone. "Mom just called. The cops have her. A park employee saw her go in the cabin yesterday." She paused, then said, "Hold on a sec. I thought I heard something." Vanessa faced the doorway and listened. Luke stayed hidden behind the door. "Guess I'm just hearing things. I'm a little nervous. Back to Mom. She sounded shaky, scared, like her drugs are gone. Where's Dad?"

She listened for a minute, then said into the receiver, "Dead? Are you sure? You know if Mom finds out what you've done, she'll squeal on us." Another pause. Luke held his breath. Then, "Hell no, I don't have any desire to spend time in prison. Do what you have to do."

Stunned, Luke decided not to reveal his presence. He pressed harder against the wall.

"Nope, haven't heard a word from Luke," Vanessa continued. "If he doesn't call soon, I'll assume he didn't survive the swim." Pause. "Yeah, that would simplify things. Anyhow, I think this operation is over here; time to move on. I'll be there in thirty minutes."

She put away her cell phone and turned around. Luke blocked her way.

"How long have you been standing there?"

"Long enough."

"I'm leaving. Get out of my way."

"No."

"You will have to hit me to keep me here. Now move."

No matter what she had done, he couldn't hit her. Instead, he grabbed her left arm. "You're not going anywhere, Vanessa."

"Let go!"

"No."

With her right fist, Vanessa punched him hard in the throat and jerked out of his grasp. Luke grabbed his neck and struggled to breathe. With tires squealing, the Camaro sped away before Luke reached the front door.

CHAPTER FORTY-ONE

Judge Anderson and Sheriff Rogers stood beside the hospital bed and watched the man struggling for each raspy breath. The doctors said the unidentified man might die, that the next few hours were critical. Charlie knew the man could provide some answers if he survived. He jumped when Aurora put her hand on his arm. "I didn't hear you come in," he said. "Is Sam okay?"

"Don't tell anyone, you two. I sneaked in. And in answer to your question, Uncle Charlie, Sam is fine. He sent for me because he remembered something important. Do you recall how he couldn't wipe the song 'Blue Suede Shoes' out of his mind? Well, there's a reason. As he lay on the floor in my parents' house, the last thing he saw before losing consciousness was a pair of blue leather sandals. And I'm pretty sure I know who was wearing them." She pointed to the bed. "That man's wife—the first time I saw her she was wearing sandals that match Sam's description. She and this man—her husband—surprised me on the dock and said they wanted to breed King with their female Lab. I saw the sandals again when the crew came to clean the house after the attack on Sam. The same woman was in charge."

"Do you know her name?"

"Sheila. She's Harold Johns' sister. Don't know her last name, though. But that man," she added, pointing to the hospital bed, "is one of those who held us captive on the houseboat. I think his name is Clyde."

"I'll throw the book at 'im!" declared the sheriff.

"We'd be dead if not for him," she said. "I don't know why, but he knocked Harold Johns down. That gave us the extra seconds we needed to get off the houseboat. That man saved our lives.

"Speaking of Harold Johns," she said to the sheriff, "have you caught him yet?"

"No, but it's not because we're not trying. Every available cop in Bedford, Franklin and Pittsylvania counties is searching for him."

"Sam trusted Harold, liked him, worked with him. Would you believe they even have a couple of patents together?" Aurora shook her head in disbelief. "I never liked him, though. Didn't like his arrogance or the lack of warmth in his eyes. It was as though he had no soul. And he treated his wife Melinda like a trophy to show off at big events to clients. No wonder she wanted to live in Paris instead of with him."

A nurse entered the room. "You must leave now," she said to the judge and the sheriff. "And what are you doing in here, miss?" She glared at Aurora.

"We're leaving. Come on, Aurora," Charlie said.

Lieutenant Conner lit Sheila another cigarette. When the phone rang, he leaned over his desk and answered it. He scribbled notes on a piece of paper and slid it across the desk to Sergeant Johnson. When he hung up, Conner looked at Sheila and said, "Ms. Perkins, I really hate to say this, but you're under arrest."

"I'm under arrest?" Sheila stared at Lieutenant Conner in disbelief. "What's the charge?" She puffed hard on her cigarette.

"Breaking and entering, burglary, assault, attempted murder." The detective read Sheila her rights.

"And just who was my murder victim supposed to be?"

"Sam Harris at 210 Spawning Run Road."

"I didn't touch the man. I just went there to help find some stuff. He surprised us. Jimmy Ray hit him with the bat."

"Do you want to call your lawyer?"

Sheila trembled. "Where's Clyde? I want Clyde."

"Who's Clyde?"

"Clyde's my husband. Where is he? I need him."

"A man named Clyde is in the hospital. He was stabbed several times." Johnson hated this; Sheila wasn't such a bad person. He didn't want to hurt her. "I'm afraid he's in pretty bad shape."

"No! It can't be! Not Clyde!" Tears ran down her cheeks.

"Aurora Harris just identified him as one of the three men on the houseboat where she and Sam were held captive. She did say, however, that Clyde knocked Harold Johns down, giving Aurora and Sam time to escape. Apparently, Clyde was knifed in the process, then dumped into a small boat and set adrift in the storm. He's in intensive care. He might not survive." He watched Sheila. She looked determined and angry.

"My maiden name is Johns, Sheila Johns. Harold Johns is my brother."

"You mentioned a Jimmy Ray. Who is he?" asked Conner. He handed her a tissue.

Sheila stopped crying and looked at the detective. "I'll tell you everything." She wiped at the streaks of smudged mascara on her cheeks and blew her nose. "But only under two conditions."

"Let's hear 'em."

"Number one: I want a guard posted at Clyde's door 'round the clock. If my brother discovers Clyde's alive, he'll kill him."

"We can arrange that. What else?" Lieutenant Conner pitied Sheila. He hated to admit it, but he respected her, too. Here she was, shaking—obviously having withdrawal symptoms—under arrest, and she was thinking of her husband. She actually loved him.

"Number two: I want protection at all times, too."

"Harold Johns is your brother; he wouldn't harm his sister."

"Yes, he would. I know too much. And don't let Red, my daughter, near me or near Clyde, either. She takes her orders from Harold. Does anything he says. She's cold and calculating, just like him." She fidgeted with her hair and wiped her eyes again. "I must look a sight.

"Hey, I've gotta have a drink, somethin'. Cain't y'all get me somethin'? Then I'll tell you 'bout Jimmy Ray."

A buzzer sounded a warning. Two seconds later, Red stepped into her Uncle Harold's lair. That's what he liked to call his secret cabin, his lair. And why not? Foxes, bears, mountain lions, they all had lairs they could retreat to. So did he, and he was just as dangerous, maybe more so.

"Welcome, Red. Meet my associate Jimmy Ray."

Jimmy Ray's eyes lit up when he saw Red for the first time. Harold bristled.

"Listen to me, both of you. Jimmy Ray, no fooling around with Red or I'll shoot you right through your ugly head. Period. Are you understanding me?"

"Yeah, boss. Pity, though." Red smiled her sexy, come-on smile at him.

Jimmy Ray looked her up and down. *This one just might be a good match for me. Maybe some other time. . . .*

"Red, get the packing materials out of the back room. You know where I keep them. Start boxing up the jewelry and silver. Jimmy Ray, you roll up the rugs, box the paintings, anything that Red's not working on. Understand?"

"Yeah, I understand. But why? We can't git 'em outa here. By now every cop on the lake is looking for your speedboat, probably the houseboat, too. Ain't you heard the helicopters? We wouldn't git a mile."

"We're not moving them by boat. We're going by van."

"If you think I'm gonna lug all them things outa this here cabin and up that there steep hill to a truck, you're nuts!"

Red laughed. "Shall I show him the way, Uncle Harold?"

Harold smiled. "You just keep on packing, sweets. I'll show 'im." He motioned for Jimmy Ray to follow. They went through the middle room and into the warehouse area.

"See that closet over there, Jimmy Ray? Open the door and go in." When Jimmy Ray stood in the empty closet, Harold pushed a button and the closet floor lifted several inches before Harold stopped it.

"Whoa! What the hell's goin' on?"

"It's an elevator, goes into the garage up top where the van's parked. I want you to load the goods on this platform, raise them to the garage, then pack them into the van. It'll take several van loads to move all this stuff, so get busy. When the first load is ready, Red will drive it away from the lake. Now get going; I doubt we've much time left."

"What are you gonna be doin'? Damn if I'm gonna do all the work."

"You'll do what you're told. I'll be making arrangements for disposing of the merchandise."

Forty-five minutes later, Red drove the white van out of the garage. Jimmy Ray continued packing and moving boxes up to the garage level. An hour later, Red returned.

"How the hell could she git to where she was going, unload, and git back here in that short a time? Ain't possible." Jimmy Ray stared at the empty van.

Harold grinned. "What if there were two vans, or three, like the one you loaded? It's simple. Red delivered the full van, stepped into an empty identical one, and returned. We'll repeat the process until we're finished. By the time Red's delivered the third load, the first van will be empty and ready to load again if need be. My associate's men on the other end are experts at unloading in record time. Ingenious, don't you think?"

Jimmy Ray scratched his head and said. "Damn right. Smart, too." Harold smiled.

Within four hours, Johns' entire warehouse had been cleaned out. Its contents now resided in a metal storage building on a Franklin County farm.

"While you were putting that last load on the van, Jimmy Ray, I checked on Sheila. The cops have arrested her."

"What about Dad? Have they found his body yet?" asked Red.

"Worse than that. They found his body, but it's still breathing."

"Then we're good as caught." Red stared at her uncle.

"Wrong, darlin'. But it is time for us to go. Jimmy Ray, thanks for your help; we couldn't have done it without you."

"I didn't help you out of the goodness of my heart. I expect to be paid what's due me."

"Of course, Jimmy Ray. You'll get exactly what you deserve." Harold smiled and stepped aside.

A bullet slammed into the back of Jimmy Ray's head. He was dead before he hit the floor.

Red walked over to Harold, handed him the smoking pistol, and looked down at Jimmy Ray. "Can you believe him? Did he really think we'd let him live? Just can't understand some folks."

"It's just you and me, Red." Harold grinned. He put his arm around his niece's shoulders and tucked the pistol inside his pants pocket.

"Just the way I like it, Uncle Harold. Let's go."

Harold pushed the elevator button. Nothing happened. At the same instant, the lights went out.

"What's the matter? Why won't the elevator work? And why'd you turn off the lights?"

"I didn't. Something must have tripped a circuit breaker."

"Well, do something about it!"

"Calm down, Red. I'll check the circuit breaker box." He lifted a flashlight off the wall beside the elevator. "I keep a flashlight beside each door for emergencies such as this. Stop worrying." He shined the beam across the room. "Wait here."

"Like I'm going anywhere!" Red hoped he'd hurry. She didn't like being alone with Jimmy Ray's body.

CHAPTER FORTY-TWO

Saturday, May 15

Tantalizing aromas wafted from the kitchen, across the living room, and out onto the screened porch. Even Sam, busy grilling striper on the porch, turned his head toward the kitchen and sniffed. King and Little Guy did the same.

"What is that delightful smell?" asked Robert Reeves.

"I'll go see." Jill rose and started toward the kitchen. "Maybe Aurora will let me sample it." Little Guy trotted after her.

"I guarantee it'll be delicious if Aurora made it, whatever it is." Charlie licked his lips. "She inherited her mother's culinary expertise. Annie and I have devoured many a meal in this house, and every one delicious. Can't believe Jack never put on pounds." He chuckled. "I'm giving you fair warning, Sam. As long as you're eating the meals Aurora cooks, you'd better be getting plenty of exercise."

"I learned that years ago, Charlie," said Sam.

Carole stopped stirring the dill sauce and smiled at Jill. "Guess things will never change. Here we are again, females in the kitchen slaving over a hot stove, while the men lounge around outside and drink beer. Except for Sam. He can drink beer and grill fish at the same time." The three women laughed.

"The guys sent me in to find out what smells so good." Jill lifted a pot lid. "They're salivating out there, Aurora."

"They're just hungry." Aurora crumbled the cheese into the salad. "But on the menu tonight is grilled striper with a dill sauce, lemon-buttered asparagus, scalloped potatoes, and a spinach salad with mandarin oranges, walnuts and crumbled feta cheese."

"Sounds yummy." Jill nibbled on a slice of orange. "May I help?"

"Certainly. Would you pull the rolls out of the oven and put them in that basket there next to the stove? The cloth liner's in the drawer next to the refrigerator." Aurora pointed to the drawer.

Carole poured the dill sauce into a bowl. "Did you make these rolls, Aurora?"

"Yes, I did. They're made from Mother's whole wheat recipe. You've always loved that one. Thought you deserved something special." Aurora handed Carole a roll.

Carole grinned and took a bite.

"How'd the promo Aurora made for you turn out, Carole?" asked Jill.

"Great. I've booked nearly eight rentals through October, and sold two houses. All because of the promo. Aurora is a genius with her cameras."

Aurora pulled the scalloped potatoes out of the oven. "Thanks. I'm glad I could do it for you, Carole."

"Have you thought of doing more promos here at the lake?" asked Jill. She put a stick of butter on the butter dish and rummaged in the drawer for a butter knife.

"That's a wonderful idea," said Carole. "Aurora, I have lots of contacts in the area that I know would jump at the chance to use you." She grabbed Aurora's hands. "Please say yes!"

Aurora laughed. "You two are good for my ego. But I can't. I missed Sam like crazy while I worked on Carole's promo. I couldn't stand being here for long periods while he's in Augusta."

"I understand, but it surely would be fun having you here. Now, what else can I do to help?"

"You could put ice in the water glasses. They're in the cabinet next to the window."

Jill waved her left hand in the air and brushed the hair off her forehead. "Have either of you noticed anything different about me?"

Aurora and Carole shrieked when they saw the large diamond ring.

"It's gorgeous!" Carole leaned toward Jill for a closer look.

"The ring belonged to Robert's great-great-grandmother. Can you believe that?"

"It's beautiful, suits you. I'm so tickled for you and Robert." said Aurora. "Have you set a date yet?"

"The sooner the better. We've missed some wonderful years together. When the police accused Robert of embezzling funds and murdering Lampwerth, my world flipped upside down. I realized then that I'd never stopped loving him. He's more important to me than any career could ever be."

"So glad you and the accountant proved him innocent. Has the press grabbed hold of that story yet?" Carole snitched a walnut from the salad bowl. "This is one they'd kill for. It's got everything: intrigue, murder, embezzlement, decency, passion."

"No, Robert doesn't want Bob Tinsley's wife to know her husband was a gambler and an embezzler. She's not well. Robert will side-step around the embezzlement facts as long as he can." Little Guy whined and Jill patted him on his head. "I'll quit my job as soon as I find a replacement. During the week, we'll live in Robert's apartment in Washington and come here to the lake most weekends. And you know what surprises me? I'm looking forward to cooking. Even cleaning. May need recipes from you, Aurora. I could count on two hands the complete from-scratch meals I've cooked in the last nine years.

"Robert and I were hoping, Aurora, that you'd be willing to keep Little Guy with you for a while. We both think he'd be happier here than in the middle of the chaos that always comes with moving. Didn't you say you'd be here a few more weeks?"

"Yes, I will. And yes, I'll keep Little Guy for you."

"Thank you so much. Robert and I appreciate it."

"Aurora, the striper's almost done!" Sam called from the porch.

"We're coming." The three women gathered up the rest of the meal and carried the dishes to the porch. Aurora didn't miss the way Luke and Carole looked at each other or the way his hand caressed her arm when she sat down close beside him. She caught Carole's attention, raised an eyebrow, and glanced at Luke. Carole nodded and grinned. So that's the way it is, thought Aurora happily. King stretched out beside her chair.

"Can an old man make an announcement?" asked Charlie.

"Of course you may," Aurora and Sam replied in unison.

"I turned in my resignation today." He set his fork down and wiped his mouth with his napkin. "I'm quitting the legal system. Gonna play golf with my retired buddies. Plan to enjoy the meals my widow neighbor brings over, might even suggest she join me." He looked at the faces staring at him. "Whaddaya think? Am I nuts?"

"Of course not. I believe you made a wise decision. Time for you to have some fun, Uncle Charlie. Dad, Mom and Aunt Annie would all agree with me." The others echoed Aurora's sentiments.

"A toast to Charlie." Sam held up his wine glass.

"To Charlie."

"This striper's the best I've ever eaten, Sam." Robert took another bite.

"I agree," echoed Luke.

"Thanks. I think Aurora's sauce makes it, though." Sam smiled at his wife.

"Luke, I apologize for giving you such a hard time. I was wrong about you. And thanks for helping Aurora and Sam. You put your life at risk for them. If ever there is anything I can do for you. . . ." Charlie looked at Luke.

"You were just doing your job, judge. There's no need for an apology." Luke smiled.

"Kind of like poetic justice, don't you think?" Sam said. "Here Harold spent untold amounts of money designing his state-of-the-art hiding place, put all kinds of walls, hidden rooms, even an elevator, everything operated electronically by remote control, into his cabin. And a simple, perfectly-timed power failure was his downfall. Red's, too."

"Excuse me, Sam, could I have another piece of fish?" Robert passed his plate.

"Of course." Sam put some striper on Robert's plate and continued. "The two were stuck there, with Jimmy Ray's dead body, until the cops arrived hours later at the exact time the power came back on. Imagine Harold's and Red's surprise when they rode the elevator up to the garage and ran smack into the cops."

"What caused the power to go out?" Robert reached for the scalloped potatoes and another roll.

Charlie laughed. "The power went out—this really is hilarious!—because a common gray squirrel knocked out a transformer." King jumped up and cocked his ears. Little Guy whined.

"It's okay, guys. There's no squirrel," Aurora whispered. Both dogs relaxed.

"But didn't they have a key?" Carole asked.

Sam laughed so hard tears streamed down his cheeks. "Keys were seldom used because all the locks in his cabin are on remote control. Remember, Harold's an electrical engineer and a genius. I'm not surprised that all the door locks were electronic. Only one key opened the doors, so as a precaution, Harold had ordered Clyde to have two duplicate keys made only a week before. Clyde did what he was told." Sam doubled over with laughter. "Clyde took—he took the one key with him, had duplicates made, but hadn't gotten around to giving them to Harold." The others laughed, too. "When Jimmy Ray stabbed Clyde, he tossed Clyde— along with the keys that were in Clyde's pants pocket—into

Luke's boat. You could say that Clyde is responsible for their capture."

When everyone's laughter subsided, the judge asked, "Want to know more about Jimmy Ray?" Everyone nodded. "Sheila led the cops to Harold's cabin, and once the electricity came back on," he snickered, "Harold and Red were apprehended. Sheriff Rogers found Jimmy Ray, dead from a gunshot in the back of his head. The guy was a sicko, got what he deserved. But you'll never guess what they found in his pants pocket." He took a swallow of wine.

"What?"

"The diamond and ruby necklace Aurora took off the grebe. Jimmy Ray must have swiped it when he was loading the van. The man just couldn't stay out of trouble."

"Pass the asparagus, please, Robert." Sam dished some onto his plate and said, "You know, I still can't fathom the criminal activities Harold was involved in. He had brains, social status, a high-paying job. Why did he do those things?" Sam shook his head. "I thought he was my friend, but he tried to kill Aurora, Luke and me. And he was responsible for Jack's death. Guess I'll never understand."

"Me either," said Aurora. "As much as I despise him for what he did, I'm intrigued with his mind. The operations center in that old boathouse and cabin required a lot of thought and work. I think Harold enjoyed the complexity of it all." She stuck a bite of salad in her mouth.

"I agree," said Uncle Charlie. "The idea of different colored flower pots on the docks was ingenious, too. The green pots signified those homes were wide-open targets; the orange ones urged caution; the red meant danger, stop, leave alone. That's why you saw the pots on your dock and Robert's dock change colors two or three times." He tossed a piece of roll to Little Guy. The terrier caught it in mid-air and waited expectantly for more. "Aurora, you cramped their style when you showed up unannounced for Margaret's funeral."

"Harold wasn't perfect, though. Dad found out what was going on and was murdered in the process. Thank goodness he took pictures with his Polaroid, or Harold would still be operating." She shuddered at the thought of her father dying such a horrible death. "Then again, I guess the pictures are what got Dad killed."

"I'm confused on a couple of things, Charlie," said Robert. "How did Harold use Jack's dock as a holding tank for stolen objects?"

"Sheila explained to us how Harold had an elaborate underwater system of ropes and pulleys just under the boathouse. At night, Clyde and Jimmy Ray would put the stolen articles in waterproof bags, hook them to a rope, and drop them in the water. The next night—or whenever they wanted—Clyde, Jimmy Ray, a man called Snake, and sometimes Sheila would retrieve the bags. Then Red would deliver the stolen items to a metal building on a Franklin County farm. I'm guessing that's the activity Aurora noticed in the boathouse those two nights.

"Their big troubles started when a plastic bag full of jewelry accidentally fell off Jack's dock and into the water."

"Is that the bag that was stuffed inside the rubber striper?" asked Aurora. "The one Dad photographed?" She spooned more potatoes onto her plate and passed the dish to Carole.

"No, this was the first of two bags that fell in the lake. They were removing the jewelry from the fake fish and Snake's foot knocked it off the dock. Harold couldn't just let the items go; they were worth hundreds of thousands of dollars and he had orders from wealthy, unscrupulous customers for most of the pieces. The water is fifteen to twenty feet deep in that spot, which presented a problem even for experienced divers because visibility is so bad. The bottom is soft, so a bag of jewelry could easily sink into the muck." He buttered a roll and took a bite.

"According to what we've pieced together from the Polaroid pictures Jack took and from what Sheila and Clyde told us, they started diving during daylight hours to take advantage of any light they could get. That's when Jack first saw them and became suspicious. Jimmy Ray got greedy and heisted a mink coat for one of his girlfriends."

Aurora frowned. "Jimmy Ray tried the coat on himself. Dad got a picture of him wearing it." Sam squeezed her hand. "Right, Uncle Charlie?"

"Yeah, he did." He smiled at his niece. "Jimmy Ray transferred the mink from one of the underwater bags to the black boat during daylight hours. That's when Jack saw Jimmy Ray and photographed him trying the coat on. The next day Jack maneuvered closer to the boathouse and snapped a picture of a painting one of the men took from the bag.

"The last straw, and the incident that sealed my brother's death, happened early one morning when Jack took it upon himself to investigate the boathouse. After all, something suspicious was happening on his property; he had a right to know what. Wish he'd called the police or me, but he didn't. That was a mistake. He carried his camera with him to the boathouse, discovered the pulleys, and pulled up the one that held the fake striper."

Robert interrupted. "Excuse me, judge, but I just can't understand the significance of the rubber striper. What purpose did it serve?"

"It was a ruse to make outsiders think Clyde and Jimmy Ray were fishing. From a distance, it looked real and gave them a reason to be in the boathouse." Charlie dropped a bite of roll on the floor. Little Guy wolfed it down and looked around for more.

"Anyhow, as I was saying," Charlie continued, "when Jack yanked up the pulley and saw the striper, he unhooked it, placed it on the dock, and photographed it. He noticed the zipper on the fish's stomach, unzipped it, and found jewelry—including the diamond and ruby necklace—concealed inside a clear plastic bag, the same type of bag that fell in the lake days earlier. Curious, he opened the bag, photographed all the jewelry, and put them back into the bag.

"Jack hurried back up to the house to think about what he'd just seen. According to what Clyde told us, Jack didn't hear the fishing boat glide up to the dock. Unfortunately, Jimmy Ray and Clyde had seen Jack through binoculars when they entered the cove. When they saw him taking pictures, Clyde used his cell phone to call Harold for instructions. Clyde still remembers the anticipation on Jimmy Ray's face when Harold ordered Jack's murder." Charlie looked at Aurora. "Are you all right, Aurora?"

"No, I'm not. They didn't have to kill Dad." Aurora, a hand over her mouth, left the porch. Sam excused himself and followed her. He knew his wife couldn't bear to hear any more. King whined and padded after them, his toenails clicking on the wood floor.

"What happened next?" asked Luke.

"The first thing Clyde and Jimmy Ray did was cut the telephone lines so Jack couldn't call the police. We believe Jack had been in the middle of dialing when the phone went dead, and then he noticed the two men outside. I'm sure he knew he was in deep trouble, so I'm guessing he put the message 'phone line cut' on the picture frame at that time, then hurried upstairs to slip the five photographs in the back of the Wyeth painting. After hiding the pictures, he wrote 'ask Wyeth' on the other frame.

"Clyde believed Jack would attempt to escape by car, so he and Jimmy Ray waited in the bushes in the front of the house. Jack evidently saw them and sneaked out the basement door, probably intending to take their fishing boat. He would've made it, but another boat pulled up to the dock. Poor Jack, he didn't realize the man in the boat was also one of Harold's men. Jack asked him for help. The man—the one named Snake—responded by slamming him in the head with a paddle, then hollered for Jimmy Ray and Clyde. We believe Snake opened the bag to check the contents and accidentally knocked it and the necklace in the lake at that time."

Carole nudged Luke and pointed to the bottle of wine. He smiled and filled her glass. "So a total of two bags of jewelry fell in the lake?" Carole asked.

"Yes," answered Charlie.

"What happened then?" asked Jill.

The judge cleared his throat. "Johns devised the plan to murder Jack and make it look like a drowning."

"Poor Jack." Robert reached for the striper.

"I know. My brother deserved better." Charlie's voice broke. He took a sip of wine.

"I can't believe I'd actually planned to marry that monster," declared Carole. "He certainly fooled me."

"He evidently fooled a lot of folks," said Jill.

"But not Aurora. She never liked him." Charlie pulled a handkerchief from his pocket and wiped his eyes. Then he smiled at his niece as she and Sam returned to the porch.

"Where did Sheila come in?" asked Carole.

"Sheila is Harold's sister. She and Clyde, bankrupt, moved to the lake and went to work for Harold. At first it was legit, but once Harold hooked Sheila on drugs, well, neither she nor Clyde had any choice but to do as Harold ordered. Johns owned a reputable cleaning company, had Sheila manage it, and she learned which homes contained valuable items."

"Sheila's the woman in the boat who wanted to breed her female Lab to King. Bet she doesn't even own a dog," Aurora said.

"You're right," continued the judge. "When Sheila cleaned homes, she hid a tiny digital camera in her pocket so she could snap pictures of valuable objects. Harold would then send the pictures over the internet to his contacts, and soon buyers lined up to purchase the stolen goods. Harold also bought Tom's Tidy Lawn & Lake Service, which gave him an easy way to mark houses. You know, the different colored flowerpots on the docks. Biff, the yardman, had no idea the pots were signals. He just put them where Harold and Sheila ordered him to."

Aurora drained her wine glass. "I hate to even ask, but where did Vanessa fit into all of this?"

Luke spoke up. "I can answer this one. Vanessa, called Red by her parents and her Uncle Harold, is Clyde and Sheila's spoiled brat of a daughter. Her job—and I have to admit she excelled at it—was to bedazzle and charm men. She'd worm her way into their confidences and hearts and then pump them for information about wealthy people on the lake. The proposed victims—or targets—could even be prospective property buyers, not just owners. Once she knew where and for how long they were staying at the lake, she'd pass on the info to Uncle Harold, and a 'chance' burglary would take place."

Luke raised his glass to Aurora. "You warned me she wasn't what she seemed, but I was in love." Taking Carole's hand, he added, "Or so I thought. Now I know what love really is." Carole leaned over and kissed his cheek.

Charlie pulled out a worn pipe from his shirt pocket, then extracted a half-full pouch of Sir Walter Raleigh pipe tobacco from his pants pocket. "Do y'all mind if I smoke?"

"No, you go right ahead," said Aurora. Charlie lit his pipe.

"The aroma from your pipe reminds me of the Sunday evenings long ago when you, Aunt Annie, and Mom and Dad would gather in the living room and sing along with the records all y'all had collected over the years." She closed her eyes, blocking out the present, and smiled at the memories of melodies from the '40s and '50s and the four adults harmonizing perfectly with one another.

"I'm sure that's why I love the Big Band sound, rock and roll, and beach music so much." She looked at Sam. "Not many people my age appreciated music from older generations, but you did. That's one of the things I love about you, Sam." He reached over and squeezed her hand.

"What will happen to Clyde, Sheila, Harold, and Vanessa?" asked Aurora.

"Sheila will probably get ten to twenty years. Clyde is another story. He'll probably get life, but since he played an important part in your survival," Charlie nodded at Aurora, Sam and Luke, "his sentence could be less. My guess is that Harold and Vanessa will get the death penalty. I certainly hope so."

Sam put his arm around Aurora's shoulder. "So who was the third victim? I know about Jack and Lampwerth. But who was number three?"

"Actually," said Charlie, "number three was number two, a fellow known as Snake. Don't know how he acquired that name, but some folks around here say it's because he couldn't be trusted. Anyhow, Snake helped kill Jack. He's the man who hit Jack in the head with a paddle and knocked the necklace and the other jewelry in the lake." Charlie puffed on his pipe. "But he got drunk in the Bucking Stallion Lounge and bragged about the killing. Lucky for Johns, everyone Snake bragged to was also drunk and either thought Snake was bluffing or didn't remember it. Unlucky for Snake, his best friend and drinking buddy Jimmy Ray heard him and shot him in the head the next day per instructions from Harold. Snake's body was the one we first thought was Lampwerth."

"That's the one I fell on in the lake." Aurora rose and gazed out at the shimmering water. "All these murders! How can I ever enjoy the lake again?" No one answered.

Sam stood and put his arm around her. "Your lake didn't kill them, Susie-Q. Greed, evil, hate, and madness are what took them. Don't let Harold Johns win by taking your lake away from you."

The others nodded.

"Thank you, Sam. He will not win." King whined and gazed up at Aurora with adoring eyes. She put her hand on his head, then sat back down at the table.

"I hope all this talk didn't dampen anyone's desire for dessert. If so, raise your hand." Aurora waited, but no hands shot up.

"Because we live in the South, and in honor of our soon-to-be-married Yankee neighbors Jill and Robert, tonight we'll celebrate the South with Crème de Menthe parfait."

"I'll help you." Carole followed Aurora to the kitchen.

"Me too," said Jill.

"I'll use this tray to take the parfaits to the porch. Carole, you can carry the platter of cookies and Jill can open the door."

"Yum! This is delicious, Aurora," Jill said when they were seated at the table. She spooned another bite into her mouth. Everyone agreed.

After dessert, Sam helped Aurora clear the table. He popped a beach music DVD into the DVD player. The sultry sounds drifted out to the porch and Aurora looked at Sam. He smiled and winked.

Carole nudged Luke. "Time for us to be going."

Charlie looked at his watch. "Where has the time gone? I had no idea it was getting so late."

"We should go, too, Jill." Robert stood up. "Sam and Aurora, this was a wonderful evening."

"We'd love for y'all to stay a while longer," Aurora said. Sam covered a yawn with his hand and jabbed her with an elbow.

"No, I think it's time for all of us to get some sleep." Uncle Charlie hugged Aurora. "Thanks again for a nice evening. Don't you kids stay up too late."

CHAPTER FORTY-THREE

Sunday, May 30

At twilight Aurora set the picnic basket on the dockside table. She folded back the red and white checkered cloth to reveal shrimp salad, boiled new potatoes, crisp-cooked broccoli sprinkled with a lemon and dill dressing, and crescent rolls. From another basket, she withdrew a bottle of Hickory Hill's Chardonnay, two crystal wineglasses, antique gold-rimmed china, sterling silver Strasbourg flatware, and a white Irish linen tablecloth and napkins.

"You outdid yourself this time, Aurora." Sam set the DVD player on the dock.

"The last two weeks without you have been awful. I wanted this night to be special, Sam." She put the cloth on the table, and set a sterling candelabra in the middle of the table. Uninterested in the elegance, King curled up on the dock near them, content to be with the two people he loved most in the world. Little Guy sniffed King and stretched out beside him.

"Any night with you is special, Susie-Q." Sam uncorked the wine and filled their glasses. "A toast to my incredible wife. May we share a long, healthy life together." The high-pitched clink of their glasses echoed across the water.

"Happy anniversary, Aurora. Ten wonderful years with the only woman I've ever loved."

"You haven't been bored?"

He moved his chair beside her so they both faced the lake. "Bored? Are you kidding? You're an exciting woman." He smiled. "But let's cut back on the excitement of the past few weeks. Deal?"

"It's a deal. Sorry I nearly got you killed. Twice." She filled his plate and set it in front of him, then served one for herself.

"They nearly killed you, too. So we're even."

"Remember the first time we sat on this dock together?"

"Of course. Thirteen years ago, and our first date. I knew then that I adored you, Aurora. I wanted to marry you, spend the rest of my life with you. I hoped you felt the same."

"Sam, I loved you the first time I saw you, when you were lost and asked me for directions." She popped a spoonful of shrimp salad into his mouth. "By the way, whatever happened to the gorgeous brunette who was hanging all over you—and hanging out of her bikini—that day?"

"I've no idea, can't even remember her name."

Aurora touched the slight scar on his forehead and leaned her head against his shoulder. "I couldn't stand it if anything happened to you. And you came so close to dying."

"Hey, I'm tough. Besides, I had too much to live for to give up without a fight."

"I'm glad."

"This shrimp salad is delicious. I've missed your cooking, Aurora."

"I've missed cooking for you." She sipped her wine.

"Susie-Q, how would you like for 210 Spawning Run Road to be our address?"

"What?"

"Would you like to move here, Aurora? Permanently."

"It would be a dream come true. Why do you even ask?"

"While in Augusta this week, I talked with a real estate agent. If you say yes, she'll put our house there on the market next week. It's up to you, Aurora."

"But what about your job? We can't just live on love." She grinned. "Although we could try."

"I talked with the president of the company. He's thought a lot about expanding and thinks the Roanoke, Lynchburg, and Bedford area could be the perfect spot to open another engineering office. He's asked me to run it." He dished some broccoli onto his plate. "You've earned a national reputation with your travelogues. Couldn't you produce them right here?"

Aurora threw her arms around her husband and kissed him passionately. "Is that the answer you need? If not. . . . "

He nodded and pushed the "Play" button on the DVD player. "Let's dance," he said in a husky voice as "Only You" by the Platters mingled with the night air.

"Sam, I think I'm ready to try for another baby." He smiled and hugged her closer to him.

As they slow-danced on the dock, Aurora thought, "What a perfect evening." King whined and Little Guy barked.

Sam pointed to the churning water. "Look. The stripers are spawning."

A light breeze ruffled the water's surface. Under a full moon, Aurora and Sam embraced at the edge of the dock and watched the dance of the stripers in Spawning Run.